Aunt Pol

Sylvia Jackson Clark
© 19th April 2013
Dedicated with my love to my Sisters
Joy & Dawn
For their expertise in Digital Art.
(Public Domain Images)
Thanks to my son Paul for his technical assistance
Many thanks to my Sons Paul and Graham
love as always

Thanks to Carol and Doug Mogano
Thanks also to Ruby and Philip Mc Cormac.

An original emotional and heart-warming portrayal of the life of Emma who moves to be in service in Coventry at
"Aunt Polly's Parlour"
Leaving her loving parents Albert & Ada in Stockingford to make her way through the turmoil of growing up and becoming a woman.
84,660 words

1912

"Aunt Polly's Parlour"

Prologue

I was fourteen when Mum said it was time for me to go into service, of course I didn't want to, it meant leaving home and the large family I had grown up with.

Mum said I was lucky, because it was to my Aunt Polly's I was going. It might well have been a stranger. I knew nothing of my Aunt she lived in Coventry, which was a long way from the Ford. I couldn't afford tram or bus fares so it meant a great deal to me. There would be no nipping to and fro, once at Aunt Polly's I would be there to stay. I was shipped off with the clothes I had been allotted until Aunt Polly told me what she wanted me to wear.

Chapter 1

I arrived at Auntie Polly's shy and not wanting to say very much. She took my Bags saying,
"Glad you have arrived safe I am just going to have a cup of tea, would you like to join me?"
I followed her to the sitting room where teacups and small pretty plates were on the

table. Aunt smiled at me and said,
"I want you and me to be good friends. We have many things to teach each other. There is plenty of time we will get to know each other as we go."
I wasn't afraid but I was full of apprehension. It would be a very different life for me now. The name of this Road is Park Road. There is a very small Park at the very end of it, other than that it houses shops. Many times carriages stop opposite Aunt's shop to let customers down, it was good for Aunt as it brought the customer right to her shop door. I wanted to know as soon as the shop was mentioned just what it sold. I couldn't ask I was only going to be in service. In my heart, I would have loved to have shop work but I had no experience.

Tea over, Aunt took Emma to look around her new abode. As they went up the staircase Emma noticed how elegant it was caressing the soft glow of the well-polished banister as she went up. They went along the corridor until they came to a cream coloured door.
"This is your room dear," Aunt Polly said Emma looked inside and saw a dressing table. It had three angled mirrors and drawers down both the sides also a wardrobe just for her.

"I don't know what I shall put in my wardrobe Aunt but I am happy to have one, I never thought I would."

Aunt Polly looked at Emma; delight was showing in her face. Aunt Polly said,

"To start you off here is a new nightie and slippers too I like pink so I have bought you pink, all shades of pink eh? May I ask do you have a corset? If not we will get you measured for one. I will leave a makeshift one, shop bought you understand, you can wear that until the measured one is ready."

"I don't wear a corset Aunt," Emma exclaimed.

"You are in a different environment here dear there are rules of fashion to be met. You will soon be able to sense the priorities; so do not go losing sleep over new things all will be dealt with. I am here for you to ask if you want to know anything."

Emma now in her room went around touching her new things. A hairbrush and comb was on her dressing table and a round box with a fancy lid containing talcum powder and puff for just her. She tried on her new slippers. Aunt watched her with interest. What a pretty girl Emma is Aunt thought she holds herself well too, Emma was engrossed in what lay all around her. Looking out of the

window being delighted to see the carriages, the sure-footed horses and elegant ladies being helped down to the pavement, it struck Emma just how fine that small detail was. The Gentleman's hand held up to her so that she would safely reach her foot to the footplate and get down from the carriage. Courtesy! Aunt could see Emma lost in the world outside her window, so she drew Emma's attention again to continue showing her through the house.
"We shall go to the bathroom next, follow me along the corridor, here we are."
Stepping inside, never having seen a bathroom before Emma was delighted. It was a huge bath. It was much bigger than the tin one they had on the hearth dragged in from the yard for a fireside bath at home. This room was entirely for bathing a separate sink and toilet. The bath had a geyser at one end of it Emma didn't recognise what this was.
"Aunt Polly, what is the round white thing at the end of the bath does it serve a purpose?"
"Oh, yes dear it heats the water, no humping buckets and bowls and if it gets too hot, you simply add some cold water to it and have the heat you chose. I will show you how. Of course, Ada doesn't have this facility in her home, I don't know what I would do without

it and you can wash your hair at the same time as bathing. You will find it very relaxing."

Emma's mind was full of exciting new beginnings didn't know what she liked most. She would explore everything when she was on her own. Aunt Polly preparing to leave her said,

"I shall leave you now to unpack, there will be tea when you have finished." Aunt Polly turned and went. Emma flopped on to the bed. The puffy eiderdown gave way to her youthful charms. She stretched out and enjoyed. Emma's Mum Ada had sorted out this position for her dear Daughter. Always the best for her girls, there would still be the close bond of Mother and Daughter nothing could change that ever. Emma wondered if she would have to wear a formal pinney with cap, she decided to put on the tidiest thing she had amongst her few clothes hoping it would do. Putting her hair into a neat look, she went down to her Aunt. There was a smile to greet her.

"Sit there Emma don't stand on too much ceremony, I feel a bit awkward myself. We will soon get to know each other you will see." They sat down and ate a piece of white fish, followed by fruitcake then cleared to

wash up.

"Did you make the fruitcake Aunt?"

"Yes, did you enjoy it? As you see dear, I have a gas stove. To tell you the truth I would always prefer to do my cooking on the fire, the hob with the oven does most things I need to do." Now sitting by the cosy fire, the talk turned to what would be Emma's duties.

"We shall share the housework Emma, I do not want you to think you have to do it all on your own, then I hope you will learn how to tend the shop, do you like the idea of shop work dear?" Emma tried not to show her bubbly enthusiasm. To work in a shop had been but a dream, shelved for lack of opportunity, was the dream starting to take shape as reality? She was thrilled, thoughts tripped through Emma's mind, she was not only a maid she was going to work in a shop as well. Learning would come into it; Emma didn't mind that. You quickly learned how to do something if you wanted it badly; this was to be her life. Pocket money two shillings a week, plus bed and board. Money, in her own pocket, never had she dreamed of such a thing. So, off to bed, Aunt followed Emma up to her bedroom to show her the way to turn off the Gas Mantle.

"Now look, turn this flat brass knob right

round, when you hear it go "Plop" it means the gas is out. You will soon get the hang of it, goodnight dear."

Emma in her own room felt strangely calm. Aunt as an afterthought had brought her a steaming cup of cocoa. Her flannel nightdress was laid out on the bed all being at peace. Going over to the dressing table she picked up the brush that was there and let her hair down. She had long dark hair and bewitching blue eyes. It was clear to see she was going to make a beautiful young lady. Up to now, there had been many ups and downs. "Not to expect too much" that is what her Mother had told her, yet what was happening to her now was far and away more than she ever thought would happen. She started to get undressed, then she remembered the corset Aunt had left her; she was expected to wear it tomorrow. I had better try it on. Undoing the solid row of metal hooks and eyes that did up down the front, Emma put it around her waist oh it would be so tight. Trying to do up the hooks was impossible. Taking it off again Emma realised the lace crisscrossing at the back was so that you could make the corset larger. She let it out a few times trying it each time, at last it fit her somewhat, her bosom pushed up to make a very daring cleavage.

Mum told me about this kind of underwear, I am sure she said busk fronts with laced backs, ha, never thought I would have to wear one. Trying once more, she put on the corset. She looked in the mirror it certainly wasn't a thing of beauty. Throwing it back on to the bed she looked at herself as she was naked, cupping her small pert and pretty breasts in her two hands then smoothing down her waistline, approving of her own reflection she thought, corsets are for fat old women. I do not need one. Yet, she didn't like facing Aunt Polly in the morning without wearing it. Fashion yes, comfort no. There had been nothing like this to wear at home. Ah, well as long as I can breathe. Picking the corset up from the bed she put it into the wardrobe with a toss of her hand, she had very little respect for the garment. Undressed and into bed, just relaxing under the clean white cotton sheets, she thought, Oh drat, the Gas Mantle is still on. Out she got, as her Aunt had shown her she turned the metal knob until the gas went off. There was a distinctive "Plop" when it went out altogether it was unmistakable, so you knew it was safe. She lay there thinking but in the flick of an eye, sleep had claimed her.

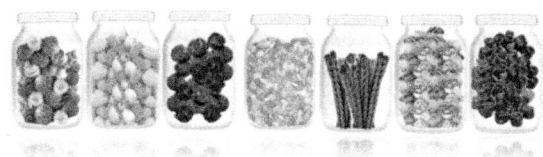

Chapter 2

Another day, all was well; it was a bright sunny morning. It was 7.30am and breakfast was at 8am then their daily duties would commence but this was Sunday. Aunt Polly said Sunday was for doing as you pleased. Aunt intended to use this Sunday to show Emma the shop. Emma couldn't wait for breakfast to be cleared and washed up she was full of excitement. Her eyes gleaming she said to Aunt,
"What kind of shop is it? I have been trying to picture it while lying on my bed. It has already been many different styles I still don't know what it really is."
"I am not telling you, we will be there soon enough." Aunt laughed with Emma.
At last, her wait was over. They went through a couple of doors a short corridor and she was in Aunt's shop. A whole display of wonderful sweets and chocolates met her

eyes. They took Emma's breath away. Placed in rows of glass jars were colours shapes and patterns that Emma hadn't seen before. At one end of the counter there stood a Glass Display Cabinet, this contained scrumptious delights, cakes in containers that the Customer could see through. These would be ordered a slice at a time, Emma liked the look of the chocolate and walnut cake, it had made her mouth water she didn't know what to say she was overwhelmed. Looking at the counter front polished and gleaming in a shaft of sunlight beaming in from the window it all looked very inviting. On the counter a pair of scales stood a balance scale with two round brass scoops either side suspended from brass chains. Alongside the scales was a row of brass weights 1oz. up to 1lb. pristine and polished. The money till had a handle you pulled forward to open the drawer, there to get change. To serve and measure these delights wasn't a job it was a privilege, how lucky she felt. For small amounts there were corner shaped bags, also larger pink bags with "Aunty Polly's Parlour" printed on them. These bags with handles would hold several smaller bags inside, the atmosphere of delicacies and the sweet aroma's that filled the air. Emma couldn't believe it, all of it was

what she had dreamed of when scrubbing the kitchen table at home. This new and wonderful scene she was to be part of. Sometimes dreams do come true, she said to herself. When Emma came down from the clouds and was thinking calmly Aunt said,
"I have another thing to tell you, it will wait until you have had your breakfast."
Clearing off the table, Emma wanted to know what it was that Aunt was going to tell her.

"I think you know the shops go on all down this road selling all sorts of merchandise. I would like you to meet my friends at the shop next door, just two ladies, Hettie and her Daughter Sally. Hettie lost her husband four years ago. It was her husband's business he did tailoring, and when he went, Hettie had to think of something that her Daughter Sally and she could manage. Alterations were made in the shop. They called it "Stitch in Time" it is a Haberdashery shop very popular too, you can buy anything from a packet of needles to a single button, I love going in there. They have gone from strength to strength ever since they opened. The cabbies that bring their fare to the main thoroughfare drop them off just around the corner of Aunt's shop. It is good for us because the ladies look first in our or Hetties

windows. I must say though there is sometimes pandemonium going on in the Road. There are the brand new motorcars, the horse and carriages not to say about delivery vans and cycles. Now we have two-seater horse and carriage to take paying ladies and gents to the destination asked for. That has taken me off my tale. Where was I, oh yes I was telling you about next door."

"How old is Hetties Daughter, what is her name?" asked Emma.

Aunt Polly smiled Emma's open enthusiasm lit up her face, it made Aunt feel young again, it was a long time since she delighted in that feeling.

"She is eighteen years old, her name as I have said is Sally," said Aunt.

"I would be pleased to meet her and would love to look at their shop, when can we?" asked Emma.

"We will go as soon as possible I know you would love the kind of merchandise they sell. I will see Hettie and ask if she has an evening free this week we could call."

"I look forward to that Aunty."

"How do you think you will do in our shop Emma?" Aunt replied.

"Oh, I will love it, for the short space of time I have been here already I am tuning myself

in, and practicing how to deal with the customer and where things belong. I want to learn as fast as I can. I really hope to be an asset not a drawback."

"I thought so, when you have got the hang of it I shall leave the business in your hands Emma, then Hettie and I can sit in the back yard while you and Sally keep each shop going."

"Oh, I am not that ready Aunt, but I will be delighted to do so as soon as I can."

"That is a good reply Emma dear. I was only seeing how you felt, it is important to me to have the customer's needs well cared for. I will let you know when we are to go round Hetties. You can turn the door sign around to say, "Open" now, I think we, are both, clear as to what we want." The meeting to see Hetties shop was arranged. After closing "Aunt Polly's" they would go to see the Haberdashery shop next door then Emma could meet Hettie and Sally.

"Hello Hettie, here we are, this is my niece Emma" they shook hands. Hettie said,

"Sally will be down in a minute she has gone to change out of her shop attire."

Sally came into the room. She had on a brown dress matching her brown eyes, with brown shoes. There was very little impressionable about the sombre look. True she was probably as down to earth as she looked. Sara thought it would have been nice for her to have one redeeming factor. There was nothing attractive about Sally.

"Sally this is Emma, you will be seeing a lot of each other. She has come to stay with Polly to help her out with the serving in the shop"

The girls didn't shake hands they just smiled and said it would be nice to see each other. They sat and talked, mainly about Emma coming from the Ford and how the traffic would be so different for her to get used to. Sally said,

"You must be very careful when crossing the road. The new cars with their loud hooters, frightens the horses. There are not many car owners but the person driving the new "Tin Lizzie" thinks he should have more of the road than the driver of the horse and Carriage. They sound their hooters so loudly, not only do they frighten the horse, the people too. Barging their way trying to get the carriage to give way and let the car pass. The car driver seems to care nothing for the carriage driver who has reigns in his hands and a living horse to consider, trying to keep his passengers safe at the same time. I call it a "Free for all" It is up to the individual to

take care so please do." Emma wasn't too keen on the lecture although she knew it was meant in the best intentions.

"Do you think I could see your shop Sally?"

"Yes Emma, you will be mesmerised with the variety of things we sell, come this way." They went down the corridor that opened into the shop space. There were counters running none stop down both the sides. These were sectioned off into pigeonholes some larger than others, some oblong, some square and in each section dwelt a different piece of merchandise. All very neat and tidy, not wall space, flat counter level spaces, all were full of the accumulation of so many different pieces it stretched the mind. Emma wanted to ask how they made a living selling such small items but thought the better of it, after all this was the first time they had met.

Chapter 3

Sitting talking before they went to bed, Emma asked Aunt Polly the question she had wanted to ask Sally.
"How do they make money on such small items Aunty? I had a good look and saw to name but a few, elastic by the yard, buttons of every description held in transparent tubes with one button left out on top of each lid to identify the contents. If you wanted one button, one button is all you had to buy, one or twenty-one no matter, needles, bias binding, lace edging, knob pins, cotton reels

of every colour, machine needles, oh such a variety. Sally told me a little story, carried on Emma, "Apparently an elderly lady took in her cardigan, her own knitting then tried an enormous amount of single buttons held to the wool to see which ones suited it best for size and colour. There was no ending to the choice and it took a long while to decide. Another instance Sally told me was about an old and gnarled lady who had lost a button but looking through the vast stock there wasn't one to match, so she complained. The button had been taken out of stock and wouldn't be replaced. The lady was very angry the cardigan must have been ten years old no wonder there was no spare buttons for it. Hettie and Sally have a lot of patience Aunt Polly, I admire them for that, I wouldn't know where to begin to help a customer like that. Would you like that sort of shop Aunt Polly?"

"No, it isn't for me it is tedious work one must be dedicated to give so much of oneself for such a small reward." Emma replied,

"My Sisters Annie and Ruby would be good customer's they make hand decorated items in embroidery, Hettie does sell silks doesn't she?"

"I wouldn't exactly know, but they do say,

e it we have it." Aunt Polly said.
f them laughed. Emma said,
"...... in the not too distant future my Sisters will be here to sew and sell."
Aunty looked shocked
"That's the first I have heard of it!"
"Oh I mean in the future Aunt," said Emma "they are very good at what they do so you never you know. I don't want to be mean Aunt, but my opinion of Sally is she is a very straight laced and a very serious lady. I would like to get to know her but I think it would be hard to do that." Aunt knew what Emma meant. Really the girls were like chalk and cheese, their personalities separated them. Aunt said,
"Well you needn't make a close friend of her, but it is good to have a neighbour that is about the same age and I thought introducing you to Sally would fill the gap that parting from your Sisters has left."
"Of course, but no one is ever going to fill that gap," replied Emma. The time was flying by things went on in a satisfactory way, learning fast as one does with anything one wants to learn. Emma dusted and polished when there wasn't anyone to serve, Emma wanting to keep the atmosphere the exact same way it had enthralled her in the first few

days. Now she was getting more familiar with the names of the customers, also the sweets. Instead of pointing at the chosen jar she would put a name to them saying,

"Is it the sugared almonds, you would like, or the mint imperial?" She offered bulls-eyes, lemon sherbet, chocolate nugget and treacle toffee. The children loved liquorice, red shoelaces and sherbet dips. They would have just 1oz and lucky to afford that, but they would stand for ages just looking into the window to make sure they had made the right choice before buying. Off they went smiles all over their faces, sweets in their hand and a game of "Hopscotch" to go and get involved in, a simple world with love involved. Children were quite happy with what was really, very little. Chatting and skipping along the way to school telling each other of the adventure that was theirs for the making. How Grandma had given them an extra halfpenny for the errand they did for her. Building "Igloos" when it snowed, Dad would make a sledge to take to the hilly parts and play sliding down the slopes, hot bacon sandwiches, wrapped tight between two hot water bottles to keep warm, a feeling of just being together no money could buy. Of course it wasn't everyone who shared in this

kind of family closeness many families were made up of too many children with not enough money. Emma's own family shared the best and the worst of what their life had become. They didn't know any other way it was fact, they dealt with it daily. For Emma to come out of that life into the life that Aunt Polly now offered her was nothing short of a miracle. Emma quite understood that, she could hardly believe it even now. Any task she was asked to do she did with pleasure. She was becoming very useful without knowing it. Her Aunt Polly also thought so and kept an eye on Emma that was far more loving than need be, a great advantage to them both. The days skipped by, Emma had her sixteenth birthday she was becoming quite a young lady.

Her Aunt sat at the breakfast table and greeted Emma as she came in.

"A Happy Birthday to you my dear," said Aunt Polly bringing a parcel from under her chair to give to Emma.

"Thank you very much." her niece replied, not at all familiar with anyone buying her a gift. Emma wanted to keep it wrapped up, just to look at the parcel made for her, but she knew her Aunt wanted it opened so slowly as if precious gems were about to be revealed.

She took off the brown paper and string thanking her Aunt as she did so. Her emotion made her speechless, for in the gift wrap was a pretty new handbag made in red velvet with draw strings to hang from the wrist, a red scarf that matched having beaded tassels at each end and a red muff with a little beading to match the scarf. Emma fondled the tassels lovingly she was enchanted. It was the first real fashion item she had owned.

"I can't believe my eyes Aunt Polly this is a lovely gift I could use them to go to visit Mum and Dad, or a walk about town, I love them. I suppose the idea is to keep your hands warm and the bag on the wrist safe, clever as well as pretty. I will just have a cup of tea, with a slice of toast Aunt Polly. I am too excited to eat," Said Emma.

Her Aunt reading between the lines smiled saying,

"You have a restful day today Emma, it is your birthday after all. I tell you what, I will run a bath for you, go on and I will follow you, I don't think you have got the hang of the geyser yet. You can then put on a dress that will tone with your Birthday present. Maybe a cape for your shoulders, there is a keen wind this morning and then we will go for a walk to show what a lovely girl should

look like. Do you really like the gift Emma?"
"It is the loveliest gift I have ever had with the matching scarf and muff too. I will never be able to say thank you enough dear Aunt Polly."
"Oh! Go on then, away with you I will wash up this morning then I will run your bath. You can go to see if there is anything else in your wardrobe to match the outfit." As she left Aunt Polly, Emma flung her arms around Aunt and kissed her cheek. Polly felt a tear in her eye she loved Emma! Emma flew up the stairs into her bedroom. She preened herself in front of the mirror trying on the scarf, holding the handbag in different ways where could she go in such finery? It didn't matter they would lie on the top of her dressing table so that she could see them whenever she came into her bedroom.

Running along to the bathroom, she was excited. It was still new to her having a bathroom. Opening the door, a soft waft of steam rushed towards her with the tang of bath perfume. Her smile rewarded Aunt who was in the bathroom filling the bath with warm water she went towards the door to leave so that Emma could have her privacy. Is this really me? Emma thought. Hmm the water smells heavenly, I feel like a Mermaid but my hair is dark. I think Mermaids have blonde hair, well I will alter the rule I will be a dark haired Mermaid. She laughed at her own silly banter as she stepped into the scented water, picking up handfuls of soapy bubbles and lying in the soft soapy water, the pretty bathroom decor all around her she began to relax. A smile on her face, her young slim body caressed by bubbles alone in a private world. The bathroom full of steam turning to water globules as it slid in droplets down the mirrors. Emma was in her element with so many things that were entirely new to her. The Ford had offered a true and loving family. Aunt Polly's world a new dimension so much to encounter that had not been part of her life before. Her Sisters Ruby and Annie just had to be given the same opportunity. Emma's thoughts always included Annie and Ruby. I think I will wash my hair. Just as the thought entered her mind there was a knock on the door.

"May I come in dear?"

"Yes, I am soaking, covered in bubbles."

"I have brought you this jug to fill with clear water for rinsing your hair don't spare the rinsing eh dear? The water in the Geyser is still warm. I also have brought you a spot of vinegar for your final rinse it will make your

hair shine." Bending over the Geyser tap Aunt showed Emma how to turn it on.

"I will leave you in peace now, don't rush we have plenty of time." Emma had no intention of rushing she was enjoying the moment. Soon enough Emma was dressing and feeling good. Her handbag, scarf and muff lay ready to put on for the final touch, having on a warm shoulder cape out they went. Aunt Polly said,

"Let's go and see if the Pool is frozen there will be skaters out if it is."Emma hadn't seen the Pool Aunt was referring to so went along gladly. Seeing the skaters in their bright warm colours their scarves billowing behind as they glided around was a sight that when looked on for the first time was breath-taking and filled Emma with delight.

Chapter 4

While Emma was working back in her sweet shop, she thought a lot about her family back home. Ruby and Annie being born much later than she was, Emma had quite a hand in being a good elder Sister to them, she felt the age gap gave her importance and responsibility. As Babies, she was able to give one of them their feeding bottle. Her Mum getting her into a firm corner of the arm chair and passing the feeding bottle to her and then Mum would feed the other one it worked well. Emma also took them out with Mum in a huge black pram that had a double hood. Everyone wanted to see them they were as pretty as a picture, perhaps not the posh

pram or the shop bought clothes that others had, but the Twins in their home made knitted matinee coats and pretty little bonnets too made up for that. Emma showed them off to perfection,
"These two are my baby Sisters and not crying Babies but smiling Babies."
The couple looking in at Ruby and Annie said,
"You can see how content your Sisters are, such lovely round cheeks with blue eyes, you must be very well loved in your family and it shows." Loved as were all in the family, it is strange but I think babies know when they are wanted. They settle into their niche and are well are loved all the more because of it. Growing up now they would soon be ready for the outside world. It would be great if they could eventually come to Aunt Polly's to work for her. Emma thought, I am going to concentrate to see if there is any possibility of that, surely something could be worked out. Emma was hoping they would get a chance such as she had and be as happy as she was with Aunt Polly. Emma knew her Sisters would be happy working alongside her; I am going to ask Aunt if she would consider having Ruby and Annie to work for her. A few alterations would have to be made. I will

find an opportune moment to have a quiet talk.

As time went by Emma found herself often thinking about the Twins. At the back of her mind, she was laying down a plan. The more she thought of it the more she wanted it to materialise. Biding her time not wanting to say anything to Aunt Polly as it might upset her, she went forward slipping into the conversation suggestions about what she wanted to do. Soon things would become a proposal she would ask Aunt Polly if it was at all possible that her dream could materialise and that Ruby and Annie could be working with her. Could it become as real as in her daydreams? She must wait a while for Ruby and Annie to get to the age of fourteen. Having put much thought into things, the well-devised plan could then be discussed. Who knows Aunty might think it was a good idea. For now it had to be laid aside while Emma did everything in her power to please her Aunt, which wasn't hard to do as Aunty did not ask the impossible she was already well pleased.

There was a pleasing in manner very polite and good looking young man coming into the shop to buy sweets for his Mother, twice a week he came. After a few encounters

he plucked up his courage and said,
"I think I have seen you before no not in the shop, you are the girl I admired at the Ice Pool a few weeks ago. I remember the flash of red that you were wearing so proudly, I thought how pretty you looked."
Emma blushed to the roots of her hair not knowing how to accept a compliment.
She didn't remember seeing this Gentleman before.
"Yes, I was at the Pool, but I don't recall having seen you."
"Oh no you wouldn't I was back and forth on the ice. I took advantage of the bright icy day and took a stroll down to the Pool to see if the ice was thick enough to skate on, obviously it was. The pale sunshine and the dash of ice beneath my skates my heart was aglow, do you skate?"
"No, I am afraid not, it isn't that I wouldn't like to. The scene enchanted me that day, it was my Birthday and the red you refer to was my Birthday present from my Aunt Polly, who was with me."
"If there is a chance your Aunt would allow me to teach you I would do so gladly."
"That is kind of you but I am not allowed out without a chaperone yet."
"Well, bring your Aunt, she can sit and

observe that we are on the ice I mean you no harm."

"I will mention it to Aunt, see what she says. I can't see her letting me skate while she sits at the edge of the Pool, for one thing she would get perished." The shop now was getting busy so he touched his hat in a complimentary fashion and left.

"Damn it, again I didn't ask her name, next time I will not forget."

Walking back to his Mother's house he could not get this girl out of his mind. He went in to his Mother to tell her he was back saying,

"You will find me in the study if you need me, I have some important work to do I shall be finished by tea time."

"All right Son don't study too hard, you need to rest your mind, you can overdo it you know Neil." He felt a bit guilty telling an outright fib, he wanted his privacy to think about the dear little shop assistant who he was falling in love with.

Emma also had a vibrant impression of the young man that had paid her such a pretty compliment. Talking to her Aunt as they sat having tea, Emma said,

"I had a compliment paid to me today Aunt."

"Did you dear, who gave you that?"

"A young Gentleman, he came in quite early

for cigars and sweets. He said he had noticed me on the Sunday, when we went to see the skater's on the frozen Pool."

"That is because you looked very pretty in your red, who could fail to notice you. I must issue you a word of warning though Emma, there will be many a young man who would gladly have you on his arm, you must be choosy, not take the first comer."

"Oh Aunt I won't do that, this man, I do not know his name cheered me up, he didn't say anything you would not approve of." Emma omitted to say anything about seeing him to learn how to skate she kept quiet. The subject was dropped. Emma still had her beau in her mind and he did have a certain appeal. Next day he came again, he wanted to buy a large box of chocolates as a gift. Emma showed him the pink boxes that were made for special occasions. She would gift-wrap the box tying pink ribbon to finish it off and a card to say they had come from "Aunty Polly's Parlour" This suited him fine so he chose a large box and one by one picked the type of sweets to go in it. Some very fine jellies, sugar coated almonds, cream toffees and a selection of Cadbury's chocolates, all cushioned on the pink tissue paper that lined the box.

"Thank you, the chocolates? Are they from the Cadbury that is the new comer to the town?"

"Yes they are being asked for now and I find them truly delicious." *It all looked scrumptious the way it had been laid into the pink box with the pink tissue enhanced its appeal he said,*

"With the brooch I already have I am sure Mother will be delighted with this gift. One more thing your name, I have been meaning to ask you I always seem to forget until I am on my way again, will you tell me?"

"Of course, my name is Emma and you are?"

"I am Neil, thank you again Emma, I shall be in to see you." *Now he went on his way, the beautiful box of sweets held gently so as not to spoil the placed items. His face had a smile and his step was light. He now knew her name was Emma would she ever be his? In his mind she already was, his mind was working overtime, his first step had been taken, what about the future? He was prepared to wait and see. He wanted her he had to make her want him, and he would make all the right moves to draw this in the right direction. What can I do to let Emma know she is so special to me? I can hardly bring roses I would frighten her off and she sells chocolate, I will think of something.*

Chapter 5

Back at the Ford the remainder of her Mum's family were also growing up, in fact the Twins would be now thirteen years old. One more year, when they were fourteen, Emma would be going on nineteen, nearly twenty it would be time to put Emma's plan into action. She had been studying it all in her mind, but not yet told her Aunt Polly. Maybe her Aunt wouldn't like the idea, in which case Emma would be disappointed. She had thought for what seemed ages about her plan. It would benefit all around and so she wasn't going to give up easily. For now though it still had to be just in Emma's mind, they all had to be the right age before it was dealt with.

These days when Emma was in the shop she was noticing the passers by more than usual. The scene in the street became so busy, the horse and carriages, the new addition of motor cars, all weaving in and out of each other, the clothes and hats people were wearing awe inspiring mainly the ladies, some with hats so big Emma wondered how they kept them on, all being very elegant. She wondered if she would ever have a hat like that, they must cost a fortune. Some with feathers held high, curls peeping out to frame the face. They always had a carriage and a Gentleman escort. If the weather turned grey or snow was in the air they would go into a tea shop, protected then from the storm, the carriage would come right up to the tea shop door to take the lady home, this way they could come out to show off their lovely finery without getting the clothes or hats spoiled. They being a very much pampered set of upper class Ladies, their Men did everything to see that they had all they needed. Emma couldn't imagine how they would cope with the type of background she herself had lived in. She was learning all was not equal in the world. Thank goodness for her Aunt Polly, she had shown her one or two things as they went daily about their work. Emma was now able to identify with the way things had to be, not that she approved there simply wasn't a choice, she hadn't the learning from an education, so simply couldn't compete even if she wanted to. Emma was a bright girl though she could turn her hand to many things, her general learning being picked up as she went along her way. There wasn't much that passed Emma's eye, that wasn't stored for later use.

All the time she was in the sweetshop the business kept growing. New lines brought in so that even the "well to do" ladies stopped for a look and then began to come in and order. Emma got used to saying,
"Good morning Madam Can I help you in any way?"
They wanted their orders delivered. Emma found herself with baskets of sweets walking through to the Posh Houses to deliver the orders placed the day before, this was not for just the odd quarter pound, the sweets she

delivered were expensive boxes that contained chocolate, with fancy ribbon wrapping and pictures of the loveliest scenes on them. They were sometimes too heavy for Emma to carry so she and her Aunt Polly devised a little wooden trolley with wheels, painted pink. The weather of course was the deciding factor. Of course, if the weather was too bad the ladies sent their servant in a carriage to collect their parcels it seemed to work quite well.

"Aunty Polly's Parlour" began to be a name well known. More and more people called in, the shop had a name for quality and service being pleasing to the eye as well as the palette. When Emma was delivering she was also learning she was asked into many a Grand House. What would her Mum think now to see her Emma in such grand surroundings? It was about time Emma went to see her Mum, it was a long way and she had no travelling companion. It made her think twice, much could happen to a girl on her own and she knew it was best to just write. Her letters were eagerly received being devoured by the rest of the family especially Ruby and Annie. They thought their Sister very lucky indeed; they talked for days between them about the letters. Emma told them little things that happened in the shop.

They even showed off to their friends too, telling them about the shop Emma managed, it being a Sweet Shop relaying all the delights that Emma had told, retelling the stories time and time again. Ruby and Annie not only loved their Sister they admired her too, which commanded great respect. Mum would sit with the girls to talk by the fire on a cold winter's night. There never was a lack of subject all bringing their own point of view, peeking in on Emma's world. Ruby saying to Annie,

"I wonder if we will ever get a chance like our Emma, how wonderful that would be. Just like Emma we would see posh horses and carriages carrying the ladies of the town passing by the windows" Annie replied,

"Don't forget the new motor cars Ruby, I think that is what I would like to see they are getting to be as many as carriages, pity they are all black still as you say they are not as elegant as carriages. We have to get a job first with Aunt Polly."

Mum didn't think that was highly likely, her Sister wouldn't have room for them, she wouldn't let her girls go to just anybody it had to be family or a well-chosen friend.

Aunt Polly was now free and easy about Emma, she couldn't think of a time without her, she thought how fortunate she was to have such a good happy relationship going on without any fuss and Aunt not having children, this was surely a blessing. Seeing the way Emma conducted herself, how other people found her so obliging, it surely was a good day for her when Emma arrived. She knew she would never want her to leave. Aunt Polly knew of the young man who still called in the shop. Not wanting to think too deeply about that, it was cast aside for the time being she would deal with that if and when it became a problem she didn't want to meddle, he was a customer at the moment nothing more and perhaps it would remain that way. He popped his head in, he was Emma's friend and this reassured Aunt that all was well.

Aunt Polly went to see Emma in the Sweet Shop Emma said,

"Hello Aunt Polly do you want me for anything special or is this a tea time visit shall I go and make tea?" They sat in the corner just behind the counter. The tea and biscuits brought a genial atmosphere to the air, it was nice. Between them they had good conversation going in no time. Aunt Polly had her reassurance Emma was settled and motivated. As to her future, there simply

wasn't anything to worry about. Her ward was growing into a very sensible young lady happiness glowed from her.

The Shop looked lovely, the counters were polished, the brass scales stood proudly, the sweet jars all tended. The cake display always looking mouth watering good and the cakes were never in there long they were too tempting. The colours of the sweets coordinated to show them to their best advantage. Displayed and arranged to be admired it was at the best when the smaller flowers such as Lilly of the valley, Primrose, Forget-me-nots and the smaller Daffodils were in bloom, in their turn they were put into a small flower vase and placed where they could be seen at one end of the counter On her own again, Emma had a flood of Customers, she liked to be busy, as usual in came Neil.

"Will you wait a while Neil, she asked, just while I serve these customers?"

Until the shop emptied a bit, Neil watched her easy manor dealing with the public she couldn't chat to him as they usually did so she directed him to the chair at the back of the counter. He had the pleasure of watching as she served, how polite she was and nimble. Up the set of small steps she went to take a firm grip on the chosen sweet jar weighing the amount requested, popping the jar back safely. It fascinated him he could have waited for hours just watching and admiring Emma. Soon she had her job finished.

"Sorry about that Neil everyone came at once, what can I get for you?"

"My usual sweets for Mum please" and something he had to say.

"Do you think Emma you would like to come and meet my Mother? I have told her lots about you she would like me to take you to tea, now please say yes, or I will be very disappointed." He looked at her with the fondness he felt. Oh dear, Emma thought, she knew that Neil lived in the posh kind of house that she only lately had been delivering sweets to, how could she possibly go to tea? Not knowing what to say realising she wasn't answering his request she tried to give a negative reply without offending.

"I am afraid it can't be just yet Neil Aunt Polly has been talking about going to see my Mum, Ruby and Annie. That will use up all my hours for leisure, perhaps soon we'll talk about it." With that, she put his order on the counter into a bag ready for him to leave. You could tell he was reluctant but what else could she do. If she went to meet his Mother,

he would then want to meet her Mum. The Ford, oh she couldn't take him to her Mum's house she didn't want him to see where she had formally lived and how many Brothers and Sisters she had lived with. He would know nothing of that kind of life. What would he think, it would embarrass her terribly but she did not want to hurt him, far from it she was so used to him coming to the shop she would really miss him. He turned his head, so as she couldn't see the disappointment in his eyes, he was going to talk her around if he could, but Emma always a sensible girl must have a very good reason, apart from the "Time off" denial, so he tempered his feelings with sanity. There would be another day, he could wait and the truth known it was more him, than his Mother that wanted Emma to Tea.

Chapter 6

Now things had moved on in Emma's small world, Neil asking her to meet his Mother had taken her by surprise yet she almost knew that someday it would happen. It was always tomorrow, not right now, she hoped she had let him down lightly, her thoughts ran on. I will get Aunt to go along with my idea of getting more into the classy side of customer so that the ladies of the town use our amenities, perhaps then I would go up in the world. It would be easier for me to accept Neil. I must get this straight in my mind in case he asks me again, he more than likely will make a second request for my company what can I say that will not be taken as a rebuff? I do like Neil, certainly I don't want to offend him, how can I do it without the formality that a visit would mean? Thinking long and hard about this and soon coming up with the answer, the thing was it would mean getting Aunt Polly, Ruby and Annie all focused on the plan she had been working on for years. That being getting the Parlour turned into a second shop. This would be for Ruby and Annie to work in with their needle and thread. They were so good at making items to wear and embroidery, they would soon be making items to sell and so make money for Aunt Polly. Thinking about Neil Emma must admit it was only because of him coming into the shop so regularly, that she had him as a friend there was no understanding between them. His asking her to tea had come straight out of the blue. Nothing will happen if I don't speak up and ask Aunt about altering the shop. I must have courage be positive that is how I must advance.

The next evening Aunt Polly said,

"I think we will have tea in the parlour Emma it is a nice evening we can watch the carriages go by. Have you noticed how the motor car has been on the road so much more lately? They frighten me every time they sound their hooter, I suppose we have to get used to the things as they progress, that's what they say, but the roads are not built for such contraptions, to cross the road these days is an experience, I fear going out on my own, with the road as busy as it is."

"Yes Aunt, a car only has to tootle its hooter and I jump out of my skin. Looking at the numbers that are increasing daily I suppose they are here to stay. I really don't know how the car and the carriages travel along together. Roads will have to be made bigger to accommodate the busy traffic. I prefer the horse and carriage it is far more elegant and romantic, ladies look elegant as they step down, with their men offering a hand. I wonder if one day I might live like that."

Emma was in her own little dream now,

amusing her inner self with the thought that would last.

"Do you want the table setting properly Aunty Polly?"

"Yes dear, it was one of your Uncles whims. When in the parlour all must be observed and set out with correct cutlery, napkins too. I didn't really think it was necessary but I did it to humour him. He was a grand partner in life the children didn't come so we looked after each other and were satisfied."

Emma could see her Aunt getting agitated so she changed the subject.

"Why, do you call this room, a parlour Aunt? She asked, really it is a reception lounge isn't it?"

"Yes you are right, replied her Aunt, it was a name that sort of got used and stuck to."

"You know Aunt we could make it into a totally different area."

"Yes, I suppose we could I have never given it much thought, it is all right as it isn't it?" Aunt Polly removed the pretty, pink tea cosy and poured the tea.

"Now you get on with your tea Emma you will have a bad tummy if you talk, as well as eat." Emma did as she was told, perhaps after tea she would bring the subject up again in small doses she thought not wanting to

offend. Tea was cleared, after a while they went back into the kitchen where there was a fire burning in the black- leaded grate. It was much cosier in there the light wasn't as stark. Emma preferred it to the parlour where there were too many drafts. She also had to be on her best behaviour in the parlour, which really she always was, but the relaxing fireside and the comfy well-worn chair; suited her so much better.

"Did I tell you about Ruby and Annie Aunt? They sent me some lovely things they had made themselves they are so good at sewing and embroidery. I have no doubt they will be snapped up when applying for work, turning their hand to all sorts of needlework they will be an asset."

"Ruby and Annie" declared Aunt surely they are not old enough to be offered for work. I know it is a few years since I saw them but I didn't think of them as young Ladies yet, goodness me how time goes by."

Emma softened her approach.

"They are lovely well behaved girls Aunt Polly. People who know them locally are always singing their praises. I don't suppose Mum wants to let them go, the time is approaching when it will only be fair for them to leave, as I did. The thing is, I came to

you, Mum knew I would be looked after, I wish you had a position for them, I don't suppose there is a chance of that is there?"

"I wouldn't have anything for them to do Aunt replied. We get along and see to almost everything between us, I thought you were happy in doing that?"

"I have a plan Aunt Polly, will you listen while I tell you? It has been growing in my mind for many years I feel it is the right time to see if it could work."

"Go on my dear you seem to be in control, I would like to know what your plan is, not that I can make any promises mind you." Aunt Polly sat back in her chair ready to listen.

"Of course, it involves Ruby and Annie and the work that they do to perfection. I thought given the chance you could open another kind of shop."

"I haven't the room for another shop Emma, even if I wanted to the Sweet Shop is doing so well I don't want to change it. I am surprised at you even thinking about changing the sweetshop."

"No Aunt I wouldn't do that, what I would do is change the parlour into a shop. Here Annie and Ruby would sell the work that they do, arranging to see the ladies of the town, doing individual sewing, embroidering to order, it

has good space and we could give it some finesse. It would be in line with the same shaped window, as my shop the only thing is it would attract a different class of customer. Actually, my thoughts go beyond that, I would take down the joining wall that separates the stairway from the parlour it is not a load-bearing wall it could be done without fuss.

Then in the spacious hallway, I would have three tables each having three chairs, all done in pink with pink frilled table clothes. Here we would serve tea and cake."

"Oh my word you have been busy in your thoughts. I don't know if I am up to all that change, we couldn't run it on our own and I don't want outsiders in. I know I am a bit set in my ways, but at this time of life I don't invite problems, you are so young, I suppose it is as nothing to you, I appreciate your thought, perhaps it would be to my benefit, you'll have to let me think about it for a day or two." Emma was thinking, now did I put that to my Aunt Polly correctly? I suppose as she says it is a lot for her to think about. Dear Aunt Polly of course was getting old, that fact was overlooked as she and Emma had a really, good relationship. Emma would leave it until her Aunt brought the subject up

again. Aunt Polly asked,
"What would you like for tea tomorrow Emma." Changing the subject carefully Aunt wanted to think in her own time, although she couldn't get the plan in her mind. It would mean alterations, giving up her parlour, yes she could find room for Ruby and Annie she had a double bedroom spare they would have to share but being Twins they always shared everything anyway, it was a fairly large room and would accommodate them both quite well for now, Aunt finally thought, that was enough thinking for the time being and picked her head up to hear Emma say,
"I don't mind a boiled egg and some bread and butter would suit me Auntie."
"Yes dear, that would do me fine too. I will make some fairy cakes and ice them and we will eat in the kitchen. The glowing fire, the aroma of whatever Aunt had been cooking lingering in the air Emma loved eating in the kitchen and then in the evening to go into her room and find a book, another day over and she had talked to Aunt about the alterations she wanted to commence. Satisfied and tired she read her book.

Chapter 7

Eating tea next day the conversation strayed into the shops again. Aunt herself brought it up and asked,
"What is it you intend to sell if we had the additional shop and how would we get supplies?"
"Oh, that will not be a problem it is plain to see I have not been keeping you up with news of Ruby and Annie. Aunty Polly you should

see the work they do at home. I don't mean housework, they are the finest embroidery and stitching girls, I have ever known. They make all kinds of things from a plain piece of cloth to the finished piece. They sell the things now but only make to order because at Mums there is just not the space, the products are fit to be offered in a shop window. I will go upstairs and fetch a small item they did for me not long ago." Rushing away in her enthusiasm, Emma flew upstairs. Aunt was listening it was getting exciting and it was Auntie not Emma that had brought the conversation up.

"Here look, Emma exclaimed, it is only a small piece but you can see the stitching is of fine quality, I would wear anything that they had made." She held across to her Aunt a round pink sundries holder, such as ladies have on the dressing table placing odd bottles of perfume, compacts of cream in them, they were elegant and very feminine. Aunt took the item scrutinised it under the light it was of very high standard. The frills and ruffs looked neat and stitched to perfection the colour also pleased her, pink with satin ribbon in a deeper pink for the ruffle, a fine satin material for the rushing. Layer upon layer of fine work now completed fit for

ladies as Emma had said. Aunt Polly was very surprised the girls had grown up without her even noticing and it seems doing such fine work. Now she was wondering what her dear Sister would think, as she hadn't taken a great deal of notice of the girls.

The parlour was now going to be transformed into something special, yes she would give this some thought. Shall I give Emma a full head of steam and tell her to get on with completing the idea?

Aunt Polly hadn't the time to brood over past events, the sorrow of losing her Husband trying to remember only the good things she found that her mind was full to overflowing. Now with the new prospect that had been offered to her through Emma, Aunt was being drawn in to approve of her Niece's plans, this was really beyond Emma's years but she was such an enterprising girl, if she thought it would work, it probably would. Then Aunt Polly started to realise she wouldn't have an "input," again she started to brood, what could she do that would be saleable? She wasn't very adept in anything; she would talk it over with Emma. There were so many things to talk over she would have to give Emma some time off to simply draw out her plan and then they could both decide what to do. Drowsy now, although it was still early Aunt was ready for bed, she had thought hard all day it had wearied her, Aunt Polly filled the stone hot water bottle retiring for the night. Emma too was very excited she had gone up even earlier than her Aunt she flung herself on the bed thinking about the brand new scheme about to be put into progress. Time was right for it, the sweet shop had taken off very well and in fact they were becoming established in the area. Everyone knew where "Aunty Polly's Parlour" was, finding the tempting sweets and chocolate hard to resist, the pictures on boxes displayed giving much pleasure. The cake displays a delight.

"Goodnight Emma is there anything you need before I go to bed," called her Aunt.

"No, I am so exhilarated I won't be going to sleep yet. I will put a few thoughts as to where this plan should go. I will tell you in the morning if I have come up with anything special."

"Well don't lie there all night getting cold and not sleeping, I have a hot water bottle to take with me, should I get you one dear?" Hot water bottle! I should say not for Emma was on cloud nine and raring to go as are all young people with a future in mind.

Neil had resumed his normal time to come and chat in the shop, Emma was glad of that, but didn't want any closer arrangement not at the moment, the immediate future also her deeply thought out "way to go" had to be as perfect as she knew how. She had to give Ruby and Annie all the guidance she could, they wouldn't know very much of how to treat Gentry. The way to conduct themselves in public was important too. Emma had taken on so much to do even Aunt Polly was looking to Emma for guidance. Waking up at 7.30am, the previous night reflected on her mood, she had a vivacious smile on her face, happiness shone from her, this hadn't been a dream she had talked to her Aunt and she seemed to be in favour, or was it Emma that had conjured the thing all up? Was she going to be disappointed at the end of the day? She was sincerely hoping not. Emma pulled her clothes on quickly, joining Aunt for a cup of tea she tried to imagine what the tables and cloths would be like in the new area and would everything she had considered come to plan?

"Aunt Polly I must ask you, I am so eager to hear you say yes to my proposal, has my idea shocked you, or do you think it could work? I can assure you I will give it my all. Ruby and

Annie will also be doing their absolute best to make a good impression." Aunt Polly replied,
"That is the trouble what can I do to be a part of this adventure, at the moment I can't think of a thing. I am not very good at sewing I do what I have to and am always glad when it is done. All night I have thought, to come up with nothing! In fact I am ashamed of myself knowing so little." Emma smiled.
"Well if that isn't an understatement, there are lots of things, you can do." Aunt was quick with her reply,
"Tell me what then? I would be happier if I was going to join in and sell something I had made myself."
"You would be so involved Auntie, wait until I tell you about the colours and the name of the new shop. This I tell you right now, who knits the tea cosies for our own use? Yes of course, you do a very good job there are many people that would buy them for their own use, or as a gift. They could order so that the colour choice would be individual. They could be packaged with six teaspoons in a pink lined box or lining could match the chosen cosy colour. They would make a lovely gift. Also you could make the pots of tea as they were ordered; we could have a pink scene going on. Ladies of the Gentry

love that kind of thing. I can assure you there would be very few dull moments for you I have only touched on the things you, me, Ruby and Annie could get involved in. Do enjoy the moment Aunt Polly, we would be a team and have such fun." Being swept up in Emma's enthusiasm Polly was beginning to see a realistic picture. At her age, Aunt Polly had to melt to the idea. She was like putty in her Nieces' hands. Emma had put her case so matter of fact and it was hard not to get involved. Yes, she could do the tea cosies and serve tea, she fancied herself doing that, her homely manner made her right for the job. She was going to be a part of this exclusive plan, she could see that quite clearly now. A feeling inside of her trickled through, was this exuberance passed on with Emma's excited way? She guessed so it was a very long time ago that this feeling was part of her and she found she liked it. Emma had come back into the kitchen to speak to her Aunt saying,

"Is there anything I can do for you Aunt? The Shop is all neat and tidy it is early so perhaps we could go to look at the space we intend to use. Of course, that is if you will let me, it would mean a lot to me if I knew you approved. I could plan out in more detail and

lose less sleep." Emma smiled at herself. Polly caught the glance as if to say, come on Auntie it could all be done in the wink of an eye, if only you will let me get on with it." The two of them had this bond of trust, there wasn't much Aunt Polly didn't know about Emma including her forthright manor, her go getting ways, what is more she approved. So Aunt went into the shop area to see what was going to happen, because she knew by now she was indeed going to say yes, why shouldn't she enjoy the experience? Put her mind in whole-heartedly and let it happen. Emma knew she had her Aunt's undivided attention she looked wistful, would Aunt say yes?

"Ooh! Auntie Polly please let me hear you say yes there is no place we couldn't reach if we did it all together."

"Yes, I can't think of any nicer girls to come here, they won't be like strangers, but my Sister Ada has to approve I don't want her to think I am stealing her family away from her. Ada will have to come to stay twice a year. She could sleep in my room either in with me, or I would put a bed up especially for her, my room is quite large. I could give her some private space for the clothes that she brings with her, it would be nice for all of us, and we

could go on a couple of outings together. I have never seen enough of Ada, she has been so busy with her family, now they are growing up it will be a fine opportunity to get to know her all over again" Auntie Polly had gone into one of those moments that carry you away with the sweep of emotion and delight; nothing could stop them now and again they were in this together. A future lay ahead; wise old Father Time beckoned them forward.

Chapter 8

Their plans soon were put into practice Emma could see the shape of what was to come. The staircase could now be seen through the open arch being very impressive. Soon the builders would have done their job and it would be time for Emma and Aunt to finish it off decoratively. This made a splendid opportunity for Emma; she jumped at the opportunity of putting a personal touch to finish the job.
"I have to say Aunt it has all gone along very

well, now we can shop for the tables and chairs then the carpet are you excited?"

"Yes, but not like you I shall be glad enough to get the whole change up and running. To be honest with you Emma I didn't foresee the cost of it all." Emma's face had dropped, the truth be told she had no money in-put. She hadn't thought of her Aunt and the bill's that kept coming. Aunt noticed Emma go quiet and said,

"Don't worry Emma all will be found it is just the time it is taking to get settled, I need to get things balanced, tomorrow we will go and order the furnishing and see if we can get the carpet we want." I find the changes exciting. Now please dear let us go into the kitchen for a break I am exhausted. She fanned her face with her hand, to emphasise the fact. Emma, softened to her Aunt's request, she did tend to forget her Aunt carried a few years. I must remember to take things a little slower in future Emma chastised her own behaviour knowing that Aunt needed time. Slower though wasn't in Emma's vocabulary she lived always planning tomorrow thinking today was almost over tomorrow was yet to come. Sometimes she was even ahead of herself and had to correct the speed her mind travelled at and rest. The kettle had boiled the

pink pot was filled and completed with its cosy. The snack of toast sent its aroma around the kitchen. There was this slot in time that had a natural peace, nothing disturbed the two of them, the fire burning bright, the butter slowly melting on the toasted bread this you could not buy, it was priceless, they were priceless the whole situation was of reality and love. The respect they had for each other commanded happiness. Just that, it is what it was in the purest sense of the word. Sipping the hot tea and crunching the toast, Emma was the first one to break the spell.

"Let's have the whole theme in pink, very feminine pink parasols to hang over the tables and pink tablecloths too. This evening I am going to get my letters written, one to my Mum and Dad one to the girls. I must tell them their future is with you and me, explain what you want them to do. I dare not tell them earlier because I needed to see how you felt, now though everything is to go ahead, I shall deliver the exciting news." Emma's words tumbled out, the time had come, her heart beat a double rhythm in the knowledge of what was to happen. Loving her Sisters, she would be their shield against the world and help in all that she could. She felt

nothing could stop her now, with Ruby and Annie beside her, and her Aunt to see all was well, her own constant enthusiasm and the future bright to be walked towards with confidence. It was meant to be, she could hardly wait, a new life for the four of them was being created, dear Aunt Polly their reliable and loving Aunt. Emma sat until midnight writing the letters to her Mum Dad and the Twins. Her own excitement on the page, she told them of all the things they had discussed. The reason for being asked a bit before they were fourteen was explained. There were things Emma wanted them to stitch before coming over. Finally she was so tired she undressed and got into bed. She was quite sure she wouldn't sleep things were running through her mind non-stop but when her head rested on the pillow she went out like a light into a deep sleep.

Next morning she was glad that she had. The daylight had brought another chance to get a bit nearer her goal setting herself the task, a deal not to be entered in lightly. Aunt was down first getting the black kettle over the fire she greeted Emma,

"Did you get your letters written Emma?"

"Yes, I did it took me a while but I have them ready for posting now. I may go to the Post

Office in the dinner break today I want them to get off right away because Aunt Polly, I can't wait for the replies." They both grinned at each other. Finally, something was being sorted. A strange contentment was written in their faces and this was really going to happen. It was no longer just Emma's mind full of thoughts, her Aunt knew all about it and was chipping in doing the planning alongside her dear Niece and she was enjoying every minute, thinking she only had her late years to come with all the trials it brought. She was an old lady but she wasn't feeling so, she was invigorated at the prospect of new things to come, being part of the newness gave her life itself. No longer wanting to get her "Will" sorted but seeing if she had enough money to carry through these recent plans, keeping her nieces in work, paying them pocket money, Aunt Polly had her work cut out financially. It would take support while the new shop was gradually getting established. To get the business going would take time, nothing happens overnight, yet nothing happens at all if the thought wasn't put into action. Polly was proud to be a part. Never having her own children, how lucky she was that Ada's girls were going to be part of her life. She mustn't forget Ada as if she would! There was a fine line between Daughter and Niece she must see that she didn't cross it. Giving Ada due reward for the clever girls that she had allowed to come to stay and work beside their Aunt Polly and Emma. Ada, Polly's dear Sister always she wanted that to be so. Aunt had no intention of coming between Ada and the Twins, always remembering the job of early teaching had taken a great deal of time out of Ada and Albert's married life. Ada and Albert had taught their Daughters how to live how to be fair and how to love. Aunt Polly only hoped she could carry on in the same manner.

Chapter 9

Post! Ruby and Annie shouted through the house, it looks like our Emma's letters." It always brought a thrill of excitement when Emma wrote to them telling of all the different things in her new life, wishing they too could get a position half as good as Emma's. Nearly fourteen they wanted their independence girls at that age all had to find jobs it was the thing to do. Finding the right one was a puzzle for girls. Parents wanting the best, wanting them safe wanting them happy, it was a very anxious time. Mum could hear the call of delight and knew it must be a letter.

"Is there one for me? Bring it in here please I will read it when I have done this job," said Mum as she folded the clothes from the line ready for ironing. She was particular about her washing and ironing. Even if the clothes they afforded were not very special, sometimes from the jumble sale, they had to be presentable.

They always were, being good with a needle and thread Ruby and Annie often made their own dresses. They would go to market with

Mum to choose the fabric; of course it meant the dresses cost a fraction of the price that they would be in a ladies dress shop. So really it left the boys to buy for, their shirts had to be bought economically, they didn't have many, boys though don't count the cost for clothes and as long as they fit and are comfortable, that was it. Trousers had to be patched to last as long as they could. They were always clean and tidy. What more does a boy want! Grinned Mum laughing to herself as she said,
"What more do I want, my family are the world to me."
Ruby and Annie could not contain themselves any longer they burst into the kitchen.
"Mum, have you read your letter yet? Oh stop folding the clothes and read. We can't wait for your answer to Emma, go on Mum, go on they shouted excitedly."
What can be as important that won't wait a minute? I am nearly done and then I will read the letter." Mum knew that something had occurred out of the ordinary. What was in the letter to get the girls all fired up like this?
"Pass it to me, there will be no peace until I know just what you are talking about."
Reading the letter Ada's eyes filled with tears.

It was good news she knew that, but her girls would have to be parted from her, she was trying to put off the evil day. She had hoped to find some work for them as Seamstresses, locally, so that they didn't have to leave home. Their eagerness at reading their letters and the enthusiasm from them to comply had dropped a bombshell in Mum's lap. Knowing she would never be able to talk them out of the adventure that this offered, what is more Mum knew in her heart it was wonderful of Aunt Polly to offer such a place of work, rather they went there than to some other vacancy she knew nothing about. They would be looked after Emma had nothing but good things to say about her own position. Mum would talk to Dad they would come to a decision.

"Mum please say we can go, we never dreamed of having a chance like our Emma now it seems we have, we are going to do what we love most, our stitching, making things to sell in the display window and shelves, all part of what we would be doing a shop to sell our own work, isn't it exciting. Please Mum please," they chanted.

"Now don't press me any-more, I shall speak to Father before I say another word. I am not saying it isn't a wonderful chance for you but

I didn't want you to leave home so soon. It is inevitable that you would have to live in at Aunt Polly's, I don't mind that really but I shall miss you so, my dear girls have you any idea how I love you both? It was Ruby and Annie's turn to fill up with tears. They hadn't thought about the downside of the proposition they had been caught up in the moment and all the good it would bring. Another thing they noticed, Mum had called Dad, Father which was a serious thing to do, it was only high days and holidays that Dad was called Father, bringing a sort of solemnity to the idea. Dad wouldn't be in until after work in the evening, this would be when the subject would be discussed so the girls knew they had to make themselves scarce not flit about like a couple of moths caught in a flame. They had to show the responsible side of themselves so to impress Father.

Chapter 10

"What do you think Emma, does this fit in with what you wanted the tearoom to be like?" Aunt was showing Emma a picture from a coloured magazine.
"Well, yes" Emma replied, but it hasn't got the class that ours will have, there will be only one in our design and we will be unique."
"Sometimes Emma I would like to creep into that mind of yours."
"I see it all very clearly Aunt, if you can't stretch your imagination to see it with me. You will have to wait for the end result I assure you there is not disappointment to foresee." Now they waited for the return letters, they were slow coming. Pouring tea, Aunt Polly commented on the fact that no letter had arrived.
"I do hope everything is all-right at Ada's, I would have thought we should have a reply by now. I suppose taking their time is the right thing to do we don't want any, "ifs and, buts" do we? It has to be taken seriously they are not a couple of kids any more, their decision has to be permanent, I can't see

them turning the offer down but I will be glad when we get the replies and the thing is settled."

"Don't worry Aunty it will be that they all haven't chosen the right course to take. Discussions take forever in my family, I remember my turn. I thought they were never going to give me the go ahead but finally they did and I have never been happier. Be patient, it will be all-right you'll see." Emma reassuring with confidence put Polly's mind at rest they continued their tea together. Yes, Emma was right, commencing in Ada's kitchen there was a lot of argumentative persuasion going on. To have Ada's girls leave home for work was almost too much, Ada only had the boys at home then. She loved them, but couldn't hold the same kind of conversations as she did with the girls, thinking deep into what was about to develop her mind was at a crossroad. Emma had got on so well at Polly's, she knew Polly looked after her so she would with Ruby and Annie it was just that she would be lost without them. Surely, she said to herself this is selfish where else would give them such a good position in a good home? She certainly knew the answer to that. Now to speak to Albert he was not enjoying this fuss. Thinking now more of

Albert than Ruby and Annie, Ada thought, I will speak to him tonight, she whispered it to herself.

"Hello Albert tea won't be long, poached eggs on toast tonight dear."

Albert looked up, Ada's attitude had changed.

"That's fine Ada have the family eaten then?"

"They ate early tonight, I wanted to have a talk with you without them being here, don't worry I am not going to read the riot act," she said with a grin .Albert said,

"I suppose then it is about our girls and their offer of a position with Polly. You know in your heart Ada it is the best way for them to do their final growing up. Polly won't get all the good side she will have to watch them, keep them safe from harm and tutor them. As their Mum, you have done your part, loved them, always will, taught them cooking, scrubbing, taking care of things, the difference between good and bad, which is the tutoring that stays for life, now etched in their memories."

"Oh Albert you know me so well, it has been the most awful time for me. I think now though hearing you say it aloud I have made my decision. We will go forward and accept even now I can't believe I am saying this."

Ada extended her hand across the table to give Albert's hand a loving squeeze.

"I am sure this will cheer you up." Albert stood up from the table with importance, drawing himself up, to bring his shoulders high.

"I my dear have been paying attention to my part of this plan."

"Don't be daft; you haven't got a part in this plan." Ada went quite coy,

"Go on then tell me it had better be good I know you when you get one of your tales going." The atmosphere had lightened, so Albert announced,

"I have been having driving tuition."

"You drive! Exclaimed Ada, you haven't got a car."

"I know it sounds odd but I think you would be happier about Ruby and Annie if you could see them regularly, if I learn to drive a motor car I could take you over there no problem."

"May I ask, what about the car? We will never be able to afford one."

"Not afford one no, but I can hire one for a day. We could see that the boys were looked after. Off we would go. It needn't be, just to go to Polly's, a picnic hamper in the back, the world would be our Oyster and yes, I am

serious. It is time we spent an hour or two on our own, the family has had to take precedence all these years. Now with Ruby and Annie going I see it as a blessing. You could see the sewing shop and all that goes with it, the things that were for sale made by our girls that would make you very proud Ada dear. I am not saying this will happen overnight this new-fangled gadget called a car will take a bit of getting used to. It is a golden opportunity though, my boss is a very pioneering man he has been set on getting this car since the first one took to the road in 1908. It has been a huge success in many parts of the world and there are millions of Ford 8's on the road now. My boss says as soon as he can afford another one he is going to get it, then hire it out for the odd day or so, a way of getting the general public to take to driving a motor car. I think he is very forward thinking, that's why I say it is not out of the question for us to own one of our own in the future. First, I must learn to drive, I have a good Teacher and I am determined so I will. The girls will be earning their own living I can start a new saving fund, shock all the neighbours! It is very good of my boss to let me have his car to learn in. The Ford 8 is very small but has four seats and is black. It is revolutionary in what it does. I am quite proud of myself learning to drive it; things are looking up Ada my dear." Ada was quite taken aback, enterprise in her Albert! She could hardly believe it; she would go along with it and thought it would help to take away the sting that had recently been delivered about Ruby and Annie.

Quietly doing her housework, Ada began to reflect about what Albert had said. She had never thought about her life in any other way, all her life contained was the children, housework, cooking, making sure that everything was as good as she could make it. When the children had illnesses she would always be at their side, never thought anything of it. Now Albert had shown her there was a way of getting to know each other all over again. She felt her attention slip away from the present and look to the future. Dear Albert he had to take place at the bottom of the list whilst Ada got on with the business at hand, always a full day, tired enough to not take notice of Albert. He was the mainstay bringing in the money they lived on. It was taken for granted he would always be there. She smiled what would she have done without him? He never complained, now he had given her this picture of a new beginning she loved him, what a wonderful thing to do.

"Ada," he whispered breaking into her daydream.

"Come on tell me what do you think? Are you going to allow Ruby and Annie to go to Polly's? We can follow our hearts then we won't have to worry about them going to some stranger's house in service. I haven't been happy thinking that is where they may land up, Polly has given them a great deal and as I have said we will go and see Ruby and Annie as often as we can." He slid his arm around Ada and kissed her forehead instilling confidence and reliability.

"See, all that worry, it never needed to be, dearest Ada, you have me by your side, so I tell you all will be well, you'll see."

He sat down in his old armchair and pulled Ada on to his lap. Togetherness an altogether beautiful entity, between Ada and Albert all problems would be sorted, one knew the other's mind even in advance, they had covered much ground and settled no fast rule, helping each other day after day, Teaching their children as they went along life's twisting road.

Chapter 11

"Still no post," said Emma, going through the letters in her hand. Emma was annoyed
"It is about time I heard from Mum, surely there could not be any obstacles in the way. It is a splendid opportunity not one to be missed, most girls would be thrilled at the prospect put before Ruby and Annie, where is that letter?" Aunty was remarking in the same way, also thinking why? Aunt said,
"We will give them one more week then we will write again, it is not like Ada to keep you in the dark she usually promptly replies but I suppose this is quite a big issue for them. I mustn't rush her I suppose if it were me that had the girls I would take a little time too."
Aunt stood up knocking the bits of crumb off her skirt, time for getting some work done. Emma had to go and open the Sweet Shop, and take off the brown paper from the window display. That was all she had done when Neil walked in.
"Good morning my dear" Neil presented himself as he always did in fine form.
"Now this week I would like a change for Mum. She wants some handpicked

chocolates, she has some of her friends calling they discuss the latest fashion and always seem to know when something in that line is going to change. The big thing I have overheard them saying during the last two weeks is that skirts are to get shorter just to show off the High Buttoned Boots. I must say Emma, don't think me cheeky but when you get up on the small steps for a jar off the top shelf your skirt rises, your elegant Boots are very nice what a shame to hide them away!"Emma felt her Colour rise but accepted the compliment gracefully.

"Do you want to choose the chocolates?"

"No you will be better than me I will chose only the ones that look good with the frills and fancies on them, yours will be an educated choice and you will know what is best for taste." Reaching a sizeable box putting in some pink tissue paper Emma began to fill and make look pretty; she certainly had a way of making the best of the chocolate, the box was filled and looking grand. The pink tissue paper arranged in frills and pleats as only Emma could do.

"Anything more today, kind sir?" she playfully said.

"There is a lot more I could ask of you dear Emma, but for now I will be about my

business. You are getting a small queue, I am in your way, see you next week." Off he went, chirpy a bounce in his step, his friendship with Emma still in fine fettle.

Her customers were three children spending a fortune, one had cinder toffee 1d worth and the other two chose 1d worth liquorice and broken bits of toffee. They were all pleased with their choice. On leaving Emma gave them some broken bits of different assortment, they gave her a lovely smile in return.

The builder had finished so Emma with Aunt Polly took the opportunity of closing the Sweet Shop to go and look at furniture shops the other side of town.

Today it was the table and chairs that they would be most interested in. It was a long time since Aunt had bought any furniture of any kind. Emma well! She had never bought any at all. So, they didn't know really how to buy, they decided if they liked the item both of them had to agree. They would keep it as simple as they could and go on looking somewhere else until finding something they could not refuse then they would buy.

"Auntie do you like the look of these chairs? Emma was pointing in the direction.

They appeal to me I like the rounded backs

on them, they are a replica of the curve in the archway what do you think?"

"They are nice aren't they, I like the cane backs and seats let me sit on one." Emma also tried the chair. Aunt said,

"Oh yes, they are I think just what we need, how clever of you to pick them out, we will have nine. Now see if there is a table that will go with them, a round table to keep the idea of the curve of course, we will want three chairs per table."

Apparently, there were only three of that kind in the store but six more could be ordered.

"Here we go Emma that is our first purchase towards the tea shop."

Polly looked pleased with herself she had mastered the art of buying, bartered with the shop owner as they wanted three tables and nine chairs and could he give them a small discount? To her amazement, she got her discount.

"Emma, I am ready for home, my feet and legs feel as though they don't belong to me. This shopping trip has given me insight and it is flat shoes and thick hose next time."

Smiling at their inadequate physique they went towards the horse drawn buggies to take them home and a delightful day was had it would seem! Getting home the kettle was put on to boil. Before they even took their coats off, they sat down, hoping the kettle would quickly boil for tea. Aunt looked at Emma saying,

"I hope we have made the right choice Emma. Looking at the new work done today, I can't think we could have done better. It is the carpets that will set it all off, I want that to go with the rich wood tone of the stairway with pink as the colour it is to be set against. I would think it would be good to have a complimentary background, solid with rich deep colour tones do you agree?"

Emma, setting the table, really wishing the subject got set aside just for a while said, "How can it be wrong, Aunty we have both given it a good deal of thought. We don't want anyone advising us, we want it to be our own idea coming to life as we planned. I must admit, it is more work than I thought it would be, that is because I have no yardstick to gauge it by, alterations in my home were none existent I have just picked up design in what I myself go for, I like curves not straight lines, personal choice that is all." She went to the cutlery drawer saying,

"Do we want knife and fork? Or shall we have a spoon and boiled egg. I really don't mind it would be less washing up wouldn't

it?"Emma shared in her Aunt's weariness not wanting to show her own weakness, goodness me there was a lifetime of years between them. Aunt needed a soft chair and cushion to rest her head, oh the weary eyes. Yes, Emma's eyes too were sore not to be wondered at, as it seemed they both had looked at most of the Town Window Displays the concentration of that alone had caused the tired feeling they both had. Emma was feeling downright worn out but didn't want to show it, so she said,

"I am going to bed early if you don't mind I am reading a book and would like to get to the next chapter. I think the girl in it is going to get a proposal, I want to see how her boyfriend does it, I hope he goes down on one knee, I hope she says yes. I like the man, the girl is a bit like me and I want a happy conclusion." Emma smiled giving her Aunt a hug off she went; knowing the peace she had left behind would be appreciated.

Chapter 12

The post came next morning Emma rushed in with it excitedly.
"This is a letter from the girls Aunt Polly I recognise the handwriting" she gave it to her Aunt.
"At last, this is what we have been waiting for." Opening the letter, she read aloud.

"Dear Aunt Polly,
Thank you Auntie Polly, we are so happy to say we have permission and we can't wait to join you and Emma. Delighted that we will be stitching, quite prepared to start making stock for the opening. Do you think we could make our own dresses? You advised us on a dusky pink with black lace at the collar and cuffs. These could be made as removable for washing, if we made two sets there would be always one to wear that is pristine crisp and pleasing to the eye. Please tell us if that suits what you require. I can't tell you the nights Ruby and I have lost sleep talking about the day we start. Leaving home won't be as bad as when Emma left because we have each other. We will miss Mum and Dad of course

but guess what Dad has told us, he is learning to drive a motor car. He will hire a car for coming to see us often. Of course, it has to be with your permission Aunty Polly." The letter went on to say all the niceties and ended in

Much love Ruby and Annie xx

Emma pleased and smiling said,
"That is just what we wanted to know I will be much more settled now. I have been worrying they were not going to come, it is I that put this all before you Aunt not thinking what would happen if they didn't want to come or indeed, if they weren't allowed to come. I must say I am relieved, now it is just a case of getting the final speed, so we can get the carpet down. The bow window in itself is ideal when it is dressed it should look very unique which is just what we wanted, something different. Oh! Aunty Polly your Parlour is about to become transformed, everyone is going to be looking, then hopefully buying, I am sure I am not mistaken." Emma's thrill was genuine the dream had been in the back of her mind for a long time, now it was about to become reality.

In the Sweet Shop, Emma was busy,

sometimes she thought there should be an assistant to help her but it was unpredictable flows of customers all or none. When she did her supplies list to restock, it seemed she would have the shop full calling Aunt Polly to assist for a short while. Auntie Polly though was no Sales Lady she wanted to be done before she had started. She was quite out of touch with the commercial side. She would if pressed help Emma do the books, under duress, then pop herself away as soon as was possible. She tried and her mind put to it managed a good job, it wasn't through choice though. Emma only called her if it was really, necessary.

At least Aunt Polly recognised that this was all part of the shop worker's job, it wasn't all looking pretty and smiling at the customer. Emma gave it her all, she was constantly reminding herself of the power and trust Aunty Polly had placed in her allowing her to do things in her own individual way. It had been the making of Emma like so would be for Ruby and Annie, wouldn't it be lovely when they could see each other talk together, exchange confidences go for a walk about town or sit in the park, all the things that Emma could not do on her own. Women didn't walk about on their own it was not the thing to do, so it took Aunty to chaperone Emma wherever she went. It did mean settling down in home quite a lot. Loving her books, or talking about things long gone, she enjoyed Aunt's company. Sometimes though she longed to be free to walk and run, to let her hair down to blow in the wind and discover her own private world that no one may enter. One day she said to herself.

Chapter 13

Ruby and Annie collecting themselves together after the excitement and suspense of not knowing if they were going to be allowed to go to Aunt Polly's, had
quietened down a bit. They tried not to be a nuisance, especially as they knew Mum and Dad were trying to come to terms with the idea.
"We had better be on our best behaviour Annie, I think it is very important to show Mum that we are grown up and can conduct ourselves the way she would want us to, we don't want her worrying all the time."
"I have been thinking just the same thing Ruby of course we know how to behave. I suppose Mum thinks when we are not around her or Dad we will not conduct ourselves as ladies should. To be fair we are only just of age I, like you feel entirely responsible to carry on and become the help that Aunt Polly wants us to be, I am very glad we are not going to strangers to be shown how to do service work, the very thought repels me!"
"Yes, me too, to do our sewing is the best thing we could earn our keep with, because

we love to do it, we are very lucky aren't we Annie?"

"When do you think Mum will let us get the material for our pink dresses? I can't wait to get started on them." Annie couldn't contain the smile that spread across her face it was infectious, Ruby too was happy.

"I think Aunt Polly is going to shop for the material herself she wants a particular dusky pink. I don't know whether it will be with summer or winter in mind, maybe we will have the two and wear them according to the weather you are either perished or cooked, anyway the weather never does what you think it will so we will leave that to Aunty." They sat stitching satin rose buds, first hemming the satin then curling it by hand, a very painstaking job, they always had a few in hand, keeping them in an old sweet tin with a pretty picture of a Lady in a crinoline dress and a huge feathered hat shown on it, a parasol too held daintily in her hand. The Twins liked to use these pretty tins or boxes it made life a little brighter, usually the tins had been kept having been full at one time and given to the family as gifts of chocolates or biscuits.

"I feel quite a chill said Ruby I must go and get another warm cardigan on. It must be

talking about the weather because I wasn't feeling cold before that, how a suggestion brings about the fact."

"Bring mine as well please you have set me off." They were so much alike people said they didn't know how to tell one from the other. Emma and the family never ever got them mixed up. They each had their own personality it was close though very close.

"Let's go and see if Mum wants us for anything, I think she was going to do some baking today, she likes us to knead the bread, she says it is getting too hard work for her alone." All the bread was baked at home, different type's batches, cottage loaves and roll to take to work; the house was permeated with the wholesome mouth-watering aroma. To fetch a tray of newly baked rolls from the oven was very special they looked as good as a work of art. Mum would let them take one and then spread it with butter eating it while really it was too hot to bear in their mouths. Mmmm delicious! The rest would be laid out in rows leaning against one another; this kept the crust crispy and allowed the roll to cool. On the days when they were freshly baked, they had them for tea with lovely homemade strawberry jam, something that was the envy of their friends. They asked their Mums

"Why don't you make our bread like Aunty Ada?" Mums soon pushed off the request it was time consuming, a required knowledge that they had not been taught. Finding it quite annoying when their Children requested them to make bread, of course Ada was aware of this fact so it became special to have homemade bread. Her whole family delighted in the fact, there wasn't much in the baking line Ada couldn't do. She made meat pies once a week. Buying a cheaper cut of shin of beef, it would taste the very best when the meat had been simmered slowly tenderising. It gave off a beefy aroma as it cooked. Sometimes it was cooked in the fire grate oven, sometimes in a saucepan on the open fire, whatever way it was done the resulting meat pie was always ate to the last crumb of pastry that is what Mum and Dad called economical no waste whatsoever.

"I thought I had been deserted Mum declared, seeing Ruby and Annie coming into the kitchen. I suppose the smell of bread enticed you in here, it won't be long." Opening the oven taking one roll out tapping it at the bottom, this is how she could tell if it was ready to come out of the oven. The sound it made by tapping the bread would be hollow, it was then declared baked then it was all

fetched out of the oven. Mum knew an awful lot of things, secretly her girls wanted to grow up just like her. She was very much loved. There was no way their bond could be severed it was written in stone, come what may Mum would always be the most loved in the land.

"Is it just bread you are making today," asked Ruby, are we having it for tea?"

"I just feel like new bread and some soup or stew, said Annie."

Mum chimed in.

"All right, it is a wonder you didn't smell that cooking as well, yes, it is rabbit stew. Dad's mate bagged a couple and didn't want two, lucky for us."

The rabbit stew had got to that stage when the cooking of it cast a savoury sweetness all over the kitchen. That and the baking bread made a unique combination.

"Did you say it wouldn't be long Mum?" Annie said, not knowing how to wait.

"Well not long, it means if you set the table and Ruby helps with this washing up we will have it ready when the boys get in, about half an hour I would think."

"Do you want me to make the gravy thickening?" Ruby asked. They liked the gravy thickened with some corn flour and

gravy browning mixed first into a basin with cold water and then adding to the stew stirring all the time it was easy. Mum said you would get lumpy gravy if you neglected to keep stirring. They wanted smooth gravy not lumpy. Now they were all busy in the kitchen each doing the selected job. This is what Mum would miss the most, the togetherness that was theirs. Come on Ada, none of that she said to herself, a tear springing from nowhere. Going over, the same ground is not going to solve anything. It was all pretence Ada was going to miss her girls tremendously. Therefore she turned keeping tears at bay back to the job in hand. The dinner was served out in time to meet the approval of the boys. The time they spent together as a family around the table Ada thought of as important, many things came to light in the banter that was passed from one to the other.

"Don't talk while you are eating." Mum knew that statement very well, yet at the table they all shared their views, it kept them in touch, didn't seem to do any harm.

A warm relaxed atmosphere went a long way towards the flow of conversation, little things came into focus like whose turn it was to use the bath and would the boys get it in from outside where it hung on a big rusty old nail.

Chapter 14

Aunty Polly was standing admiring the new alterations.
"Doesn't it look splendid Emma the new tables fit in with the decor very well don't they?" The tables they had chosen were round with a display of three ornate legs at the base rising to a central support, the chairs fitted underneath being the same colour polished wood as the wood arched frame on the back of the chairs. They were both well

pleased. The staircase also blended in, it all looked very smart. All they wanted now was a carpet.

"What colour carpet shall we have Emma?"
"Looking at the whole scene Emma said,
"Auntie, I don't think brown is going to do anything very special. I know you wanted brown but it is too close to the colour of the wood, if you really want my opinion how about a deep rich red? Perhaps a little pattern involving browns and pinks. It would have to wear well as it will have to deal with a lot of tread. Think about it, we may not get the exact colours but we could look around to see what is available."
"I knew you would know Emma you are so good at matching even in the Sweet Shop the jars enhance one another. Red also is a good warm colour we will go and shop for it tomorrow, I know a couple of places close to town, for now though I am going to get some sleep I will say goodnight Emma. Don't lie awake all night with your plans, you too want rest." Closing the shop just for the morning they headed out to town. Afternoons were busiest so they would be back to open the shop again.
"Shall we have a quick dinner time, a sandwich in town eh?" Aunt said,

"I do want to get the last details sorted it has been a decent while since we were all straight. Ruby and Annie will think it is taking forever." Emma reassured her Aunt

"I keep them in touch though, you will know from your letters they are getting on with pieces to go into the window. They have made their dresses so all is coming along fine. In fact, the exciting bit is when we actually open with the new fabrics and embroidery shop. It is getting near I would like to have the girls over here before we open, I want them to get their bearings and feel confidant before having to face the Public. It will be an ordeal for them. Aunt replied

"I truly want the Twins to feel loved and welcomed. Our Ada, will want to know that the work we have for them to do is within the realms of their capability. I will do all I can to assure her."

"Mum and Dad trust you Aunt, otherwise they would not have allowed Ruby and Annie to come to you, they are very conscious of the girls welfare. So you need not worry on that score. Annie and Ruby can't wait to start so all will be well.

Chit chatting Aunt told Emma,

"I am going the whole hog taking the carpet to match all the way into the far corners of

the hall and on into the tea room following through on to the embroidery floor stopping only at the edge of the Sweet Shop, which I don't think needs to be carpeted. It will make the space seem larger. I think that would be lovely it will be pricey though, in for a Penny in for a Pound, I am not going to have next best I want the best." Aunt lengthened her neck and her chin in the air, this was personal pride, and nothing was going to stop her now.

An early start good light for choosing colour, they felt they must make a choice today the shop needed opening, the money calculated for the renovation was fast slipping away. It was time to sell not buy so that expense could even up a bit.

"Hey! I like that," said Emma, pulling at Auntie Polly's sleeve for her to look in the shop window." It wasn't quite what they had set out to get, but it was very sophisticated. The deep burgundy carpet took centre place in the shop window.

"The dusky pink accessories, table cloths, light fittings, pieces to sell in the window would all dance off that very well, let's go in to see what it feels like and how much it will cost. It isn't going to be cheap I can tell that from just looking at it. We can always say no

if we don't think we can afford it."
In the shop a young Gentleman came towards them smiling and polite he said,
"Can I help you Madam," Aunt answered,
"Yes you can tell us the price of the burgundy carpet you have displayed in the window." Aunty was a little over-whelmed she didn't like having to ask prices, it was a must though and it would cost a fair old copper she thought. She wasn't wrong, already Emma and herself had fell in love with it. The two of them had a debate and so it was ordered to arrive for fitting in two days time. Not stopping for lunch in town feeling guilty at their self-indulgence buying the expensive carpet, off home they went. Putting her feet up, Auntie declared,
"That's done it, I didn't really want to spend that much. I expect it will be worth it, you get what you pay for at the end of the day. It has a classy look, being Wilton too it will wear like iron, can't wait for it to be fitted now, it is all going to be rather grand isn't it Emma?"
This "Rather Grand" description had been well used Emma thought.
The day had come; the carpet was to be delivered. Looking through the shop window Emma and Aunt Polly were straining their necks to see if the van was coming. Emma

said,

"During the time I have been here with you Aunty the scene through this window has changed. There are more cars than horse drawn buggies now, I don't know if I like it or not. I know cars are all the rage of the day but the horse and carriage has such elegance about it. I wanted Ruby and Annie to see it as I did, they won't will they?"

"No I am afraid not, times are changing very fast that doesn't mean to say though they will be disappointed. I don't think they will see many cars in the Ford except the one your Dad is talking about hiring. I wonder how he is getting on with his instruction. The trouble is he will have a clear road to learn on in the Ford. The burning question is will he be able to drive on the roads that are getting busier every day over here? There are more motor vehicles than ever before honking and tooting, making a darn good racket. The peace of the horse drawn carriage is fast going much to my regret." She was right, still though hoping that whoever was going to teach Albert included the busy roads. Aunt said,

"No-one learns in a village then comes out to drive around here, it is expecting too much.

"Here's the van," called Emma who had

moved into a better advantage position to see into the oncoming traffic. A small brown van with gold letters on it pulled up in front of the shop, the letters said "Johnson & Son." ever so posh! Polly was as proud as peacock!

"Ah Aunt Polly said. You have come to time; we have been looking forward to this day. Come inside do what you have to do we won't get in your way, give me a call when you would like a cup of tea, we will make ourselves scarce in the kitchen," Off they went.

"Well Jim, it is up to us now, the sooner we get started, the sooner we'll finish. You fetch in the tools we shall need and I will decide which end to start." Jim replied,

"Ok. I think it must be the landing and stairs we do first, it is a big area to cover.

See what you think? We might not get it all done today." Jim went to the van for the tools, Jim had worked with Clive the owner's Son for a long time now, he knew the job as well as Clive it was Clive though that made the final decisions. Clive didn't take long to agree with Jim so out to the van he went to help bring in the underlay for the stairs. Even this was heavy, they were not looking forward to getting the actual carpet in as it would weigh a ton, even with their expertise there was no way to lay it easily. Working on the landing where Aunt said the carpet was to start from, they soon wanted a cup of tea, this was thirsty work and the inevitable fluff off the material they were handling made the throat very dry so to the kitchen they went.

"Hello there," said Jim you told us to come back here for a cup of tea and we could do with one please."

"Of course come in we are in a bit of a mess in here it is due to the alterations we have been getting done, we feel the end is in sight when you have done the carpet we are going to get nice and straight again. We couldn't wait for you to come now we can't wait for you to be finished and go." Emma answered. She laughed at her own forthrightness. Where was the shy maid, who had come to Aunt's at fourteen years of age? Her manor, her knowledge, easy posture and freedom of speech made a positive picture of how Emma had matured. No one would know her now and she just would not fit in at the Ford.

Clive and Jim had sat down in the kitchen, unwrapped their snack and tea was set before them.

"You have a very nice place here, said Jim, it looks as though it has been a big ordeal for two ladies to plan, a big decision to make."

Jim was a handsome Man, a twinkle in those blue eyes. Emma noticed straight away the muscle in his arms and his back, saying to herself, it must be all the heavy weights that he has to lift in his job that make such muscles. No not really because Clive was smaller made, not as tall as Jim, neither did he have the body structure yet he did the same job. It seemed that Jim had that certain something, personality, call it grit call it what you will, it caught Emma's attention. She wanted to get to know more about him.

Now Clive and Jim were getting on splendidly, the finished effect was beginning to show. It had taken all of the first day, now time was getting on into the second day. It was not surprising, the carpet curved and the corners were difficult. A lot of stretching and pulling to get any slack tightened so that the carpet lay absolutely flat was quite an achievement. It wasn't very warm, but the sweat trickled down Jim's face, Clive backed off from the real solid effort to let Jim tackle it. He was always at the ready though if it was too much for one man, yes that is what it was too much for one. Almost all the time they pulled and wriggled the carpet between them. Jim took over on his own getting it into the corners, they had to be neat. There wasn't room in many parts for two men to work. Jim took it all in his stride, many cups of tea were made and drank. Jim relied on his trusty curved knife that was held in a sheath on his waistband, he called it "my mate" it got round many tight fit corners and this time there was no shortage of those.

"Nearly done Aunt Polly said, cheering them on. I bet you don't get many like this carpet to put down" Clive said,

"You would be surprised, some are even worse than this one, we get there in the end." They were in fact coming to the end of the job, both Jim and Clive being pleased with the outcome. As Jim tacked and trimmed, he was hoping Emma would come in.

He wanted to get to know her a bit better before they finished and were leaving. He could hardly call her he was working. A few glances were cast over his shoulder to see if he could see her anywhere. He realised there were not many times he had found someone he really wanted to talk to, why then did he want to talk to Emma?

"About done?" Clive asked Jim, and wondered why Jim was tagging on a bit longer than strictly necessary.

"Not long now Clive" Jim answered, I could do with another cup of tea though."

Playing for time, they followed Aunt Polly into the kitchen. Jim was disappointed because he expected Emma to be in there, but she was nowhere to be seen.

"Does your niece live with you?" Jim asked.

"Yes she does, but at the moment she is out buying at the wholesalers. Did you want to speak to her?" How could Jim say yes he hardly knew her?

"I will see her sometime, it isn't important," He shifted his feet nervously. He was behaving like a lovesick School child it was so silly. A grown man all he wanted was to talk to Emma time would tell it was just that he wanted it to be this time. Climbing into the van saying their goodbyes Clive said,

"Another job well done" He always commended a good piece of work, he liked working with Jim.

"Yes it wasn't all that easy was it? It certainly looks good though doesn't it?" "Cranking the engine to start the motor, they left pleased, ready for a good meal swilled down with a pint of beer it was drying to the throat fitting carpet, Clive and Jim were always ready for a pint of beer after the job was done and today was no exception.

"Are you in a hurry to get home Jim?"

"Not really, let's go for a pint first eh?"

Chapter 15

"Oh! Auntie Polly, doesn't it look lovely," exclaimed Emma, she had come in seeing the carpet with fresh eyes, now that it was finished.
"I hardly dare tread on it I must at least take off these outdoor boots my stocking feet will be better." She tripped over it as though she was dancing, her heart light and her spirits high. Smiling because this is what she had imagined, she couldn't believe at last it was all coming into reality. Never thinking of the cost, Aunt Polly would look after that, Emma had to do her part by making it all work. Excited was hardly the word; she must write to Annie and Ruby this very night to tell them how things were coming together coupled with how pleased they were with the result so far.

Dear Ruby and Annie,
Our dream is about to come true the carpet was finished today. It has taken two full days work I can hardly believe how smart it looks; putting yourselves into the equation it will be splendid, just for you to do your work, bet you are thrilled. You have a lovely place to come to work I hope you will appreciate it but of course you will. I can't wait for it all to get under way and for you to come over, have you been making lots of pretty items to show in the window?

Now it is just a matter of Aunt and me getting straight. A bit of polish, a window clean is all we need to do; you can help with the duster when you come to join us. Please bring an old dress to wear to help finalise the cleaning. I presume your shop dresses are ready I bet they look smart, can't have you dusting in those new dresses can we. If you are as excited as I am, you will want the date set as soon as possible? Write by return post, keep well can't have you going down with something at this crucial stage.

Love as always Emma. Xxx
Love from Aunt Polly too. Xxx

How Emma would sleep tonight she had no

idea her heart was racing feeling that sleep had little or no importance. Saying goodnight off she went to her bedroom flinging herself down on her (what she called "beautiful bed") having to get up to turn the gas light off.

Why couldn't she remember to turn it off before she got into bed? There it was with a final 'plop sound' when it went out seeming to say all is well. Sliding between the covers, her head full of colour and the day's events she fell asleep almost immediately, worn out. Oh dear Emma, were her last thoughts. She could do everything but finding out there was a point when even she had to say enough. Next day feeling fresher her Aunt had started early so was working steadily when Emma joined her.

"Sorry I am a bit late Auntie Polly I had to have a bit of breakfast as I didn't eat much last night. I was too full of all that is happening around us. I am here now eager to get on, I must go to see if everything is all right in the Sweet Shop I am thinking that all the Jars will want a duster over them and the shelves, counter, and scales all will be covered in carpet fluff it will have gone over everything. It isn't really dirt though is it? It will soon come off. I hope so anyway."

"Yes you go and do that, I will continue here, it is all staring us in the face and I also want to give the banister a good waxing, to bring the lustre back to it. We won't lack finding a job for the next few days will we? Could do with the help of Annie and Ruby; did you say the sooner the better."Emma replied,
"They will know how to clean and polish they won't need training for that, neither will they be dismayed at a little carpet fluff" Aunt smiled and got on with her piece of handiwork. It all had to come together, she was as eager as Emma to see the rooms straight again even though the alterations had been done for them. The casual work it had left behind would take a few days if not weeks to rectify. Brick dust, Carpet fluff here being a generous amount of both, the shop window display covered with brown paper but the debris had found its way through to the items in there. It would be more than enough work to get back to normality.
"By the way Emma, did you know Jim was looking to speak to you before he left?
I asked if there was a message, he said it would wait."
"I wonder what he wanted." Emma blushed as she said it, she would have liked to know, it was too late she sighed. Perhaps it was just as

well; there was too much going on right now to have anything else to think about.

They both worked like there was no tomorrow, in the evening having sandwiches to eat, they were worn out.

"Where does that leave us Auntie Polly?"

"Our next job is to put the tables and chairs into their place, we seem to have been cleaning for weeks there can't be much dust around now. I don't know about you but I can't do any more tonight. I don't think I shall even be reading my book, early bed and a fresh start is what I intend doing. Fill the kettle again Emma, I could drink another pot of tea." The kettle filled and soon singing on the hob of the open fire all was peaceful again. By the time the tea was in the pot, Emma had to give Aunt's shoulder a little shake. Her head had fallen on to her chest she was half asleep.

"Come on Aunty, here is the tea you wanted, Aunty, shaking her again, tea."

Oh! I was almost asleep, asleep sitting up? I could easily do that tonight, but bed is best." Taking her cup from Emma, she sipped it in appreciation.

"Thank you dear. I don't know what I would do without you."

Emma thought it was nice to be wanted, had

another cup of tea for herself then as her Aunt was going to do she went to bed. Lying thinking about tomorrow, she couldn't get to sleep. It was an exciting stage they had reached, bringing in the tables and chairs seeing if it all fit as planned, maybe getting a reply to her letter from Ruby and Annie. It felt like a milestone had been reached. What if, no she would not go down that road nothing is ever perfect, it would be as perfect as they could make it. Wondering too about what Jim had wanted her for? That was another mystery to her. Life never had been so full, not knowing what the girls would think of it all, her Mum and Dad too.

"I have not put the gas light out again, now I have to get out of bed, oh well. The gaslight did its now familiar "plop""as it went out. Emma got back into bed exhausted.

Chapter 16

Pulling the curtains open Emma was greeted by a bright day, the excitement from the evening before stirred in her, she all but ran down the stairs, Aunt Polly was having a bowl of porridge.
"There is some left for you dear it has only just been made, I thought it would be quick and easy. I know like me you are anxious to get on, fancy Emma, this is the day we both have been waiting for. There has to be a time to finish, yet I don't think either of us realised it was coming together so soon. It has been creeping up then with a mighty jump, here it is." Emma put her bowl of porridge on the table.
Aunty was right this great day would be the final one, then all had to fall into place, Ruby and Annie had to come over to have a few days at least to learn what would be expected when they started their new position. Auntie Polly needed to get the shops opened, they had very little takings from the last few weeks and a shop does not run on its own without thought. It all had to be cared for with customers coming in to buy, the new shop needed time to get the customers interested.

The tea room too it had to be tempting, with a small menu to advice the customer just what there was to order. Emma would see Aunt about the prices she wasn't quite sure enough herself. Knowing there wasn't going to be a lot of food to offer should make it easy, it had to be good homemade food that the customer couldn't get just anywhere, enticing the palate. Surrounding decor would make it a joy just be in the Tea shop, out would come the china tea service with the rosebuds pink on white, the dusky pink table cloths with the frill around them on the round tables. The tables had spaces between the three ornate legs that supported the top so that the display of legs looked elegant. The space left between them when sitting for tea left room to house the dress that Milady would be wearing down to the ankle, then showing the buttoned boot to perfection. All this Auntie Polly and Emma had planned leaving no detail to chance.

It all had to become reality now today they would take the final step.

The tables were heavier than they thought glad there were only three of them to move, nine chairs all needing the wrapping of cardboard taking off them so to reveal these master pieces. A beam of pleasure spread over their faces. Just what they wanted delivered without a scratch. Tucking them in one by one, three chairs to a table closed the gap. When not in use it gave a very good impression of a comfortable place to sit for tea.

"I am well pleased with the effect," Emma declared standing back to admire the area. Aunt agreed and said,

"The staircase fits in as though it had been chosen from new doesn't it dear. I feel we will get some very nice customers attracted to this place. Who would have thought it, I certainly wouldn't. But you did Emma."
Emma preened herself and replied,

"I would have spoken up sooner, at my age it didn't seem the thing to do. I didn't know what you would say even at this late date, certainly now that it is done. I am very pleased. Aunt agreed and said,

"I am happy to be a part of it in its infancy, watching it grow seeing the customers, hoping they will appreciate this little gem"
Emma said,

"Ruby will have something to show off about, because the carpet colour is also Ruby's name. It is a good job they are not jealous of each other isn't it. Are we going to drop the formality and let the ladies call them Ruby and Annie? They would take it as a privilege

to bind them as regular guests, a little informality. They don't get that in many places, another good idea Auntie Polly?" Emma put on her broadest grin she knew she was being cheeky but Aunt really didn't mind it at all, good for them good for the business a working team not to be found just anywhere.

Aunt even agreed to being, "Auntie Polly" to her guests.

The next thing to do was the price list. Neither of them fancied doing that they had never sold tea and cakes before. They agreed to go to into town to see what other people charged; it would be a good yardstick to follow. They could always be a little cheaper, but then they didn't want to lower prestige because what they intended to sell would be second to none. The space already was second to none, with Aunt Polly serving and Ruby with Annie backing her up they couldn't fail. Between them Emma with Polly dusted off the new pieces, put them into their allotted spot, fetched the tablecloths spreading them out, a little tweak here and there they were complete. A glass covered candle placed at the centre of each table brought the whole scene to life.

"Do you think Auntie Polly we could have a pot of tea in here? Sort of a trial run to get

the feel of things, see if we have missed anything out?"Polly fetched the tea then the paper serviettes which hadn't been in fashion very long. They saved a lot of napkin washing. The paper serviettes were thrown away straight after use. The sugar and milk were to be in their place with a side plate for small cakes.

"Surely there can't be anything else Emma we are only serving tea and cakes, I am certain that it will be enough refinement that is what it is all about, letting our ladies rest before or after they have chosen their goods. Talking to each other could well mean another sale or they may think of something they have to get. It is the ideal way to encourage sales, without saying a thing."

"Yes Aunt I have been in that same position myself would have loved a quiet little quarter to pause to think a while before completing my shopping. All you want on days like that is a cup of tea and a sit down even if it is only for ten minutes, once you have cleared your thinking, off you can go again refreshed. Our endeavour will be received with pleasure I am sure, your home baked cakes will soon be talked about and they are delicious."

"If we are finished, Aunt Polly said, I am going to write to Ada and Albert after tea. See

if we can get those Sisters of yours over, show them the place also their position in it, it is all happening at once now isn't it?" Walking towards the kitchen, they went for their proper meal. Bedtime again Emma thought, the days are flying by it must be all things happening at once. She laid on top of her bed her eyes scanning around the room, a lovely room. She was so lucky, yet just lately she hadn't felt very settled wanting to discover new territory, a bit more company, going to bed when she decided, not her Aunt. The big thing on her mind to be truthful was Jim of all people she couldn't stop thinking about him. His contoured body his strength his vital behaviour, there was a spark in him that drew her like a magnet. I have only seen him when the carpet was put down, I can't pretend to know him at all. He hasn't asked to see me, there is no date made. Probably he thinks nothing at all of me, indeed how could he but there was that sparkle in his eyes when he looked up at me as he was tacking the carpet down. She made herself laugh, how romantic, Jim doing his job and she doing hers. She just wished on returning to the shop he would still have been there. During the last day that he had been there Emma hadn't seen much of him she was annoyed having to go to fetch stock but Aunt had insisted. Emma had no idea what Jim wanted her for. From that moment, he hadn't been out of her thoughts. Sliding the bedclothes back, tucking her feet underneath them pulling the pillow around her neck, quietly she rested before sleep Jim still on her mind; her imagination took her away into dreamtime.

Chapter 17

The smell of bacon being fried awoke her. Yawning stretching, another day had arrived. I wonder if Aunt Polly wrote to Mum and Dad she thought, I must ask her the sooner the better now, anyway if Annie and Ruby are about to arrive, I wouldn't have time to think about Jim. I would be thinking of the girls. She knew she needed a diversion from thinking about Jim. It was just plain silly. She wasn't usually a silly type of girl nor never had been. She was practical and very pretty.
"I'm coming," she called downstairs hearing her Aunt call her.
"How is that? A bacon and egg breakfast at last, we have had so many odd meals just lately I thought I would surprise you, sit down you'll have the tea cold."
"Thanks very much Auntie Polly I shall really enjoy that, whoop! Fried bread too you spoil me." With great satisfaction, they sat together and enjoyed a really, nice meal.
"Did you write to Ruby and Annie?"
"Yes I did, the letter was short as I was so tired but they will know that we want them over as soon as possible, whoops!! That will

be four breakfasts to get; we shall have to take it in turn, won't we?"

"I have been thinking Aunty, a Parasol over the top centre of the table dainty in pink could look very nice as a finishing touch, obviously it would serve no purpose it would though cast a pink glow down on to the table as if the sun was shining."

"I will think about it during the day, you do come up with some unusual ideas, I don't know how you think them up, Parasol's indoors indeed. Just for effect you say ha, ha." Aunty Polly walked away, still smiling to herself. There was no end to her niece's decorative suggestions, one thing she knew, no one in this vicinity would be able to match her in the tearoom, small it might be, second to none in the artistry it had. The design was made for a "Lady about Town" with her ankle length skirts, high-buttoned boots, tall feathered hat and her elegant sophistication with style.

Ruby and Annie would be almost unique too; there were not many if any identical Twins in this immediate area. The hand stitched items, the embroidery they could do also made them special.

"PINK PERFECTION" yes Auntie that sounds about right. Does that suit you too?

"Yes dear quite so, later on in the week I will get the sign made. It is all costing a lot of money, I am sure all we have done will bring returns and so pay for itself, enough thought has been put into it." Aunt also thought the money that I give Emma for her pocket has to be looked into, a little more for all the extra work that has taken place. Aunt's mind rambled on in a most practical manor. It would all be sorted. Emma came tripping in,

"I have put the lock on the shop for a few minutes. I have been thinking about the Parasol idea we can't have a support in the middle of the table because the wood is solid, may I suggest suspending them over the tables, hanging on plaited satin rope, from the ceiling they would keep dignity in the tearoom. They would be higher than the usual we could have them just as high as we thought they would look best, the suspension would be interesting. What do you think?"

"I think it would look very pretty but Emma I must say it is the last thing I shall be buying. Again, we would have to get someone in to do it properly. Couldn't have them unsafe, yes we will go into that later on."

"All right, I will go back to the shop again now, don't get me any lunch today I want to go a little browse around the shops, is that

alright with you?"

"Of course it is I shall take the opportunity to get my feet up for an hour they deserve it the work I am making them do. I want to get myself rested, in order to greet the girls. I don't want to appear worn out. They will take a lot off my duties. Also I want Ada to see me looking sprightly, I don't see my Sister often enough, so I must give a good impression."

Emma didn't want anything from the shops but she thought she might see Jim working somewhere in the vicinity. She hadn't thought if he was encountered what she would say to him? Not wanting to seem as though she was chasing him. Oh! No, she could not have that. With that thought coming into her mind she began to feel guilty of what she was thinking saying to herself, I am not chasing Jim he can go to blue blazes for all I care. It brought her chin up as her pride took over who did he think he was anyway? Emma was still looking as she walked along the shop fronts she had her eyes trained looking out for Jim. She had only turned her head to look for a clear road when she looked the other way there he was, Jim large as life talking to another young lady. What should she do, pretend he wasn't there, cross the road away from him or stand her ground to say Hello? Her heart was pounding the palms of her hands sweaty, she swiped them down her dress, not very lady like, she was sure her hair was a mess and her hat on crooked. Why wasn't she prettier at this moment Emma longed to be pretty so that Jim would be drawn to her. Face flushed to see if she could find him that was one thing, but introducing herself into his company was entirely different. Now suddenly Jim was in front of her, well only a few steps away and she wanted to run. Come on Emma! She had missed her chance, he had not seen her and had gone into the place where he was working, and she couldn't barge in. Again, disappointment swept over her, what she wanted couldn't happen. She must step back and find another way to encounter Jim without him knowing he was on her mind. I might as well go back to the shop. Perhaps I will have a cup of tea and a bun at that tea room over there it will feel as though I have been out and give me something to say to Aunt Polly who always asks me where I have been. A little walk after, then my time will be used up, so my sweet shop awaits me. Emma's sweet shop never lost its magic, the glass jars the lids with the bobble of glass on top that did a little chunk when placed on the counter a chink when put back on to the jar. It never ceased to please her.

Chapter 18

In the house at the Ford, they were packing Bags. Ada wished they had some suit cases not wanting the dresses they had so carefully made to wear in the shop crumpled. Bags are all they had so they had to use them. The loving care they gave to each piece of clothing signified the respect they had for anything new.

"How excited are you Ruby?"

"Me, I can hardly contain myself I keep saying is this really happening? You and me a job doing just what we wanted to do, of course it is Emma we have to thank as well as Auntie Polly. Fancy we will have a bedroom to share a proper bedroom with separate beds. I wonder what the view is outside looking from our bedroom window. Wouldn't it be great if we could see the cars and carriages, see the posh ladies in their finery? Oh, I had better shut up we'll see when we get there." Mum walked in,

"Nearly finished girls? Don't forget to put a separate pair of boots in, one for best, you are going to meet people, I want you to leave a good impression on them. I have tried to teach you etiquette you must take every bit of knowledge I have given to you. I knew some day you would need to know many things that have not been practised in this house, I am very glad now that I took the trouble to help you with your education. Dad said it was all baloney that you would never need it, yet look at you now needing every bit of information, pity I wasn't able to teach you more." Annie said,

"I have been practising have even said words

out loud to Ruby, sentences too."

Ruby agreed having done that with Annie, Ruby went even further saying

"We have helped each other you know we always do, we have pretended to be very "La de da and practised at being posh ladies, we have finished up in laughter, enough to make tears roll down our cheeks."Ruby finished with a big grin strutting up and down the room like a posh lady strolling with a furled umbrella .Mum smiled and said,

"You haven't asked your Dad yet if he is taking you, he has to get permission to borrow the car from his friend. I am glad he has his driving license he hasn't any driving test to take. He handles the car with ease, it is the Coventry traffic I worry about there have always been horse drawn carriages and more two-seater horse drawn cabs on the roads, now there is the motor car to contend with. I only hear it from our Polly, in her letter's she says to cross the busy road is like taking your life into your own hands, there are a many accidents. I don't know how the driver's cope, we certainly do not want to cause any accident it is a very busy thoroughfare. We must be careful not to talk in the car Dad must have his wits about him." This they all agreed on.

Emma had gone back to the shop opening it. Not seeing Auntie Polly, she did not have to tell her where she had been, somehow she was glad of that, thinking her face would give her away if leading questions were asked, get on with her job that is what she must do. The window wanted rearranging, she had some lovely chocolates wrapped in pink cellophane that looked good, sticks of coconut wrapped in green, they would look good together, pink mice, lemon sherbets, mint humbugs, Turkish delight, nougat brought fresh from the wholesalers a couple of days ago. Doing her window, she heard a tap on the glass turning her head she could see it was Neil.
"Oh I don't want to be bothered with him."
As soon as the thought entered her head, she felt guilty. Dear Neil, he being a constant friend, but Jim was all she could think about, she didn't yet know Jim.
Neil was refined and gentle always there to confide in, but no, her attraction was towards Jim. It made the conversation with Neil droll this afternoon so when he had chosen his sweets he left. Emma was only too glad to see him go, there had been an atmosphere awkward to say the least, hoping he hadn't recognised this fact for himself, she certainly didn't want to hurt him. Oh! Blast, she said

under her breath.

There wasn't a part in her body that Jim was not included, all the while she tutored herself to stop it, he probably didn't think of her at all, she mustn't give way to the girlish pipe dreams that would not stop passing through her mind. Back to work, so to the window. It looks pretty, she thought as she worked putting some ruffles of tissue paper in between the items selected. The light was fast fading, closing time almost arriving. She decided to stop now to leave the work in the main shop until tomorrow. To be honest her sap had all run away, feeling drained after seeing Jim earlier even that was only from a distance. That was the effect he had on her she had no idea why. Feeling as she did, she was trying to curb the conversations with her Aunt not wanting her to know about Jim that was just it, there was nothing to know! Emma was afraid of making herself look ridiculous.

She didn't embark anywhere near to bringing Jim into the conversation, the talk between them rested with Ruby and Annie, and when they would arrive. Emma wished they would arrive shortly it would give her mind a chance to think of other things instead of Jim. Aunt interrupted Emma's dream pattern saying,

"I have seen the men who fitted the carpet Emma, I thought they would know who to ask to do the Parasols, I want them doing properly or not at all, they said they could do them. They are letting me know when they will have time. As it is just a small job, they have to fit it in. Anyway I can order them now so that when the time comes all three will be ready to hang, mustn't forget the twisted satin to suspend them on." Emma replied,

"That's good we will be opening soon and we want everything ready don't we?"

Emma's thoughts ran away with her, Does that mean Jim will be coming to work again in Aunt's tea room? As Emma went along with her work the very thought of Jim made her shiver this feeling remained unspoken of. Aunt and Emma had tea then Emma excused herself saying,

"I am reading a good book, if you don't mind I will go upstairs early also I want to manicure my nails they always get broken when I do the window it must be the positions I have to get in to reach that further bit."Aunt looked convinced, saying what she always seemed to say,

"Don't forget to put the light out when you have finished, goodnight dear."

Aunt Polly' wasn't as daft as all that, she

knew there was something on Emma's mind, but if Emma didn't want to share it Polly would leave well alone. When she was ready, Emma would tell her. Although curious, it must wait. All girls had their secrets it was part of growing up. Emma though was twenty now quite a young lady.

In her bedroom, Emma thought very deeply about Jim coming in to do some more work. Could she face him, knowing what was set in her mind? Then come to think what was set in her mind? Saying quietly referring to her own thoughts she quietly whispered, look at me, no-one is going to bother two jots what is on my mind, I am being silly but I really want to be looking good for Jim, I should be prettier, wear better clothes and do my hair in the up-swept modern look. I could if I tried, I have long hair and a curling tongue I could make my appearance look much more attractive. Abandoning her reflection, she knew there was nothing to be gained from self-criticism and pulling herself to ribbons. If she really wanted Jim she must somehow find a way of letting him know how he was attracting her, maybe he would return the interest, then they could see what happened. Emma felt haunted try as she might this man had made inroads into her very private world.

This had never been so before she didn't particularly like men so why did this one stay in her thoughts?

"Would you like some hot chocolate," Aunt called up the stairs.

"Yes please, do you want me to come down for it?"

"No, I am coming up, I will bring it." Aunt Polly was a good soul she had a way of making you comfortable even when things were not quite right. Emma jumped up and scrambled over to her little bookshelf, she must have a book in her hand reading this is what she was supposed to be doing. This one will do, she had read a few pages already so knew the plot so if Aunty asked her what it was about she could bluff her way through.

"I am putting it down here Aunty said, don't want you spilling it all over your book do we?" Auntie was glad to see Emma with a book perhaps her concern over Emma wasn't justified. Aunt was feeling better about things and her thought her concern wasn't necessary, she said,

"I will leave you in peace now I don't read much these days there was a time when I went through a book like wildfire not any more I am sorry to say, it is nice to see you have the same tendency, there is a lot of

pleasure in reading."

Emma agreed, even though she hadn't read more than a couple of pages, it was read months ago it wasn't that good so she had skipped read it. Glad it had done its job she sat drinking her cocoa.

Chapter 19

Ruby was in, Annie was in, and Ada was in, all with their bags packed at their feet, a little cramped to say the least. Dear Albert was having a whale of a time cranking the engine up to start the motor. It needed a very deliberate swing, then it would start up, or fail, you had to know your engine, this was not Albert's car, he was finding it offensive and hard work! His friend called the motor "Tin Lizzie" it was too true! At last, just when he was about to give up the engine turned over, hearing it spit sputtering with a splut splut splut he was satisfied,

"Be good, be good," Albert said to the motor car willing it to settle down after the fight he had to start it going. He jumped into the driving seat and away they went.

The curtains of the neighbours were twitching eager to see Albert's failing attempt to start the vehicle, but they actually saw the family drive off heads held high waving to the boys left at home. Phut-phut-phut the engine was raring to go,

"Sing to me," Albert said laughing. He wanted to get going he was not too sure of driving especially in traffic. The quicker the better he thought, putting the car into gear manoeuvring the steering wheel to show his family he was boss not the car!

Ada very proud seeing her Husband at the wheel and said,

"Well Albert you said you would do it and you have, I feel like Royalty, sitting here beside you I am going to be so proud of you when we reach our Polly's, she would never think of us driving up to her front door, I can't wait to see her face." This was a red-letter day and all of them would remember this day for a long time to come, in fact forever. The traffic as they approached

Coventry increased Albert said,
"Don't talk to each other I have to have my mind on the Road, I wish I had studied the map a bit better, I don't know where the turn is to Polly's shop." They all did as he asked understanding the serious side of car travel, it was no picnic in the midst of carriages and motorcars, Albert needed his wits about him, but they had every confidence in Albert. He now, took pride of place as he weaved in and out of the traffic.

Not being too sure Albert drew the car into a parking space. Leaving the engine running (he didn't want a repeat performance of the morning) he asked a Gentleman for direction. "Yes, second right then a left turn should bring you to the Road you have described to me." This was where Aunt Polly had her shop. Soon they would be there delighting them all. They proceeded on the last part of their journey Albert had to wipe the sweat from his brow he was well and truly in line for a cup of tea!

"How grand," Ada said nodding her head toward the outside of the shop with the sign that said "Auntie Polly's Parlour." Inside Ada there was a spark of pride at her Sister's achievement. Albert glad to have arrived safely said,

"Being able to park here is a good thing, we can all get out of the car bags an' all, very convenient." Ada remarked,

"I didn't think our Polly would do as well as this, the shop is in a nice area too." Ada glanced around at the other shops. Ruby and Annie started to get apprehensive, would they be able to fit into a posh place like this. There was only one way to find out so they alighted from the car ready to go into Aunt Polly's Annie said,

"Does Aunt Polly know we are coming?"

"No, I thought we would get here a couple of days earlier to surprise her and Emma." Mum had a twinkle in her eye.

"Have you got all your things?" Dad was placing the bags one by one on the pavement, so they could see which was whose? Mum said,

"There are some boots under the front seat don't forget them will you?"

If the truth is known Dad would be indeed glad to see this journey and all it entailed over, not that he wanted to see his girls go. It was the paraphernalia of it all that he didn't like. Whereas the Ladies were enjoying it. They were excited giggling giving knocks and winks to each other and swapping bags, to get the right one.

"Is this bag yours?" The question kept coming up. Ada was fluffing round like a prize hen, straightening the girls' hats and coats, tucking in a stray curl or two, wanting Annie and Ruby to look at their best. They did, two pretty girls with their eyes shining ready to tackle the world as soon as they had been accepted. They must mind the way that they spoke it was a good job they had practised their manners, their speech too they could see why it had all been so necessary. Now they had to put their work into practice, getting to know Aunt Polly, also Emma, they hadn't seen Emma for a long while. Mum smiled at her girls contented with their appearance and said,

"Come, on my dears, it is time you got acquainted with your new home."

Dad took his share of bags which was almost all of them and went towards the shop door.

"Should we go in this way Albert?" Ada thought it was a bit forward to go into the front shop door.

"Yes I am not standing about ages while you decide which way to go in, it is only your Sister, this is not Buckingham Palace."

Ada knew he was right so in to the front shop door they went. Emma was up the steps so to reach the top jars of sweets. She had her back to the counter,

"I will be with you in half a moment, this won't take me long." She glanced back to see who it was she was keeping waiting.

"Oh! Ruby, Oh! Annie, how did you get here what a surprise," coming down the steps and opening her arms crossing the floor to greet them.

"It was quite a few days before I reckoned on you arriving it is so lovely to see you. I must fetch Aunty Polly, what am I saying! I mean come through we will find Aunty in the kitchen." Dropping the latch on the shop door, they were led forward. Ada's eyes took in all the assets placed in her mind, all the things that Polly had told her about in her letters. Polly hadn't exaggerated; the place was done so finely that Ada felt she would have to leave her shoes at the door next time she came in. The new carpet smell and fresh paint, new furniture, counters polished, the whole atmosphere of new things all weighed up to make this a special place to be.

"Fancy our Emma has been working here in all its finery." Mum was talking to herself because no one was listening.

"Aunty Polly, look who I have here. Polly lifted her eyes from the pastry board. She couldn't believe it.

"Well! Our Ada Ruby and Annie!"
"Never mind them Polly, tell me where I can put these bags, my arms are dropping off."
Albert had been allotted the carrying of the bags so that the girls could go in to make a good impression. Ruby and Annie had gone all coy again, they were glad when Aunt offered them a place to sit they were not at all used to all this grandeur. Aunt spoke to Albert saying,
"Put the bags down Albert, we will see to those in a minute."
"Oh, Ada you too do sit down, I will make a cup of tea." *Albert smiled,*
"That's just what I want I am only just getting my legs back from the drive over."
"Did you drive then Albert?"
"Yes it was my first long trip, I am glad I got us all here in one piece, need to practise I suppose, but I have no car so it is only when I can afford to borrow this one from my friend that I get out on the road. I have a Licence, but that doesn't automatically turn me into a good driver. Never have I seen such traffic let alone drive in it, it has made me sweat. I will improve as I do it time after time, now though I need to recuperate so a cup of tea sounds good. Thank you Polly." *Ada, looked at the lovely teapot and cups to match, they*

delighted the eye. One thing she didn't have to worry about was the girls' welfare this being a lovely place to work and live. Polly offered them biscuits and asked,

"Will you be staying for tea Ada?"

"If that is all right with you we would love to. Of course you realise the girls are over now for the duration, hope we have not dropped it on you too soon, they have been on to Albert and me relentlessly to bring them so we made it as a surprise."

"That is quite all right I am just wondering what to get you for tea. We usually have our dinner at teatime. I was just making a meat pie, if I put extra shin on to simmer I could make a bigger pie, one that would be enough for us all, l can I do that?"

"Lovely chimed in Albert one of my favourites, I am getting very hungry. We will have a nice long afternoon and then leave about seven, it will be dark and less traffic then well I hope so. That will make my return trip easier, the Car has good lights that is if I can start the darned thing, I did have a spot of bother when we started out I am not all that used to driving. You could show us your new shop area Polly, where Ruby and Annie will be working. I know the girls can't wait to see it.

"That is just what I was going to say Albert I am as bad as the girls, I can't wait. Polly you have a lovely place here." Ada sipped her welcome tea, feeling very agreeable with the world. Passing light conversation all being in a good mood, Polly said,

"I know you are going to be pleased, Emma and I have planned it all with great patience plus eye for detail, well to tell you the truth Emma is the one that has brought all the new ideas I merely listened. If I thought things would be good then I agreed for her to get on with it. Emma is very good at planning things don't know who she takes after she knows how anyway. I wouldn't say it has not been without a few sleepless nights, wondering "if" by and large it has come together well. I do hope you like the colour scheme it took a little while to decide. Enough of talking leave your things here we will come back and sort them out shortly, follow me."

They did, when they got to the hall and stairway gleaming in its newness with the round tables three chairs to each, they looked so amazed. The glowing deep red wine colour of the carpet stretching through to the shop where Annie and Ruby would eventually do there stitching and on right in as far as the bowed display window. There was a work and serve counter to the side with a register till for the cash it was all just too much. Ada was thrilled for her girls.

"It is no wonder Emma has insisted that you girls should come to share in this life, where else would you get such a position?" Ada spoke words of wisdom to her girls.

Dad taking it all in seemed pleased he wasn't the one for fancy words. The smile that lit up Ruby and Annie's face with the gleam in their eyes told all.

"Look said Emma, you don't have an outside door, the ladies have to come through my sweet shop to visit you, we thought it would be a safe way of keeping you out of harm, also the customer won't be bothered by passing strangers, it will be very private while they have a chat with a cup of tea. Aunt is going to make cakes too; it will all be very congenial we are going to try to make pleasure while doing business. The fitting room too will add security, a feeling of being looked after. We intend pampering our customer, Ruby and Annie will be well versed in how to treat our ladies suggesting the right colour for them to choose, tell them of the latest fashion yes, all of that and more can be achieved. Come on Ruby and you Annie see how you will show off your expertise with

needle and thread to the customer with the love and care it deserves." Aunt Polly had a word to add,

"The screen that shields the window can be drawn back, so that you can show off your expert needle embroidery, the public of course ladies, will be able to see you working. A very new idea, of course when you wanted privacy the screen can be replaced very easily. Emma thought of that, she seems to have lots of new ideas.

Ruby had overheard Annie saying she wasn't very keen on people seeing her actually working!

"It will all be all right, you'll see," Emma said with a grin.

"Have you brought your dresses" asked Aunt.

"Yes, but they need hanging to get out any creases Aunt Polly. We have made black collar and cuff, used the dusky pink material you sent us for the dresses, shall I bring them for you to see?" said Annie.

"Looking at the finished product Emma said,

"The colour is good, it will mirror the Parasol's colour, there is going to be black fringing all around the edge of the pink fabric on those."

"Is there? First I have known about it," Aunt Polly exclaimed! They all chimed in with the

laughter that followed. So far so good Aunt Polly thought as she made her way back to see how the dinner was cooking. We can't expect them to take it in all at once. It will be weeks before we are ready enough to open "Pink Perfection." A thorough training, relaxation in front of the Public will be needed to fit the bill. They would get it, sometimes it would sting, but it had to be done.

The dinner smelled savoury and inviting, although the window was left open to avoid cooking smells lingering and settling in the shop area, the aroma sometimes permeated the whole building. Aunt had seen an extractor fan she was going to invest in having been told they were worth their weight in gold. It would solve her problem. The pie was a huge success, the six of them sat around the table together.

"Like a party," Ruby said feeling a little better now that the initial procedure was over. It had been so thrilling and tiring they were all worn out. The move made to say it was time they were off came from Dad it was now welcomed. The goodbyes were not so easy, Mum had tears Ruby and Annie were trying to sniff back their own, Emma standing in the background ready to support wherever she

was needed. They all knew this was inevitable because they loved each other. The twins hadn't been parted from Mum and Dad for more than the School hours all of their lives. It had to be done the quietest way possible so that readjustment would be less painful. At this moment, Mum Ruby and Annie all wished they were back home chipped cups and all! They all went out to wave goodbye. Dad hoped the bloomin' car would behave so that he didn't have to stand with the starter handle, refusing to do its job in firing the engine. Very embarrassing if it did, there should be a better way. When the weather was also pitching in with rain or snow the driver could get wet through just getting the engine to start. Ah! Well it was dry tonight he would be covered once he got into the driving seat. Hoping as it was dry now it would stay dry for the journey home. The engine fired the splut-splut-splut sounded reassuring. One by one, they all kissed and hugged. Lights on, car ready and off they went Albert thought how much lighter in weight the car seemed to drive.

Chapter 20

"Wahoo" Dad said I am glad that is over. It's you and me now, me darlin. The boys will be glad to see us back, I certainly will be glad to get home. It is all very well this finesse but I prefer our life with all its rough ways, it is what I call living, none of that airy fairy performance, just a good fire a nice meal some homemade bread and you dear Ada sitting opposite me. That is all I need."
"Oh Albert, you know Polly's shops are lovely, a splendid meal too, all very grand, we will never have anything like that."
"Don't want it Ada how we go on suits me fine, now that the girls are with Polly I shall have you more to myself, the boys like to be out and about. I will promise you if anything is going to change it will be the extra time we will spend together I love you old gal just as you are."
"I love you too Albert, hey less of the old I am still the girl you married all those years ago, if anyone could make my life better it would be you."
He placed his hand on hers and gave it a squeeze. The time they had together was

going to be as much their time as anyone else's. The car jogging along the cosy feeling of belonging time to look forward to togetherness, it was, all good. The smiles on their faces reflected their contentment; Ruby and Annie wanted to find their own direction. All was well in the world as far as they were able they would keep it that way. Contented with their way of life what else could they want?

Emma and Auntie Polly were now showing the girls their bedroom, a little squeal of delight when the bedroom door was opened, two beds, sitting side by side with a centre space, two bedside oil lamps stood ready to use, the base decorated in a lavender design. Identical lavender eiderdowns with pillows to match, the whitest of sheets folded back ready to get into, how could they not enjoy! They had the same as Emma had, a three-mirrored dressing table with stool, a wicker chair in one corner another one in the other corner. They could be put together with the very small occasional table placed at the foot of the bed for chatting, or tea or looking at new materials, the floor being carpeted in pink it was a dream for them. Ruby and Annie moving around the delightful room said,

"Can we come to bed right now? They were both talking at once, Aunt didn't know hardly which was which, please we are tired we would love to lie and talk to each other there is so much to say? Thank you very much Aunty the room is just what we would have chosen ourselves, are we close to Emma's bedroom?"

"Yes, you are, if you don't go to sleep and be quiet I shall be after you," Emma said good-heartedly. She smiled and continued have you seen your new night dresses?"

"No, where are they?"

Emma nodded, "In the top drawer over there."

The drawers were polished wood, similar to the wood in the staircase they both went to find what was in the drawers. Holding up the nightdresses in front of them they were well pleased.

"These are beautiful look at the lace." They each held them up for all to admire. Aunt Polly said,

"There are slippers to match in the wardrobes so I suggest you put them on, I will bring a hot drink up to you then surely you will have had enough excitement for one day. I nearly forgot there are corsets to fit you both, on the shelf in the wardrobe. They are adjustable

with the laces at the back, when I can get you measured you will have a better fit."

Emma remembered when she was introduced to a Corset, an item of torture.

"Corsets what are corsets?"

Annie looked at Ruby she had the same wondering look on her face.

"What are corsets Aunty?"

"Oh my, don't know what a corset is?" Aunty was smiling bemused.

"It is an under garment, here let me show you." Aunt went to the wardrobe and picked out, two pink items saying,

"These are the latest ready-made fashion garments. See they fit around your figure below the bust line and the hooks are to do up down the front. The lacing at the back allows your waist line to be pulled into shape, forgive me my dears but your waist line certainly needs attention you will soon get used to them."

Ruby and Annie thought that these garments looked ridiculous, how would they ever get used to wearing them, fashion had never been observed at Mums, having to please Aunt they kept their views to themselves they would try these on at their own leisure as for wearing them every day it remained to be seen.

"That is enough for one day I am very tired, goodnight Ladies, sleep tight." Aunt yawned and retreated to her own room. They all needed sleep it had been a very wearing day, that is if they could calm down enough for sleep, there was always tomorrow, it wasn't a dream but it seemed like one, their imagination knew no limits. Emma now left them promising to show them the bathroom tomorrow chanting as she went off to her own room,

"I don't know about you girls I am dead on my feet if you want anything I will be in my bedroom. You can ask for a further half hour then all will have to wait until morning, goodnight to you, both."

Emma thought she could tell Aunt was really tired, her walk along to her bedroom was dragged, her shoulders bent. Tomorrow, she would have a word with Ruby and Annie they would have to be told how to give Aunt some time of her own without her realising and after all because she was as old as their Mother, rest time must be considered. It was because Aunt was active she didn't do a lot of complaining and could talk fashion with an educated voice, even Emma tended to forget her age. She could discuss anything on trend Emma and Aunt would sit and have lengthy discussions about colours and lengths and cuts of up to the mark selling attractions. Aunt was always suggesting something new it was a delight to them both enjoying each other's company it was easy to do; now they must include Ruby and Annie. With them all wanting to be adept in their work, they could help each other.

The next day was still a little chaotic, Ruby and Annie unpacked trying to take in all that Emma with Aunt Polly was trying to tell them. A new world was opening up, all in it was up to the moment foreign, they kept checking with one another things they must remember. It was not easy but it had to be done. The window of the new shop was the object centre today. In their bags, they had completed quite a few pretty items to put on display. Aunt said,

"They might as well go into the window, just to show the sort of trade we are going to be in." The shelves in the window were not yet completed so their work was laid flat down. There was a nightdress case with lovely embroidery and a space left to put the owner's name or initial on it, a pink holder for lotions or potions to be placed on a dressing table. A pair of pillowcases with Pink Ribbon, two beautiful quilted cushions

worthy of any one's settee and a slipper holder that was to go on a wardrobe door to hold four pairs. These are to name but a few.

"You have been busy girls your work is here to be seen and I can see the well to do ladies who pay a pretty penny, being very interested, do not worry though if it is slow to take off disappointing results sometimes come before success? The people we have to tempt have their regular Houses, we must show we are better than the one they are already going to of course we are, or will be. Aunt said with a smile, we have lots of competition with the other ladies shops in the area. Emma said, "We will outshine them all."

The window was laid out with the few things that were complete, just as a tantaliser. Ruby and Annie went outside to see what the display looked like it was a thrill just to see their work shown. Giggling and trying to look dignified didn't really go; today they couldn't stop looking at the work in the window that they had actually stitched! There first achievement.

"Emma, come and look," Annie said, seeing her Sister doing the sweet shop window. Emma waved and nodded,

"In a minute, just want to finish this window" She was also serving her customer and

customers came first. Annie and Ruby must learn this one thing, it wasn't a game it was real money that was at stake. Not having much handling of real money of course it was so new to them. The till another item they knew nothing about had to be precise, whereas at home if the cash was near enough it would do. So many things to learn, they we're glad the shop was not ready to open just yet; time is of the essence that is what they needed time. At least Ruby and Annie realised that, so as long as they did a follow up day by day slowly the pieces would fall together. They would become surer of themselves and that allowed them to learn at a quicker pace. The window shelves had been put in, also the items they had made whilst learning the shop routine. Every evening something would come into their hands for precise stitching. Aunty Polly marvelled at the way they handled the expensive cloth, the patience!

"I couldn't do that Annie, you have such dainty hands and I wouldn't have the knowledge or the patience. You too Ruby you make it look easy; I know it is not, we will have something special to offer when we open."

The girls acknowledged the compliment.

"Thank you Aunt Polly, the thing is we love doing it, it is good earning our living with the thing we are good at, you see it is not work to us, it is pleasure, if we get stuck we have each other to ask."

"I see, then I won't interrupt you. Do tell me if you want more cloth or ribbon, I want you to have the best materials for such fine work." Emma came to join them,

"Still stitching? I like the colour of that Ruby, looks as though you have just started yours Annie, why can't I stitch like you two, I have no sooner started, then I want to stop, I just haven't got the staying power."

"That is just what I have been telling them Emma; if it were left to me the pretty things I made would be ten times the price, because it would take me ten times as long." They all had a titter at this remark! Aunt Polly had her own way of stating a fact.

The Parasol Canopies arrived, they had to be Canopies and as there was no handle, they were to be suspended. They looked very pretty with the deep pink and the black fringe as ordered. The suspension satin was over long, so to leave enough to hang them at the required height. Now thought Emma, the Canopies are here that means Jim will be advised so that they can be put into the position allotted for them, they are taking a lot of room on the shop floor... Ruby and Annie coming had given Emma much more to think about but Jim was never far from her thoughts. She must make sure she would be around when he came. What to say to him? Hoping he would start a conversation so she could naturally fall in. Anyway she was going to give it her best shot, it was a-must she could not go on mooning over him while doing nothing at all.

"When will they come to put up the Canopies Aunt Polly?"

"Well I know they are very busy this week, maybe the week after. I want to get ready for the opening Ruby and Annie are getting quite adept in their position, to tell you the truth I need to get some returns on my investment. I don't mean that in a hard way but there has been some whopping bills coming in lately. It is time to balance the books, and with a little extra hopefully. Can't go on forever spending with nothing coming in can we?" Emma replied,

"I understand and agree, everything is looking good, it is time we tested the water so to speak. That will be in about a fortnight's time then will it?" In her mind, Emma was counting the days until Jim was here

working. Every day a drag waiting to see him again, thinking of him while lying trying to get some sleep, he was going to be the one and only, never had she felt this way. Then Neil jumped to mind, he was always there, still coming in for his weekly chat and to buy sweets. I am not leading him on am I? Emma thought, he seems to be quite happy the way things are, but then he doesn't know how Jim has taken over my every thought. Did Jim know this? How could he? The job he had done had only taken three days, how could he possibly have noticed Emma? He had barely seen her. It was Emma that had noticed Jim it was his bright shining eyes and his manly physique that had caught her eye. Determined, she would follow her heart

.

Chapter 21

Annie and Ruby came into the sweet shop to join Emma.
"This is a lovely shop, look at all the different colours in the sweets, it is making our mouths water. Chocolates too, Mmmm which would you have Ruby?"
"I like them all wish I didn't, I have to keep an eye on my figure, I am round enough as it is, don't want to have to wear this corset any tighter, I can't breathe now."
"I know what you mean Ruby we have always

been the same, round as an apple and if we went skinny Mum would think there was something wrong with us."

"Come on Emma said, choose 4oz sweets between you, you can have just one of each kind, then tonight while you sew it will be something to look forward to."

"Go on Annie, you choose first."

"No you go on, choose a couple of chocolate ones, I like chocolate."

"See I told you, I will have whatever you have, so pick two of each kind, that will suit me. They all look delicious don't they?"

Emma could see 4oz. wasn't going to be enough so it had to be 4oz. each, it didn't matter Aunt would approve as long as it wasn't regular.

"Do you have to change your window display very often," Annie enquired.

"When I think it is getting stale or I get something new in. The boxes are not full they are just imitation, the full ones are kept in here in a cool spot, in the window the chocolate would get very discoloured."

"I didn't know that, they both chimed in together, what about the other sweets, said Ruby?"

"Some are all right others must have a little care taken and they don't stay in the window

for long. We can't have waste so it is as well I do keep my eye open. Even the Sun directly on the window will do damage, a good thick sheet of brown paper over the window contents for a little time while the Sun is high does the trick anything else you would like to know "Madam."

Emma, pronounced the "Madam" as though she was serving one of the elite. Ruby and Annie fell in with the idea all fell into laughter. It wasn't all serious things that they had to learn. It was also how to relax, to be comfortable with the, Lady or Gent they were serving. They were sure though it would be more of the feminine, unless the masculine was buying a gift there were many things that could be given as a gift. Once "Pink Perfection" was up and running who knows gifts might be a best seller. Two days yes then Jim would be in doing the Parasol work. Emma must look her best on that day, her stomach kept turning over, she felt sick all because of Jim! Hoping Ruby and Annie indeed her Aunt Polly hadn't noticed any change in her. Emma knew there was a definite change, it was for Jim's eyes only the others need not know, ordinary that is what she must seem to them so ordinary was her goal. How can I be just the same as always when I know Jim is coming, my heart will be beating and my face flushed?

"Hello Emma, busy today? It was Neil. Oh! He would come today. Not wanting to converse keeping her thoughts on Jim she forced a smile.

"This is not your regular visit is it Neil?"

"No you are right I have an Aunt coming to visit Mum. She sent me to buy some of her favourite sweets. You wouldn't like to join us would you?"

Wanting to say NO THANK YOU as it was the last thing she wanted to do she mumbled an excuse from a bowed head, Neil was so kind, she was hurting him, it wasn't what she wanted to do, but he kept putting her in such a tight spot. Talking to herself she said, Come on Emma try to keep it believable he is so fond in his ways, oh dear, I hope he doesn't stay long. Just as though he had heard her, he said,

"Anyway, I can't stay long I will talk to you later on in the week, duty calls. When Aunt comes to visit Mother likes me around, she is a bossy old soul I can keep her somewhat subdued. I rather hoped you would come, some other time maybe."

"Of course Neil, it is very nice of you to consider me at all, see you soon then."

He left the shop unsatisfied as to the answer he had been given knowing not to push things, pacifying himself he was being silly. Emma was a busy lady he hadn't the right to but in on her privacy, that didn't stop him feeling for her as he did. One day she would welcome him with open arms he could wait.

Another day, now only one day to go before Jim was here in the shop. All the time she was trying not to get worked up, I must keep calm, what if I make myself ill and can't see him at all. This was a thought running around her head, not wanting to get on with her job, this was so unlike Emma. There was always time for her shop she loved it. The words "what if" became very much used. Encountering every position that might occur "What to say" also took prime position. Practising to be word perfect stringing words together that made her sound intelligent, how did he speak? She realised she didn't know, because a conversation hadn't passed between them. He would sound manly with authority in his voice his whole countenance said so, in command and she wanted him to be hers, his enticing body and the gleam in his eyes. He had to know somewhat surely the attraction she had for him. Only how could he? They had never been together for long.

When I get up in the morning, I wonder if he will have arrived, perhaps not, really preferring not, then I would have time to dress properly. A dab of powder on my face a touch of perfume that Aunt has given me, I have been waiting for the right time to wear it. My hair will be brushed and combed into an attractive style a pale pink tip put on my fingernails. I must look at my very best, destiny is about to happen, this might last for all the days of my life a bright shining life alongside Jim. Her mind ran away with her, almost blushing at the thoughts that speedily went from one thing to another, Jim the centre of her world longing to be in his arms even though he hadn't even asked her to go walking with him!

The shop now was getting busy, she was glad it relieved her mind because she had to pay attention to what she was doing, her customers too liked a little chat, they had become well conversed where Emma was concerned making them feel more like friends than customers coming in to buy something. Emma liked it too, she knew where they were going on holiday and when a marriage was to take place, when the next baby was expected. All was confided as Emma did the routine jobs that were listed out before her. Bedtime at last, after tea and talk with Aunt, Emma excused herself and went early to her room. Once in her room the exciting day to follow took over, looking in the wardrobe for the best shop dress she had, placing things ready on the dressing table, putting her shoes and stockings to hand, she didn't want to miss a second. I am glad Aunt Polly is going to look after the sweet shop tomorrow, she thought. It had been arranged last night, that Emma would supervise the placing of the Parasols. Aunt said she would have a better eye for getting them central to the table. As they were very decorative, they had to be just so. It worked in with Emma's idea, thinking it was a bit of luck that Aunt had wanted it that way, then she didn't have to think of excuses to keep going into where Jim was working. She could watch him without him thinking that she was watching, also the conversation would be natural. Undressed now she slid into the sheets giving a little shiver as the cold cotton wrapped around her, the eiderdown soon did its job, the feathers cosy soon got her warm. Sleep did not come easily, lying listening to the horses trotting by, the new motor cars chugging along the road outside her window, coming to bed early meant the road was still quite busy, it served her a purpose, pretending it was Jim with her in a horse drawn buggy. They would go a ride round the park. He would put his arm round her; she would feel his hot breath on her cheek as he leaned over to kiss her. Maybe in such circumstances he would fetch out a box, this would have an engagement ring in it and he would slip it on her left hand. As she lay soliloquising, the hair on her arms stood up, the back of her neck too, romancing leaving the real world behind. Knowing this was how it would be, smiling to herself confidant in her estimation of Jim, she finally went to sleep.

Chapter 22

All too soon morning came, now she wished she had gone to sleep earlier she was still tired, the thought of the morning and of Jim soon bucked her up.
I am going to see Jim today, this is the day! Silently she mouthed the words so no one could hear. Dressed, tea and toast, the day had begun.
"Are you sure you will be all right in the sweet shop Aunty Polly?"
"Of course, don't forget, I have Ruby and Annie to call if I need them. As their shop isn't open, they are working at their stitching uninterrupted, but if I need them I shall call and they will come and help me. It will be ideal I can let them have a go at the till; see to a few customers a good training day I would say. No, don't worry about me, you go and get the Parasols in place, I think they will be coming about 10am, so there is still an hour for you to go and get things positioned right for them to start as soon as they get here."
"Thanks Aunt, I will do that, is there anything you want to tell me about the

positions before I go?"

"No you will know exactly what to do you did all the planning anyway. You know I only supervise that is more than enough for me, off you go."

Emma gratefully went thinking she had handled that quite well. Now in the tea room she looked to see if the tables were in the right position and that they were situated to their best advantage because when they were placed this time they would have to be permanent, the Parasols would have to be central to them or they would look quite silly. Get them right, they would have something special. The candles on the tables also central would shine up into their round cavity and glow, that would be the result as they were pink ,it would look very effective very feminine. That was how Emma had pictured it she had a good forward seeing mind to do this it came quite naturally. The van drew up. Emma's heart did a somersault looking out of the window making sure that Jim was there, he was.

She went to get the door open for them, this door was only used for deliveries and the customers would have to use the sweet shop door. It was more convenient for a van to unload straight into the ladies shop rather than walk all the way through the sweet shop.

"Hello, a nice bright morning you have brought with you. Emma said with a big smile trying to be casual. Do you want tea before you begin?"

"No, we want to get on we have another job after this we want to get both in today, Clive called, bring that measuring rod in with you please Jim."

Jim came in, Emma looked at him he was the most handsome man she had ever seen. Her legs went weak, glad not to have to say anything, because she knew her voice would resound in her throat, as she wasn't able to control how she spoke. Her mouth was dry, knowing this she avoided Jim for a moment, excusing herself about having to go into the kitchen, she promptly left.

What am I doing, I must calm down Jim will think I am always like this. Getting a drink of water, she took a few deep breaths and tried to relax. Soon as she had herself under control, she went back.

"Sorry about that I had to get a drink it must be getting excited about this finishing touch you are about to do, I can't wait to see what it will look like. I will get the supporting satin ropes for you, so you can see how to go about this job I don't think you have done this

before have you? This is my idea and so I want it to work."

It was true; they hadn't done a job like this it was a way out idea yet they agreed it could work and it would be exclusive. Putting two pair of high steps where they needed to reach with a sturdy joining plank to make a support to walk on they proceeded. Emma had placed the tables in order she had to direct the position to hang the satin rope to work in accordance, not as easy as it sounded. Directing meant talking to Jim, he had the deep masculine voice she had heard in her dreams he was very practical. On instruction Clive worked with Jim, this was how she thought it would be, gaining her composure able to talk although it was only about the job in hand, it was satisfying. The boss went out to the van to fetch his receipt book. Jim was having a cup of tea, before they left he turned to Emma saying,

"Funny thing Emma I was hoping to see you again I tried to speak to you last time but you had gone to the wholesalers, I would like you to come for a walk with me one evening after work, will you?"

Oh! Yes indeed, she would. Trying to stop trembling, she said,

"I would like that Jim, what night would suit

you?"

"Let's see, it is Wednesday today, make it tomorrow about six at the park gates."

"I will be there; I hope it is a nice evening, until tomorrow then. Emma did a hop skip and jump she had done it! Tomorrow he was coming out to see just her.

Going in to fetch Aunt Polly to see the job, her heart she was singing. It had all gone swimmingly well, the man of her dreams had asked her to go walking with him yes it was tomorrow not next month or next week, tomorrow.

Aunt Polly locked up the sweet shop smiling at Emma she said,

"Is it all done dear, does it look good?"

"Yes it does, sort of special, just like we wanted it, you'll see in a minute."

Aunt could see Emma had a spring in her heels so she knew the job had been done well. Emma was precise when it came to the end result. She knew a good job.

When Aunt saw the effect she gasped, these pretty effective Canopies complete with the long black fringe had made such a sweeping statement, the satin rope suspensions were unique, the difference it had made to the overall look of the tea room elegant and worthy of any fine Lady.

"Such a difference Emma, the pink shows beautifully, edged with the black that sets it off to a "T". I am very pleased, you're a clever girl my dear your ideas seem to always work, this idea especially so, it is unique we will be the talking point of the month. Oh Emma I just shivered, is it excitement? Or is it getting cold in here, let's go for tea get the kettle on shall we? We will discuss things while we rest"

"Yes Aunt, I have something more to tell you."

"More? I should think there have been enough delights for today," Aunt smiled.

Emma didn't know whether or not to tell Aunt about her date with Jim, she would decide while they conversed drinking there tea. Emma didn't really want to let Aunt into her private world alongside Jim, it was precious time and her very own feelings.

Chapter 23

"Ruby and Annie will want to see what has been going on; they have gone upstairs for the moment. I have been pleased with them today they created an atmosphere a bit different for the customers, they all wanted to know who they were, their home town asking if they were going to be permanent, their names too. It has been non-stop chat, I think that is why they have disappeared upstairs they would have found today quite taxing I bet they're on their beds!"

"I will take them a cup of tea Aunt, so make enough for four of us please." Emma was dying to tell Polly about her date with Jim but her Aunt went on and on about the girls, the subject could be brought up later when they sat down together.

Aunt Polly was excited she never stopped talking when this mood was on her, the Parasols, the carpet, the tables and stairway all included in the chat so not a word was spoken about Emma's exciting news, this was really what Emma wanted, she would have to bide her time to get a word in and then make this date nothing out of the ordinary, in

Emma's mind the date was exactly the opposite exciting and of paramount importance.

Sitting at her dressing table, brushing her hair, thinking, I wonder why Jim didn't say he would meet me outside the shop, outside the Park at the gates he said, he must have his reasons. She didn't like walking alone at dusk, sitting by the fire was her favourite place in the evening or lying on her bed. Not used to nocturnal gallivanting she was a little apprehensive even though this was Jim she was going to see. After tea when washing-up she told her Aunt about her date, she had to, or else Aunt would think there was something not nice going on. Aunt Polly was bemused, saying,

"Your first conquest Emma, everything is new to you as it should be, please dear use your head and don't let your heart rule. I think Jim is a good kind of man he will look after you, but come home early please or I shall be worried, I would think he will come all the way back with you, it will be quite dark by then."

"Of course I will use my head Aunt, Jim is a good solid man; he will know what is expected of him. To tell you the truth Aunt I have been looking forward to this date for

ages, I couldn't wait for him to come back to do the remaining work in the shop, I didn't say anything to you, because I would have made myself look a fool if Jim hadn't asked me out." There Emma had told her Aunt, and felt better for it.

"All right then Emma but do be sure you know the ways of a Man, I don't think you do, as yet, you haven't been in male company, situations change from a Man's point of view. I suppose at your age it would be wrong of me to wrap you in cotton wool. Again, I say do take care, I can't stress enough, I can't go with you to hold your hand, not so long ago a girl had to have a chaperone to be with a man, especially in the evening or after dark, it was not a bad idea."

"Oh, Aunt Polly, don't be silly, I can look after myself and Jim will see that no harm comes to me. Can I close the shop at 5.30 pm. tomorrow? I don't want to be late; I shall want to get ready properly too. Can I wear the red scarf and handbag with the red trim, my muff too that you bought me ages ago? I have only worn them twice they would be the right clothing for tonight as I want to look my best." Aunt Polly sighed it had arrived, the day when Emma was no longer content with just the shop or her Sisters company.

Wanting to spread her wings as well it was bound to happen; at least Emma had told her Aunt who she would be meeting. Ruby, Annie and Aunt all agreed to retire early, feeling the strain of the day.

Emma, getting ready made her appearance lovely. She had put on a little face powder, heightening the colour in her cheeks and put on one of her best skirts and blouse; the skirt just came above her ankles, showing her pretty buttoned boots, she stood back to look at herself in the mirror.

"Hmm, not so bad," She reached for her red scarf put it around her neck tying it in a simple flounce at the front, picked up her muff and put her handbag over her wrist. I know what I want to set it all off. Reaching for a red lipstick that she had bought because it was all the fashion never dreaming she would use it, she curled it out of the tube. This is me in for a penny, in for a pound she sweetly murmured .Using the lipstick to its full effect, now she would have to sidle past her Aunt Polly Ruby and Annie, she knew what they would say if they saw her with a full make up on, curls peeping out of her hat, a strictly "me" look about her. That was not going to happen knowing it was better to dodge her Aunt and Sisters, nothing was

going to spoil her evening with Jim all would be well she was sure.

She took the back way out of the house so as not to confront anyone they were still sitting talking in the kitchen as she left. She called to say bye-bye then scampered out of the house very quickly. Now on her way her heart lighter she began to feel more grown up and in charge, it was a good feeling. The gas lamps were being lit in the Park as she arrived. She thought how romantic it all looked it was her first time to see this as it was always daylight when she had passed the Park before. A cosy glow seemed to settle around her, wasn't she the luckiest of girls, her handsome Jim waiting for her? Did he feel the same?

Funny, but she didn't know, in fact there was very little she did know about Jim except that he drew her like a magnet he in her thoughts all the time. This was the first date of many dates to come, what a lovely thought. There he was, standing as he had said by the Park Gates.

"Hello Jim, I hope I am not late, it was a job to get out of the house and I didn't want any fuss so I sidled out the back way."

"I am glad you did, we don't want everyone to know do we?"

Not knowing quite what he meant by that she fell in step beside him. He hasn't offered me his arm, perhaps on a first date he doesn't want to. Emma's mind was working at full speed, everything must be correct. Oh! Stop it, I am out with Jim, I will follow him, he will know best. They were walking into the Park there were three quite separate roads through. It was odd that Jim was taking her along the poorest path, this way wasn't lit up and she had looked forward to walking under the lamplight, it was romantic. Why go round this way Emma thought. I have my best button boots on, the path will be less looked after and full of stones, she said,

"I would have liked to stroll down the centre of the Park Jim it is more lit up and the trees look lovely."

"Another time Emma, I have to be back early tonight, this is the shortest way."

That is not what Emma wanted to hear, her heart sank a little. Jim noticed her go quiet.

"You don't mind do you? He asked, trying to be a bit less abrupt. I am sorry something came up at the last moment. We have an hour, it will be dark early tonight and I expect your Aunt will like to see you back early, it will give you time for a chat with your Sisters too I am sure you will like that."

Her thoughts again ran away with her, have a chat with those back home? It is not that I wanted to do. Here was the man that had ruled her every thought for weeks now. She walking beside him hanging on his every word, but no love words were spoken, why then had he asked her out? Thinking she had his measure, she had not! Auntie Polly was right, she knew very little about men. She answered him,

"Yes, it will be all right, I did think we would be out longer, it doesn't matter though. It must be important for you to go back early, I am being silly." They went on walking. He was not walking her home and he was all the while looking at the time.

Did he want her or didn't he? Emma couldn't make him out and he was her Jim!

She arrived back at Aunt Polly's feeling down not understanding Jim, she still wanted to see him and they had made another date for the earlier time of 4.30pm It was not a good time for her, she would have to wheedle her way round Aunt to let her go earlier than her usual time. A whole week again to wait she could have seen him Sunday any time. It didn't suit him though, he had said in a very demanding tone,

"You will be here at 4.30pm next week. I will

expect you not to be late." It had added to her misery. Of course she would be at the Park gates at the given time there was no need to order her.

Aunt Polly called from her bedroom,

"Is that you Emma? You are earlier than I expected dear, the girls and I decided to take an early night did you want me for anything?"

"No thanks, I am ready for bed in fact, I am very tired." Very tired yes, very disappointed too not wanting her Aunt to start asking questions, her every being felt in disarray this was not like Emma. The old Emma had calm about her, always knew the way things had been planned knowing where she was going and who with, Jim had turned her positive thoughts into chaos, not now knowing where the planned future she had envisaged was going, would Jim be part of it? Of course hoping was the best she could do, he had after all made another date and so he did want to see her. She thought I am putting too much emphasis on tonight my mind is running on. Perhaps first dates are always like this; of course, we have to get to know one another. What am I expecting? Tonight though she had learned nothing not one solitary thing, she had not taken his arm,

there had been little in the way of conversation, she was not at all well advised about Jim. Emma wanted to be, the feeling of lack of understanding overwhelmed her. Next time I will be more relaxed less awkward. Sliding between the sheets, she knew he hadn't even complimented her on her dearly loved red scarf and her matching hand Bag. It was dusk perhaps he didn't notice, she excused him. Maybe next time he would look at them. He didn't seem like the Jim she had fixed in her mind. I must be aware to give him some space, so we can get to know each other. Another whole week to wait, oh Jim dear Jim, if you only knew my feelings for you, waiting another week seems forever.

Chapter 24

The Tearoom was proving quite a success, items in the shop that Ruby and Annie had stitched were also getting popular and Aunt was pleased. The ladies came into the sweet shop through to the tearoom, at first they would enquire,
"Is this the way through to the tea shop

please"?

"Yes, just go right on through into the sewing room, Aunt will be there, Annie and Ruby will look after you should you want to buy anything from the hand stitched range, Aunt Polly will get your tea."

"Thank you, I won't have to ask next time."

Disappearing through Emma thought how well things were working out. If it hadn't been for Jim, she would have been very happy. He still stuck in her mind.

Sitting down at the table waiting for tea and cakes, the two ladies were now chatting about the room. Annie went over to speak to them.

"Aunt won't be long, please feel free to look around while you are waiting."

"Are you Twins," this question was asked many times.

"Yes we are, I am Annie this is Ruby" they dipped a little curtsey as they introduced themselves. Not knowing if the lady was important they gave her the benefit of the doubt, few people took offence.

"What fine embroidery you do, let me look at that in your hand, what patience you have."

At this moment the ladies did not give their names, they didn't have to.

"I will certainly be coming back to see you when I need something stitched, this shop is

newly opened isn't it?"

"Yes, although it has been through a lot of changes, we are open now and getting quite busy." Ruby moved away as she could see Aunt bringing the tea with cake. It looked very tempting, the usual china teapot and a plate of small cakes to choose from. This customer was being well looked after it seemed too she appreciated it. Her friends would soon be joining her. It was going to be a very busy shop, the tearoom added to the enjoyment. Emma's plans were working well, but the question of Jim kept arising. Her personal plans were all askew, if only she could plan for Jim and herself as she had planned for the shop, she would try again.

Having tea together with Aunt, Ruby and Annie the twins were excited saying,
"Did you know Emma, there is a fair coming to town we saw it advertised on a poster, Auntie Polly, can we all go?"
"What me at a fair! Can't bide the things always thinking there may be an accident. The rides go so fast; the King and Queen boats would make me so sick. Oh! No, they are not for me."
"Well could we go? We have never seen a fair it would be something to look forward to for Annie and me, Emma too if she would want

to come." Emma joined in saying,
"No, if I went to the fair it would be with Jim, you have each other, let them go Aunt no harm will come to them, it is time they done something a bit different. What better opportunity than this."
"I will think about it I forget you are getting older. You should have more freedom you will have to forgive your poor old Aunt. Time stands still in one respect on the other hand the days fly by, especially when you get older, I can't think of you as any older than when you came, it must be about eighteen months or is it longer than that? We had to get the shop ready before it opened, that took all of six months, is it two years you have been here?"
"More than that," they both said, wanting to sound older so they could go to the fair. It was a huge thing to them living with their Aunt. In the Ford there had not been opportunities like this. Since coming to Aunt's they had saved money out of their pocket money so if anything came up they could use what they had and didn't have to ask anyone. Now they were glad that they had saved, spending a little of what they had saved, made it worthwhile saving. The week had gone by in a flash Emma wondered how

she had waited that long to see Jim again yet here it was. She had spoken to her Aunt about leaving the shop at four; she was hoping the shop didn't get very busy at that time. Aunt was willing to let her go, but it would mean closing the tea room down early, Aunt couldn't do both so reluctantly she said yes and let Emma go early. Here I go again, Emma thought, getting ready for her date. What will he be like tonight? Emma put on her best, wearing a new pair of button boots purchased from the sales. A bargain, they were a little stiff, looking for her buttonhook she decided if she was to get them on at all it would have to be by doing one button at a time. They were leather with particular fancy buttons that had enticed her to part with her money, the cold place they had been stored in their new box had made them hard to get on. Persevering making slow progress she finally had them on. Wriggling her toes trying to get them to be a better fit she walked up and down the floor bending the instep to an excessive degree, and finally decided to keep them on.

"I am going Auntie, I won't be late it looks as though it might rain it won't be much fun walking if it does."

"Bye, bye dear, don't worry I will look after

things while you're gone."

It didn't take long to get to the Park gates their meeting place. He wasn't dressed up; in fact, he was wearing a heavy overcoat. That wasn't what Emma wanted, she wanted him to look debonair and care free, like he had seemed in Aunt Polly's, this could be anyone he was so covered up. Maybe, he is cold, Emma thought, it wasn't that cold though. How could she show off her wonderful Jim as he was, in a huddle of clothes? Emma had envisaged being on his arm walking down the main thoroughfare waving and saying hello to people she knew from the shop, showing off her conquest.

"Hello Emma I see you got the time off I knew you would, we will walk along here tonight, it looks rainy there are entries along this stretch to pop into if it does rain can't be getting you wet can we?" What a feeble thing to say! why, there were shops all up the High Street to pop into for a tea, or coffee, didn't he want to buy her anything? These thoughts came to mind immediately, what did he think she was? Not someone he could treat like a passing fancy surely. Her back went up, not knowing what to think or say. Was this how all men treated their girls? She knew it wasn't, thoughtfully Neil came to mind. He

was still her dear friend never in a thousand years would he treat her so thoughtlessly. Still giving Jim the benefit of the doubt, they walked and talked. He saw her shudder,

"You are cold, he said, come into this entry I will wrap you into my coat to keep you warm." Before she could say anything, she was in the entry and stood like a parcel in his coat. They stood still for a few minutes.

"I will go home Jim, it will give you an evening to do whatever you want to, I don't like standing in some ones entry." she was pulling away, he caught her off guard.

"You must stay with me." His voice again was commanding, with his strength she couldn't do anything else but stay, she felt her body go rigid. His hands searched her body, his lips crashed down on hers. He hitched up her skirt and somehow touched her very private parts. Emma tingled all over. This was an entirely new experience, her head was swimming and she had no will of her own. Trembling she tried to stop the force that was carrying her, nature was having its own way, the desire natural. Again she pushed him away saying, in a trembling voice,

"Please Jim, I must go," His voice husky with passion answered,

"I want you to stay Emma don't be afraid, I will be gentle."

She found herself not wanting him to stop, sensations all over her body in a power that was enveloping her. I must stop him, he is overwhelming me. Gathering all her will power Emma gave him an almighty push kicking him in the calf as she did so.

"Hey that hurt, you're a feisty little madam I see you have the temperance of a young filly. I like that I will be victor Emma I want you so."

"I must go Jim, I have said a time that has to be honoured Aunt won't let me come again if I don't get back now. A feeble excuse to cover the passion that she was really experiencing for the first time, it was the only thing she could come up with, wanting distance between herself and Jim. He was swallowing her up Emma needed time to get her breath back and let the high colour go from her cheeks so to present herself normal on arriving home. Avoiding Aunt Polly again, Emma went straight up to her room. Feeling dishevelled yet strangely in a mood, she began whispering to herself. Has he reviled me? No, do I still want him? Yes more than ever. His fingers as he had touched her gave her distinct delight although she had

protested he had thrilled her entire body, her mouth trembled between the kisses, he was so near the heat of his loins transferred a message to her feelings, she wanted to be part of him it made her feel transparent. Wanting to stop wanting even more to go on, tears of frustration now fell down her cheeks had it been real? Yes, it had, why she was so frightened? He had not hurt her. What he had done was, arouse the sleeping need in her, never had she known this before Emma didn't recognise her own maternal emotion. I will be his; this is Jim telling me he wants me, now I know he wants me I will be there only for him.

This, being a sweeping statement with endless meaning, she cried herself to sleep.

Chapter 25

"Good morning Emma. The girls knocked her door loudly calling time for breakfast."
Yawning stretching her arms Emma got out of bed; must I get up so early?
"I will be down in a few minutes," she called happy to hear her two Sisters so alert. She couldn't pretend she felt the same way. Last evening had been a shock, it was bound to tell on her today but she had more than Jim to consider, it would do her good to get her feet

firmly on the ground, work had its place in life. Doing her work perhaps things would become less of a conundrum the answer to her questions would come naturally. There was no person to ask, even if there were Emma wouldn't have listened, her questions were so very personal. If Aunt Polly knew about last night she would close the door to Jim Emma knew that, then why didn't she do just that? It would be the end to her worry. Love does not let you go so easily she was bound, surely after getting to really know each other Jim would marry her then there would be no more questions asked, life would be in balance once more, it needed to be. The girls walked into Emma's bedroom, her thought pattern was disturbed she heard,
"We are going to the fair tomorrow night Emma," Ruby smiled,
"You got your wish then did you. I hope it is a fine evening for you."
"Why won't you come with us it would be fun all three of us"?
"I will see how I feel later on. I was out last night Aunt will think she is being deserted."
"No, she won't, I think she would feel better if you tagged along, she seems to think we will get whisked away, by the gypsies."
"I shouldn't laugh at that my girls, stranger

things have happened."

Giggling they all went downstairs to join their Aunt.

"What was all the laughter about? I could hear you from the kitchen." Aunt walked in and asked how did you get on last night Emma dear?" Emma replied

"You know just a walk and talk getting to know each other then it rained. Being so cold we decided to come home so we got home early again." Emma didn't dare think what Aunt would say if she knew what had really happened. There was no way Aunt would ever know. This was between Jim and Emma a law unto itself between lovers not for any other ears or eyes. That little statement made to herself had lightened her load, Jim and me are not the only ones trying to understand the human condition, she prayed she had done the right thing, she would see Jim again he had this hold on her.

Ruby and Annie had asked Emma so many times to go to the fair with them, she finally said yes.

"Shall we go on Saturday, or do you think a night in the week would be better?" Ruby asked.

"Saturday, Emma replied, we have Sunday off to get over the late night, not that I want

to make it too late, we don't want to be there when the pubs turn out do we, going about seven to be back at nine would suit me."

"That is what we will do then." Annie, wasn't too sure of this fair idea, she was going along with it to please Ruby. Emma was joining them now so that pleased Annie. Aunt Polly was also pleased Emma was going they could all look after each other. Saturday quickly came. Off to the fair they went, all with their frilly bonnets and pretty, flouncy dresses. Seeing the three of them all arm in arm, did Aunty Polly good.

"Lovely girls you look a picture now heed what I say, stay together and don't make yourselves sick on the rides."

"All right, all right, don't take our enthusiasm away all together." They laughingly said. Their hearts were light, the nights twinkling stars were out. The shine in their eyes and the skip in their toes the coins jingling in the bags they carried, no worries or troubles just three loving Sisters out to conquer the world able to take all that came their way, hopefully. The barrel organ played its tune as they approached. In the background, the round-a-bouts music outdid the organ blasting its music over the top of everything.

"How can we not be excited," Ruby exclaimed! Look at all the colours, the movement is surrounding us do you want to ride on anything Annie?"

"I only want to look for a while I will tell you when I am brave enough to go on something. They all go so fast, I don't want to be a spoil sport you go if you want to I will wait, go on Emma, go with her I will be all right and I promise I won't move from this spot." In front of them the Painted Horses that went up and down tempted them to have a ride, they were not too fast and the Horses had these nice friendly faces. When the roundabout stopped Emma and Ruby got on, it was a job to get a balance, their skirts full and billowing blowing in the breeze, as they tried to side-saddle the Wooden Horse with decorum and safety.

"Thank goodness it isn't a real horse," Ruby said.

Emma too was having trouble, the man collecting the money came around and helped the pair of them it was part of his job to see things were safe before the music and the round-a-bout got started. Off, they went, with the broadest of smiles, to the music of "Sweet Rosie O Grady." Annie waved every time they went by, she could see they were enjoying it, why hadn't she gone on too?

"Are they your Sisters?" A voice piped up at the side of her, she turned her head to see this young man talking to her.

"Yes they are we are all together." Better, say that quickly so that he wasn't left in any doubt.

"Come from round here do you? Can't say I have seen you, wouldn't miss a pretty face like yours, what is your name?"

"Why should I tell you my name? It is none of your business." Annie said.

"I could make it my business for tonight, let me show you the fair, there is lots to see and we could go on the Swing Boats together after getting candy floss."

He being full of himself put Annie ill at ease, she was glad when the round-a-bout slowed down so that Emma and Ruby would be with her.

"Oh! That was fun," Ruby laughed Emma following at her heels.

Annie turned around to see if the young man wanted to be introduced, but he was no-where in sight.

"I have been talking to a young man Ruby. He's gone into the crowd" Annie told Emma and Ruby. Emma said,

"There are a lot of those sorts of men around.

It's best just to ignore them; you did the right thing Annie. They linked arms, turned in another direction went on looking for the next item to catch their attention.

"Here you are Annie, this won't upset you," Emma was looking at the coconut shy. The man shouting,

"Three balls for a halfpenny, winner every time. Come on you girls take a Coconut home to Mum, she will be ever so pleased, or you can have a goldfish, look how nice a goldfish would look on the sideboard."

They had three balls one each, throwing them to dislodge the coconut of its stand. The stall holder grinned and said,

"Oh! What a shame better luck next time ladies all the fun of the fair." He then passed his attention to the next passers-by. Not many winners they all agreed.

Next was the "Roll a penny" stall, you rolled the coin down a slit, if it landed on the square correctly you won double your money,

"Easy", Annie said, rolling her coin down, it landed on the line that was separating the squares. No luck.

"I shall try again." Calculating as to where the penny would roll to, she let it go out of her fingers, still no luck, last one, down rolled her penny. Much to their delight, this time it

landed on a bonus square, she came away winning all of two pennies, the amount wasn't important; it was the winning that had made her day.

"The King and Queen boats," they headed for next. All of them went on this ride. They could all sit together it made Annie feel safe.

Swoooooooooosh it went up and Swooooooooooooooooooosh it came down in a swinging movement. Their dress skirts flew back when they came down showing pretty petticoats with lace and pink ribbon. When they came off, their legs had turned to jelly it took a few moments to get the feeling under control. Yes, all was well, having spent the money that they had allowed for the trip each having their own experience they were satisfied, still skipping along on the way home without a care in the world. Once home of course all talking one over the other they told Aunt about the rides, the music, and the atmosphere of the fair, she laughed with them.

Annie didn't tell about the young man who had wanted to know her name. She thought she hadn't better or next time Aunt would not let them go. The night carried on Aunt Polly had jacket potatoes in the oven the aroma was lovely. None of them could resist sitting

down with the butter dish on the table to take what you wanted. Togetherness it was for all to see. This is what happiness is made of, solid two feet on the ground and love for each other. Aunt went on to say,
"Did they use manual labour to work the rides, or did it come from steam?"
Nobody knew, to be honest nobody cared. That side of things were left to the males of the population, the pretty side that was the one that they took notice of and the pretty tunes, the coloured lights, they found themselves crooning, "Sweet Rosy O Grady" in the oddest of moments, for the next few days all the colour of the fair came to mind a real thrill.

Chapter 26

Sunday sweet Sunday, a day for doing just what you wanted to. Why thought Emma, didn't Jim make a Sunday date there would be no rush, no shop to leave for Aunt to look after, maybe I will ask him next week. Although she after had immediately thought. If I didn't have my Sunday when would I wash my hair and see that my clothes are presentable? There had to be some time allotted to these domestic duties and personal care. Emma generally took her odd sewing bits to the girls they did them much neater than she could, they didn't mind in fact they would ask if there was anything they could do for her. Trying not to be a pain, she only answered yes if it was something she really could not do herself then the offer became a real bonus. A good hair brush was well used on Sunday too, combing, brushing till her hair shone then she would put it all up in pins covered by a mop cap and this would keep it all tidy to look smart in the shop the following week. Annie tapped her door,
"Come in,"
"Have you any black hose wool Emma?"

"If I have, it is in my small sewing box over there, got over your trip to the fair Annie?"

"Just about, it was a lovely evening wasn't it? I couldn't have stayed any longer though I was really whacked out. I thought Aunt having the supper ready for us finished the evening off perfectly, it had seemed a long time since tea I was ready for supper will we do it again Emma?"

"Of course we will, we need to spend more time together. By the way, have you heard from Mum and Dad lately?"

"Ruby and me sent a letter about a week ago, we will get one back shortly."

"I am glad about that, because I don't seem to have had a minute to write. As long as they are both all right that is the main thing. Have you found the wool you wanted? Yes thank you Emma I will leave you in peace now, I have to darn my stockings, I wore a hole right through the toe at the fair and I hope I can darn it so that it doesn't wriggle into a bump."

"What with the fine work you do! Away with you, see you in the morning."

The week pressed on, it would soon be time for Emma to see Jim again she had mixed feelings about this, one way her conscience bothered her, the other way Mother Nature had taken hold she was not going to let her go, she needed Jim all her body told her so. There were no ifs or buts, Jim had laid the law down and she had to see him. He was her man, not being used to men made it more difficult to understand Jim's ways. He knew what he wanted so he got it, simple as that. Emma had been getting things in her head untangled, knowing how she needed Jim what could she do? I hope he softens is his approach towards me, Emma thought.

"Hello Jim, he was still wearing the heavy coat she noticed. What shall we do tonight, your choice, I don't mind."

It was a lie but she knew he would have his own way no matter what, it was pointless to argue.

"Our usual walk will suit me just to the edge of Town. There are some derelict houses no-one goes there and we would have it to ourselves."

She followed the way he went, neither of them said very much, Emma's heart was pounding, thinking this still doesn't seem right, she warned herself, but on they went. Arriving at the spot Jim had mentioned its crumbled appearance did it no favours. He put his arm around her they kissed, she knew his passion was eminent his hands were wandering inside her blouse then running over her hips, her own passion mounting to match his. She couldn't stop him she wanted him as much as he wanted her. It wasn't all Jim's fault she was fulfilling the most basic desire and was unable to deny him. Her breath was coming in short gasps, her body was opening to him he thrust himself inside her. It was a moment in a lifetime that could not be repeated for she was a virgin. She cried out feeling pain then there was an ecstatic moment when they joined body and soul together. The two of them as one, it was over.

Emma thought no-one will ever know, soon we will marry then I will be Jim's in everyone's eyes. She allowed herself to run her fingers over his arms then his male parts adoring him. He stayed very quiet in the after-glow of love. This is what their meetings had come to, people, if they knew, would warn Emma, but Emma knew better, she was to be Jim's wife respected and happy. There would be no need for all the hiding away they would walk proudly together showing all the world the love they had for each other, enough to last a lifetime. Emma would have Jim's children some day, in her head she had it all planned out, counting herself lucky. Jim could have been more thoughtful though, perhaps men in general didn't think thoughtfulness an attribute. Again, Neil crossed her mind, thinking of him while in another man's arms. What do you want? Emma questioned, Neil's best attributes, he is kind, thoughtful and always ready to give a willing hand, or the rugged appeal the rough manor that my Jim has. Jim didn't ask, he took. Some of the guilt has to be laid at my feet I can't help wanting to be near him. Straightening their clothes they stood up and got ready to leave each other. Jim said,

"I will be able to walk some of the way with you then I have to run I have to make some business calls." Emma replied,

"We don't seem to have much time together perhaps we could make an earlier date as well as Thursday."

"No I am so busy, I can't do that. It will have to be a week today same time."

"All right," Emma said linking her arm through his.

"Please don't do that, it ruffles the lining in this coat, I like to walk alone."

How dare he, once more his manor was stand offish, she wanted to be as close to him as she could. Again, she doubted, it troubled her mind how could he not want her close to him? He almost left her out when it came to the normal boy girl relationship. He was all too quick at making love, that sort of bond should have been approached gently it made her head swim at the speed he used. Why? She found the question coming again and again... Was Emma really loved?

Chapter 27

"Did you get a letter, Annie? Are they all well?" Emma called, being in adjoining shops they could talk that is if there were no customers in.

"I did and they are Annie called back, I will tell you the news tonight, when we all sit together." Today, Emma felt degraded it had felt like a blow when Jim didn't want her to walk arm in arm with him. I have to try to understand him better, she thought, if he is so busy, isn't that a good sign? It means when the expense of marriage comes along he will have job security he probably has plans that are too early to discuss with me. I have to stop being so pushy it is my fault; I want it all today that is my trouble, I never have wanted to wait for anything. A customer broke her thoughts

"What can I get for you today madam? No the new style box chocolates haven't come in yet, maybe by the weekend, yes they will be assorted, these are the best I have at the moment." Emma, looking after her customer, showing no sign of the heavy heart she had. She thought I have to get over it one way or

another, work is the best thing for me to do. I know it, why can't my life be simpler. Look at Annie and Ruby they don't chase after men, they are perfectly happy with each other unless it is the age gap and their needs will come later, she sighed wishing she had never set eyes on Jim, he had given her heartache.

With all four of them sitting around the table having tea, Emma wanted to know about Mum and Dad. Ruby told them all,

"They seem to be having a whale of a time now they can go out together again, we needn't worry about them, apparently Dad has a fresh crush ha, ha, on Mum; he is treating her like a Queen she is taking all she can get and loving it. Borrowing the car has been great; they do simple things like a picnic together, a ride to a different town that they haven't been before. Mum is telling tales out of school she says Dad has become her beau all over again he even buys her flowers."

"I can't wait to be married," Annie said. It must be so lovely to have someone that cares for you alone, what will you wear Ruby when you get married?"

"I haven't given it a thought to tell you the truth, I am sure I would make my own Wedding Dress, or we could do it between us Annie, I will help you with yours, you can

help me with mine, but enough of this wedding talk, it will be Emma's turn before us. She has found her Jim, come on Emma, tell us all."

Emma was in no fit state to talk about Jim, or weddings, so she laughed it off.

"Can I see the letter?" Emma asked.

"Of course you can, there is a lot more in it than I have told you, but we were messing about, having a joke, so I didn't get to the more important things in this morning."

Ruby gave the letter to Emma.

"I think if you don't mind I will go to my bedroom to read it. I wanted to have a chat with Mum this will be the next best thing."

Lying on her bed Emma wanted to feel close to Mum and Dad, they were still her solid ground. Reading the letter aloud, she gave a "whoop" of delight. Mum had asked them all to go on a weeks' holiday Emma knew they must be missing her as well as Annie and Ruby. They all were missing them. Back at the Ford Albert had said,

"All right Ada I think it is time we had our family all under this roof for a short while. I think they would love to come, have a holiday and spend a little time catching up on our news and us there news. Time has passed so quickly it has rolled into years since the girls

have been home. There has always been pressing engagements it has had to be put off time after time. I am sorry I haven't fulfilled my promise to go and see the girls often the Coventry traffic has really put me off. There is no reason though they can't come to us for a while, I will risk the driving to go and pick them up."

The Coventry traffic was the draw back as far as the girls could see, so letters were all the more important. Now they were asked to go all together to stay just for a week. Emma couldn't contain herself she jumped up off the bed ran downstairs waving the letter in her hand.

"Well, you didn't tell me about the holiday when you read the letter earlier Ruby, does Aunt Polly know?"

"Annie knows but not Aunt, we thought we would get her in a good mood before we said anything. We would love to go and by the look on your face you would too. We will talk to Aunt when next we are together. You know what it is like Emma the time goes then its bedtime, we must make an effort this evening I don't know what she will say, it would mean shutting both shops for a week." The evening came they confronted Aunt Polly with the holiday offer. Putting it in a nutshell with no

fancy words Aunt said,

"This is out of the blue, I will have to consider it and I know it has been a long time since you saw both of them, they are bound to want to see you. As you say there never is a right time, I'll tell you tomorrow me darlins."

Now and again, Aunt Polly would slip into very informal words. Annie and Ruby liked it, - it was the way Mum spoke. Emma didn't like it she liked the step up she had taken into a higher ranking community, so watched her P's and Q's.

"Has the order come in yet Emma," Aunt Polly said enquiring about the sweet shop.

"It should be here today Aunt, did you want something particular from it?"

"Yes I am going to take Ada the biggest box of chocolates they deliver, I have thought about the holiday it is a very kind thing to ask us all not leaving me out, so I am going to say yes. I shall look forward to it my letter will be in the post tonight, so you can sort out your best bib and tucker."

Emma's face lit up, Aunt had decided so quickly and the girls also thought Aunt would take ages to make up her mind. Emma called the girls in from their side of the shop, saying to Aunt, go on you tell them."

"Tell us what?"

Aunt Polly looked at the three lovely girls, pleased in her choice seeing she was about to make them all very happy.

"We are going to go on the holiday. It didn't take long to decide, because I too am looking forward to a week free from the shop. It is established enough now to close for just one week. We will all come back refreshed then we will get on with business again, I should just have said yes before, I am a bit slower on the uptake these days I need time to decide everything."

Customers were arriving so their holiday debate had to go, not that it went from their minds already they were making plans. It would be lovely to see Mum and Dad again their old room, this and that there were so many things all of which they had missed without even knowing it. One thing crossed their minds, which they had now, but didn't have at home, it was an indoor bath and toilet there were many attributes from living with Aunt Polly and of course the beautiful shop, both sweets and the stitching shop. The ladies tearoom, the fine embroidery Annie and Ruby did, all of these things were not thought about as they went on with their daily work. As Emma went on with her day, she thought about Jim, she would not be able to see him for a week. Good she thought he will miss me and then he might value me more. Meeting him this week, he had moaned and argued about her going on the holiday but she stood her ground, so he backed off. Emma thought, Have I got to take a stronger stance with him, he has backed off about the holiday, perhaps when I come back I will stand my ground again and bring wedding plans into the conversation. Her position was not ideal she needed some thinking time.

It was arranged that Albert would pick them up, to go on the weeks' holiday. He arrived without Ada.

"Ada hasn't come with me it will give you a little more room for your bags and it is going to be one of those tight squeezes anyway" He went inside to pick up the bags telling the girls,

"Aunt must sit beside me, you three will sit in the back you will have to balance your bags on your laps and I am hoping you are not bringing too much."

Doing as Albert had said, they were ready to go, he called,

"Turn the ignition on Polly."

She had no idea what the ignition was so she called back saying so.

"Sorry Albert, you will have to come and do

it."

Albert leaned into the car and turned the key.
"Now I can get the engine started," he said swinging the handle at the front of the car listening for the engine to fire. Here we go then," They pulled off to join the other traffic that was on the road. There was a lot of giggling and moving around in their seats to make their journey as comfortable as possible. Albert had a thought and said,
"Polly, Emma, is it the first time you have been in a car? Or have you young lady, (meaning Emma,) a beau, that picks you up regularly?"
Emma thought fat chance and replied,
"No this is the first time, we are finding it almost as good as a ride at the fair you must forgive us giggling, we are all a little apprehensive, we do feel very privileged though, we do thank you very much. Aunt Polly, how do you like it?"
"I am just quietly taking it all in, I won't be sorry when we see Ada though with the kettle already on" They knew she was smiling it was the tone in her voice that was conveying the fact.
"Splut, splut, splut." They chugged along, beep, beep went, the horn."
Aunt Polly didn't know how Albert had

swerved to miss a horse; the horse drawn cabs flitted in and out of the throng and it made Aunt flinch as they passed by. She thought Albert very clever to negotiate through the narrow spaces that were left for him. He had his work cut out to get them all over to Eadie Street safely, he deserved a medal. Albert was considerably satisfied he was controlling the car like a veteran. The car chugging away nicely splut splut splut, the steering wheel in his capable hands felt right and Albert was King of all he surveyed!

Chapter 28

"That's more like it," Aunt said as they walked over the thresh-hold into Ada's kitchen. Ada was tending the kettle as Polly had hoped she said,
"Hello Polly, how good to see you, the kettle is on, I have a hot meal to sit down to shortly. How was your journey?"
"To tell you the truth Ada, I was petrified. These new-fangled gadgets are not for the likes of me, give me a horse and carriage any day." They embraced and laughed. Ada

greeted her Daughters with open arms and a kiss. They were quite embarrassed it had been so long since they had seen Mum forgetting the real motherly attitude that was once an everyday occurrence. Emma looking at the table that she had scrubbed so often, the thread bare rugs, the same old chairs, the candle sticks with burned down candles, the fire guard and the stand with the poker brush and shovel hanging with it in the hearth. On the way in there were the outside privy and the tin bath still hanging on a nail that they had hauled in when needed. It was as if time had stood still, they were strangers in their own home. Morning of the next day they were all very chatty, that is except Emma.

"What is the matter with you Emma," Ruby said, you seem quiet today"

"I have a spin in my head, I am feeling a bit sick I think it is the trip over in the car, not used to it you see."

Dad, his arm around Emma's shoulder, giving her a squeeze he said,

"I can see car riding doesn't suit you me darlin.' I was going to suggest we went on a picnic in Asbury woods the Pool is on the opposite side of the road, it is very pleasant."

"No, sorry Dad that is not for me today, but you go I will be one too many in the car, it is

a quiet sit down I need."

"That's a shame I only have the opportunity today, I believe Mum and Aunt have planned out for the rest of the week and I don't want to spoil their plans do I?

"Don't worry I will be quite happy lying on my bed, in fact I prefer it, you lot can go and chat as much as you like I just need a rest today." All agreed that was the best thing to do. Mum started to pack the picnic just a light lunch with a flask of tea, they all crammed into the car and Emma waved goodbye, then went to lie down. Looking around the room it was surprising to see nothing had changed, there her slippers were, an old dressing gown worst for wear, hung on the door peg, the old lino curled up at one place, the curtains hung pitifully thin. Nothing of an extravagant sense was to be seen. Did I put up with this as my bedroom while I lived with Mum and Dad? Of course I did, I didn't know of anything different. Her eyes closed to relieve her headache she was thinking of Jim. He was never too far away from her thoughts for this week though her own feminine side could rule, not having to do anything she did not want to do, being with the family putting solidarity in all things she had been taught from Mum and Dad to the fore. Why then did

she have to bring Jim into the picture? Did she really intend bringing him into her lovely family? Marriage that would change his status he would then be part of her family is this what she really wanted? Trying to sort out her conundrum, she fell asleep.

Opening her eyes hearing noises downstairs, she realised the others must be back. She straightened herself up swung her legs to the floor to get up. Still feeling giddy, she slowly combed her hair; she would leave it just tidy for tonight, anything to relieve her head, and she knew she didn't have to stand on ceremony for her family. Forcing a smile to her face she went to join Ruby and Annie.

"Hello, did you have a nice picnic?" Emma greeted the girls, she did have a smile albeit forced. They looked as though they had enjoyed the afternoon, having bright ruddy faces, and smiles a mile wide, there was a basin of blackberries in Ruby's hand, and Annie was holding her bonnet letting her hair free. Aunt pushed her way forward, to put the kettle on it was always her first thought, saying to Emma,

"It was lovely Emma very different to our usual days in the shop, I wish you had come, then again, I don't think the car would have held you, we were like sardines in a tin."

"Don't say that old girl or I won't ask you again." *Dad said in a playful mood as he grinned. It had been lovely. Next day all of them had a day of lying around just relaxing, chatting, catching up on the family news, messing about and getting nowhere our Mum called it. As they or she didn't get much time for doing just that, all enjoyed each other's company. Discussing the next day, they decided to make bread. It was a long time since the girls had helped Mum with this; it was a special thing between them. It brought them together, made them feel real again, it was grounding for them. Their life in the shop now, was somewhat pretentious and they didn't have to say "yes Madam" to Mum, they all laughed talking about it.*

Wednesday was for bread making, all eager to start the table had been scrubbed. The wood was almost white doing this job over the years had bleached it. On the table two bowls were placed, two bags of strong flour, a jug with tepid milk and water in it, to start the yeast working, and oil in moderation Sugar was used in the sweet bread mix with sultanas. Pepper and salt for savoury bread a tad more of oil, and cheese if wanted.

"Come on, let me put the ingredients in," Ruby said, pushing Emma out of the way.

Annie was behind Ruby, they all wanted to get in on the act.

"What you! Emma replied we want bread not concrete. All gathered around Mum, she stood like a surgeon going to do a big operation; Mum was the head of the team. Putting the yeast into the milky water then standing it near the warmth of the oven, she split the flour between two bowls then added all the dry ingredients to each bowl one sweet one savoury, Mum said,

"You can have a go now and split the liquid half into one bowl the rest into the other.

Annie and Ruby did this.

"Gently mix" Mum's instruction always there.

"Emma came forward, what can I do?"

"Don't worry, there is plenty of elbow work to do, yes you can all have a go when the dough is ready to knead, it will save my poor arms."

They all sniggered.

"Is this the right consistency?" Annie picked up her hands from the bowl they were stuck with the mixture. Mum said,

"I don't think so Annie it is too wet, Ruby's is better."

Annie looked at Ruby's it was quite dry. Annie then added some flour left over for this purpose the dough then became more pliable.

"You know girls the times you have seen me doing this, I would have thought you would have remembered how to do it for yourselves, how are you going to look after a Husband and family if you can't make bread?"
Polly looked over their shoulders.
"Oh! Ada, you shame me, I am not too sure about making bread, I wait to see the batches when they come out of the oven before I know they are going to be eat-able, they usually are, but I always breathe a sigh of relief when they are good. I am watching you and I might pick up a few tips hey? The trouble is I don't get the time, the tearoom has a consistent flow of customers and I treat them with great respect. I do make the small cakes and the fruit cake that is enough for me." Mum smiled,
"I know Polly, I wasn't trying to torment you, I just thought, the girls have seen it done so often they should have remembered some of the routine." The dough was turned out on to the clean table. After Mum had shown them, Annie and Ruby took charge of the kneading, pulling and thumping the bread flattening and rolling bringing together then doing it all over again till their arms ached and their backs bent. Annie said,
"Here you are Emma it is about your turn."

Emma didn't mind watching saying,

"I thought you were doing it so well, I didn't want to disturb you, There was a smile lingering as Emma said this, anyway, I still haven't got rid of my headache properly." Aunt joined in the conversation saying,

"That headache is lasting a long time Emma we'll have to get you to a Doctor to see what can be done about it.

Mum joined in knowing a Doctor was not what Emma required in her opinion Emma just needed rest. The bread was left to prove for a couple of hours with a loose cover over it. It was now ready to be punched in the middle flattening it, a second time of proving and when it had risen again, it was ready to be shaped and baked.

"Now flour your hands, roll the dough into small balls encouraging the air to stay in, gently dear, gently. Two baking trays full of individual batches were now put in the oven, they would cook until risen and golden then be taken out and placed on a cooling tray. There is not an aroma in the entire world that would take the place of baking bread, especially made lovingly in the bosom of family. It permeates through the home our senses pick up the vibes and we know we are

loved.

Chapter 29

The week had gone so quickly it had been a dream. Now leaving Mum and Dad it was the wounds of their first departure that made solemn faces as they packed into the car again to go back to the shops. Emma was hoping the trip didn't make her feel sick, Aunt had some mints in her bag for that very purpose. Again the curtains were twitching in the street, this time though Mum was proud of her family, three of the prettiest girls all dressed beautifully holding their heads high, confident, that is why they went to Aunt Polly. Ada knew she would be able to start them off into an adult world better than she could herself. The boys still being with Ada and Albert and working with them they would teach them, and mould them into the life a male had to face. How much they had to learn to pass on to their children, the grandchildren still to be born Ada and Albert's grandchildren, just as wise and loving as they themselves had been. The last kisses, the last waves, they had gone out of sight. On the road back to the shops, everyone was quiet in the car. The return even though they loved the life they now lived with Aunt Polly hadn't the essence of home.

The journey back seemed shorter. When they walked into the front door of the sweet shop, Emma could distinguish the smell of chocolate, mints and éclairs, she was back.

"Have you got all your belongings Emma? Dad called. Don't want to be leaving anything important I have to return the car as soon as I get back. Don't want you saying you have something missing, I can't bring it back easily, you all please check your things." Dad always made a big fuss over seeing to all of this, he was only looking after

his girls, it was just common sense and sometimes sense is not so common! Albert went into the shop to see if things were all safe inside, no break in or damage while they had been away, all was well.

"Dad, the kettle is on, tell Aunt to come and sit down for a cup of tea before we all go to bed. Are you returning tonight Dad?"

"Yes, I wouldn't be comfortable if I left my Ada alone overnight, the car will travel light there will be very little traffic, so it shouldn't take me too long. Don't worry about me you get your beauty sleep me darlins'." Albert had brought his precious cargo safely back to Polly's, now he had to take gifts to Ada from Polly and the girls. All the girls and Aunt Polly had gifts for Ada, they were to be taken by Dad in his trusty Ford 8. Emma said,

"We do worry about you though Dad, so drive safely, better to get there later than not to get there at all, there is a hamper that we couldn't get in the car going over, take it tonight. Mum will be pleased, it will be safe on the back seat and there are no perishables in it." At last the car was packed, Dad remarking that it was full to the brim. Finally they all sat together and drank tea. Sipping their tea glad of the moist warmth it put inside, they talked to each other, exchanging

conversation before Albert went into the night. This family was poor, but rich in family love, to be envied for all to see. Aunt Polly now in that circle, she didn't feel how she used to feel after she lost her Husband. She was caught in another web, happily joining in, feeling secure being part of a close-knit thread, which gave her security.

The girls were now in their shops the next day, getting a little dusting done here and there. Ruby dusting and placing the items for sale at a better angle in the window said,

"You can't believe there is dust collected in so short a time."

"No" Annie replied, even the counters are dusty I think it is the traffic, it is fairly busy around here isn't it, we do like it busy, so we shouldn't grumble." Emma was in her sweet shop glad to see her old customers and again directing the way to the tearoom.

"It is a pity" Aunt said, I didn't have more room it is a very popular teashop. I think Annie and Ruby draw our ladies they always chat to them, they follow on buying something that catches their eye I said that would be the case I didn't expect it so soon. People seem to love the pink atmosphere, the glow from the Parasols, the elegant way it is set out, not saying about the privacy that

comes quite naturally. Having the week away has been good, not only for us for the business too, we have all been missed A pleasant look on Aunt's face informed the girls that Aunt Polly was satisfied. If the truth were known Aunt liked serving the tea, it gave her a sense of importance and kept her active. Emma showing a customer one of the largest boxes of chocolates, recently delivered said,

"They are assorted madam, the chocolate is a very fine brand, I am sure when you open them you will see that the presentation is second to none. Even the colours in this lovely picture tell you that this is distinguished merchandise, I do have cheaper brands." The lady held up her hand saying,

"Oh no, I certainly don't want anything cheap these will be just the thing for Mary I see there are different pictures on the front of them mind you I am having a job to choose. I declare to pick the best design, is difficult." Finally choosing one with a thatched cottage on the front lid, they were duly wrapped into a pretty, pink parcel, with Aunt Polly's name on it. This was one customer who would advertise "Aunt Polly's Parlour," wherever she went this morning. In fact, the pretty, pink parcel actually set off her garments and

toned with the colour chosen to wear today. Annie came in to see Emma,

"Do you know what we have just had?"

"No, should I?" Ruby joined them just for a minute. Annie went on,

"We have definite orders for embroidery from the collar to the waist at the back of two coats, for Lady Faversham. We were amazed when this fine carriage drew up. The person that alighted came in; well into your shop door actually, didn't you see her? She looked very grand. We are to embroider the V section running from the wide shoulder to the waist, with just one Red Rose with stem and leaves running down it. The second one has to have a Gardenia with leaves, in a pale creamy pink. We are thrilled, so is Aunt, you would have known about it sooner but you had a good customer yourself buying boxed chocolates. What do you think of that our Emma?"

Faces full of glee they returned to their own work. Of course, it was thrilling news, Emma was as proud of them as they were themselves. Emma loved her Sisters dearly she loved the smiles that lit up their faces when the achievement that they had been aiming for were realised, all through the years it had been this way, it was no effort at all to be with them looking after their best interests, Emma was so pleased a happy moment for them all.

Chapter 30

During the week Emma thought about Jim a lot, she again was so looking forward to their meeting. I wonder if he has missed me, I have missed him he seems a part of me since we made love together. I would marry him. Perhaps he wouldn't use me so brusquely if we were together all the time. I am thinking time is of the essence if he had more time that would be the answer he seems always in a desperate hurry. Soon we will talk it over and make some final plans for my peace of mind this has to be done. After a busy week in the shop, Emma was now getting ready to go on her date, looking tidy and smart, but not so elaborate. It was a waste of time, he messed all her dresses up fifteen minutes after meeting him her clothes would be of least importance she was as bad as him longing to be near. Loving him with all her heart, she couldn't be close enough to him.
"Hello Jim, have you missed me?"
"Come here you rag a muffin, I will show you how I have missed you."
He embraced her kissing her wildly, she responded. All the gentle warning she had

told herself was blown away. Now in Jim's strong arms, all precautionary measures took flight. Wanting him desperately pulling him ever closer to her he entered her body, ecstasy in the movement making her breathing fast, her mouth open she was his, this was real, no control for either of them in a bond of love so deep it was all that mattered.

"Jim, my darling Jim," she uttered, it was lost in the ferment that was taking place, the place she wanted to be forever, now she was sure all doubts gone. Their wedding day would be a beautiful conclusion, to be his forever this is what Emma wanted.

"Jim, come on Jim, he had nestled his head close on to her bosom still fondling her.

Darling are you all right," she said, gently moving his weight. He being a big man, swamped her forgetting how small she was, how fragile like a china doll so easily broken. Yes all of those things she may be, but inside there was a resolution with a determination that matched Jim's own, knowing what she was all about and aiming for her goal, this was Emma. Getting there clothes tidy enough to be seen they chuckled and smiled, did that really happen? Each one asking the other with their eyes making the contact, no words were necessary. In loves young dream they

went forward although Jim still didn't want Emma to walk arm in arm, she dismissed it as just a quirky way he had. She supposed there would be a few quirky ways she would have to get used to. She had a few of her own for him to get used to. Smiling gently, walking slowly, they prepared to leave each other.
"I am not going to kiss you out here Emma people are too nosey and I want my business kept private, as I suppose you do."
"Me Jim, I could shout our love from the roof tops. There is nothing to hide in the way I feel for you but as you wish."
After making another date they walked in different directions, her heart was light and she felt very happy.

Emma didn't go into the kitchen, her own room was the place to go. Going over every move Jim had made to re-live the ecstasy the belonging the love there was between them. Soon she would tell Aunt Polly Annie and Ruby, they would be so excited for her, the girls would make her wedding dress themselves, two bridesmaids dresses, or should that be "Maids Of Honour" they were too grown up to be bridesmaids. Now, Emma thought, pink would follow on from the choice of pink in the shop. That would be nice for Aunt to know that I have enough consideration to choose pink maids. She smiled to herself, but the pink wouldn't have, "Aunt Polly's Parlour" written all over it. It would be elegant pink so lovely with crinoline skirts, Parasols, button boots in white, or a pair of white satin shoes. Yes, at last Emma was making plans even if they were only in her own mind. She would be prepared when the time came not undecided and fidgety. Being mistress of all she surveyed, she was ready to go ahead, Jim would like that. I of course will wear white although I am not still a virgin Jim is the only man I have ever known that my body has invited in, to share our love as I am marrying that man it will be all right. Shall I have a Parasol too or a bouquet? We have plenty of time to think things over no need to rush.

She rolled over her bed in a casual manor, flinging her arms up to the ceiling feeling light hearted almost drunk with the thoughts that were running through her head. It was all really going to happen, the biggest passage in her life. It is ME not the girl down the street, not a friend, just ME. Jubilantly she stood in front of the long mirror, I must keep my hair in good order, use the cream I had given me for my face, hands too they are important. I want to look my very best for

Jim. I want to take his breath away when I walk down the aisle on Dad's arm to join him. We will remember the day and the attire all the days to come, when we're joined together before God. We will make memories of our own putting down our roots and maybe someday having a baby. All my life I have waited for this moment, I mustn't waste it. I must keep all of this a secret. Jim will tell me when the time is right to tell the family I really don't know how to wait, but I must.

Another very busy day in the shop, Emma didn't have much time to think more of her own future it had to be shelved for the time being. Looking out of the window to rest her eyes from the gaslights, a carriage stopped the lady alighting from it looked very grand. "This" thought Emma must be for the girls, the coats to embroider hung in dust bags over her Man Servant's arm, they walked through on the way to Annie and Ruby.

"Good evening Lady Faversham, Emma said dropping a gentle curtsey. Please do go through, they are waiting for you. Emma led the way and said Ruby here is Lady Faversham is Annie in here too?"

"Yes, she will be she has popped into the back for moment, she won't be long would you take a seat Lady Faversham?"

"Thank you my dear, I hope this is a convenient time for you, I would like to get this work started, I shall be in to supervise the embroidery from time to time I hope that is in order?"

"Yes of course, we will start it first thing in the morning, Oh! Here is Annie now." Dropping a quiet curtsey, Annie said,

"Good afternoon, sorry I was out in the kitchen I hope you haven't waited long."

"No, and I am not staying I know it is near to your closing time. I don't want to delay you; your Sister says you will start embroidering first thing in the morning that will be fine. I will leave you to it; I just want to get some chocolate before I leave, goodnight."

"Emma was standing behind her counter ready to serve.

"Just a small box of chocolates please, now what is your name, ah, Emma of course. Cadbury if you have them, I have heard they are all the rage."

"Yes, Madam, if I show you the two smallest boxes you can chose the one you want."

"Yes, that one will do I don't want to put on weight just when I am having my coats done do I?" They both laughed and away milady went her servant just behind her.

When she had gone Emma closed the shop.

In she went to see Annie and Ruby saying, "She seems nice enough, doesn't she? She was ready to have a smile with me about putting on weight, some wouldn't do that and they think they are far above that sort of thing. I can see her becoming a regular that will please Aunt Polly.

Chapter 31

Emma went to see Jim again on Thursday she almost knew what would happen, it did infuriate her sometimes, but she didn't say anything. He still played at laying down the law the more hold he had on her the better he liked it. She still hadn't found a loophole to broach the subject of marriage. Sometimes she worked herself up to the point of tears which was no good, she knew that. Why the delay? Emma couldn't fathom out why. She wanted to tell Annie and Ruby. There wasn't a day went by without her almost blurting it out and then she would check herself and remain quiet. Why did men have all the deciding to do, if it had been left up to her own choice they would be in their house by now, it wasn't up to her it was definitely up to Jim he would be the bread winner, the head of the family.

Next afternoon a young Gentleman was looking in the sweet shop window. He came in to buy but there was no one in the shop. A dainty bell was on the counter he rang it. Going closer to the counter he could see something lying on the floor, he stretched over the counter to see what it was. He ran into the embroidery shop declaring,

"I think your Sister has fallen, she is on the floor, I don't know what to do."

Immediately Annie and Ruby ran to the spot. By this time, Emma was coming to life again. They cradled her in their arms saying soothing words Ruby tried to sit Emma up

Emma tried,
"No don't do that Ruby, we don't know if she has broken a bone or anything serious has happened."
The young man stood there feeling useless.
"If I can help I will would you like me to go to fetch a Doctor?"
"No, Emma replied, in a hesitant voice, just give me a minute, I will be all right." Annie said,
"Fetch Aunt Polly Ruby, she knows better than we do."
"What on earth is going on Aunt bustled in taking control. My dear Emma, what has happened to you?" Aunt Polly hadn't much more knowledge than the girls and said, "Drop the catch on the door Annie customers will have to come another time we have to get Emma into the kitchen."
The young man came forward to help with Emma. He picked her up in his arms; fragrant perfume was in the air as he moved her.
"Show me where you want me to take her."
"Through here please."
In they went to the inviting kitchen.
"Sit her on a chair if you will, I think she is slowly coming back to herself, we are sorry we bothered you."

"No, not at all, I will leave you to it now things are under control. I am just sorry it happened. I will call in another day, to see how she is, that is if you don't mind."

"You have been a great help to us, thank you. I will come to let you out of the door, then lock it again. We shall be sorting Emma out, don't know even now what could have happened the main thing is she seems to be all right."

In the kitchen Emma was pulling herself round not knowing how to look at her Sisters or Aunt Polly feeling an explanation was due but she had none, there was no fixed excuse. The first thing she remembered was taking stock then suddenly opening her eyes on the floor and the kind Gentleman picking her up. Aunt Polly full of concern said,

"This is the second time you have had a giddy spell, the other one was when you were at your Mums the day we arrived. If it carries on you will have to see a Doctor, for now we will help you upstairs, I will bring you a sweet cup of tea. When you want to eat, you will have to let me know. Just at the moment you won't want anything but your bed." With that, Emma's Sisters either side of her got her upstairs and into her bed. Emma was glad of that, because at once she felt safe. Trying not

to think too much her eyes closed and she soon slept. Next day still feeling a bit strange, the sweet shop lock was opened insisting the work would not be too much for her, feeling a bit silly over yesterdays' episode. Emma said, "Of course I can manage Aunt there is nothing wrong with me."

"Well if you are sure, if you feel you need a break let me know, I will stand in for you don't want any more frights like yesterdays."

Aunt Polly was as good as gold the welfare of the girls being paramount. She knew fussing wasn't the right thing to do so normality was the way to go. Annie and Ruby were left to see Emma from time to time, just so Emma was reassured, they could pop their heads in without anything being amiss stand to chat for a couple of minutes, this way keeping an eye open in case. All seemed well, getting on with the day perfectly normal, of course Emma was trying to explain the episode to her own satisfaction but nothing came to mind. I best forget it now, a storm in a tea cup. It had passed, she would tell Jim about it when she saw him why? She didn't know, just a feeling that Jim had to know anything and everything about her. Ruby came in asking, "Is everything all right Emma?"

"Yes, I am quite well thank you. You needn't

trouble yourselves to keep coming in; it was just a fluke it won't happen again I am feeling quite normal now" Ruby said,

"We have started Lady Faversham's embroidery. We have decided to do one between us at a time. Sometimes I am better at a certain stitch sometimes Annie, so we thought if we do the one together the best of our work would be seen, we want it to be good obviously. Lady Faversham will show it off, we could get more orders with the elite if our work is admired."

"Yes, that is so, your work is always pristine I wish I could stitch like you, I am a duffer with needle and thread." They parted ways. Normality was coming to the fore. They were not so worried about Emma now she seemed in fighting spirit that was a good sign. Going back to Annie, Ruby told her all seemed well.

"Emma says not to keep going to see if she is all right that she will be. Nothing happened really, she says she just had a dizzy spell." Annie and Ruby got on with the embroidery for Lady Faversham.

"Annie, that piece of the rose looks really lovely, shall I have a go now"

"Yes Ruby, I have been on it for some time my eyes need a rest. I will sketch the gardenia on the other coat so that it will be ready when

we want it."
Ruby and Annie continued their work, Emma seemed to be well and they wouldn't worry about her.

Chapter 32

I will see Jim tomorrow I have a lot to tell him Emma thought. I would like to go into one of those tea shops in the High Street I could talk better in there I would be resting too, we'll see. Knowing how Jim opposed the idea of going in anywhere, a part of her wasn't sure. She knew she would have to suggest the idea, what if he says no? Not seeing a reason for him to object other than him wanting to rule, it seemed so silly. When was he going to bend a little, they should know by now where they stood. Still she couldn't fathom Jim and his ways, she had tried, nothing made sense. Love was an all-consuming passion, he always wanted her in his arms the minute he saw her, not a bad thing but it meant the general getting to know each other got shelved. Each time she met him resolving to tone the passion down so that they had time to talk, it didn't happen. Once he had her close in his strong arms she was lost, her own feelings got the better of her and there she was again doing exactly what he wanted her to do. The shop bell interrupted her thought pattern.

"Hello, how are you?"

Recognising the young man Emma said,

"I am very well thank you, it was very kind of you to help me yesterday, after a good night's sleep I am much better"

"I am happy to hear that you gave us quite a shock you know, I am glad I came in at that moment at least I was able to help."

"I am in your debt, you were very kind. What can I do for you today?"

"I would like the tobacco I came in for yesterday."

They both laughed, the tobacco was put into a bag and he offered her the money.

"No, please have that as a thank you, I am much obliged, I bet I was quite heavy to pick up from the floor."

"Not at all, I was a bit anxious in case I hurt you but you were as light as a feather no worries there. Are you sure, you want me to have the tobacco? I didn't come in with gain on my mind you know."

"Of course, it is little enough, thank you again."

He left the shop well pleased, thinking what a nice girl Emma was.

"Is it tomorrow you see Jim?" Aunt came in to see Emma they were not going to leave her on her own much today, Emma knew

their kindness and was glad to have their attention, it made her feel safe.

"Yes Aunt, I shall see him tomorrow, do you want him for anything?"

"No, I just want to know you will be in safe hands and of course you will."

"Just take care of yourself Emma dear." Off to see Jim, nothing else untoward had occurred so Emma was feeling confident. She walked with the usual spring in her step, Jim her darling Jim; soon she would be "Mrs Enderton." She had practised writing it as a signature it looked good. Emma Enderton. It had a ring to it she was happy with that, any day now he would ask her to marry him, knowing he had a lot of work money would not be a problem, what else could hold them up? Aunt Polly and her parents would bless the union yes things are coming along nicely. I will still work in the shop the extra money will buy some well-chosen furniture, maybe a holiday, fancy us two lying on the beach, Jim showing his well-developed muscles, me in one of those beach suits that are all the rage. These thoughts thrilled her; she was soon at their meeting place. Seeing Jim in the distance, her heart began to race again.

"Here I am darling." She touched him on the shoulder.

"Are you a bit late? I like you here on time, I don't like standing about waiting."
Not a good start to their date as Emma had planned it. She could see he was not in the mood for chat and she realised was he ever?
"I wasn't well yesterday Jim." She thought getting it in early would make him want to know what had been wrong with her he said,
"You are always moaning about something, you are well now aren't you?" His brusque reply hit her like a ton of bricks.
"Yes I suppose I am I thought you would like to know what happened to me Jim. I collapsed or fainted not sure which but I was very poorly."
"You make mountains out of molehills I thought all women had odd spells like that." Again, he had no words of compassion.
"I don't have spells like that not unless something is wrong. Don't call me woman it makes me feel as though you don't care about me."
"Forget it, let's go to our usual place, my time is short tonight I need you."
Taking her hand pulling it in the direction he wanted her to go, she felt used. She knew once he had started his passionate advance she would be lost in the ferment of love. He owned her, that is what he thought anyway,

then why didn't he marry her? The question in her mind was arising time after time. Surely, by now, he knew he was the only man for her. She loved him and that is why she wanted him and kept longing for him.

They had found the place he was leading her to, he didn't give her chance to talk his lips crushed down on hers, her head was swimming, his hands moved down her body caressing her, removing her clothes as he went. The passion full and apparent, feeling the hardness of his male parts, the need in her again she was his. This climax was filling both of their being. She was lost in his arms his breath shafting down her neck made her shiver. The swift kisses all over her left her helpless, locked into a place where there was no return, leaving all decision to him, nowhere to run, a spiral that had to reach its peak. Life around them didn't exist, just the two of them that wanted to become as one, the passion subsided and guilt became Emma's problem. If Aunt Polly ever knew, what would she say? Emma knew what she would say very well, dear Aunt, never in a million years would she allow someone to take advantage of Emma and it would be her worst nightmare. Thoughts travelled in Emma's mind, Jim has to marry me soon, how long can I keep doing this without telling my family that I love Jim and soon we are to be married?

"It is getting cold now Jim, I think next time I see you, it would be good if we went inside."

There she had said it, being on her mind to say for the last few weeks never picking up the courage. Jim said,

"When we go inside there will be people, I don't want people around us. Where do you think we could go Madam" mimicking her aspiration of grandeur. She knew he wasn't going to comply the very look on his face told her so.

"A bit of cold weather won't hurt you Emma when I get my arms around you."

He expected her to smile, but she didn't. It was no smiling matter; of late the fact that she had not been well hadn't moved him at all. He had dismissed it as nothing. In a hole, a deep pit, that is where she was, not knowing what to do? She would lose Jim if she made a fuss he had the upper hand still. The thought had crossed her mind more than once, what would he be like to live with? Perhaps he needed security to slow him down. She looked at him standing next to her. He was so handsome his body so desirable she would be so proud to have him knowing he wanted her, why the delay? Another thing, he had never asked her to meet his parents, Emma didn't know where they lived it struck her senses to realise she did not even know Jim's address. She said,

"Jim, I should have your address dear, I have just thought, I can't send you a letter or card if I need to." The excuse was feeble it was the only one she could think of for now.

"You don't need to send me a card Emma and I shan't be sending you a card or a letter so don't expect me to."

Again, he had turned it around putting her at fault not him. She was too tired and too cold to discuss it any more, she abandoned the idea. Feeling defeated, walking home on her own, things in her mind just wouldn't come right. Soon it would be Christmas, what would that bring she wondered.

Chapter 33

Aunt was in one of her best moods saying, "It is time to put Christmas decorations in the shop windows we don't want to look drab against our neighbours do we? I didn't tell you but I have bought a Rocking Horse for the embroidery window. It should look splendid; all there is to do then is to drape some red ribbon with green enhancing it. Preferably you could display something you had made, Have you got anything that will fit the bill?"

"I am sure we can find something, Ruby and I often do small pieces to please our own choice and Aunt you could knit a red tea cosy and display green table napkins. They would all make good Christmas gifts. Aunt replied, "Yes that would be effective girls."

Later in the week, having tea around the table, Aunt Polly said,

"It is time to hang a stocking full of colourful items in the sweetshop window, a few hanging out at the top with a pretty Christmas card, a large one so it can be seen, there we have it. Do you think that it would be all right ladies? Emma please display any red or green sweets we have in stock and of course the pretty chocolate boxes. The winter scenes pictured will be part of the Christmas scene" Emma Annie and Ruby exclaimed,

"We can't wait to do it perhaps a little tinsel as well would set it off?" Aunt said,

"Emma, I also have a Father Christmas with reindeer and sleigh, for the sweet shop window, lots of children stop to look in that window, I think that will please them. You can arrange the sleigh in any fashion you think it would be best against the red green emphasis, a little cotton wool for effect, does that sound about right?"

Emma looked happy at that saying,

"Aunty Polly we would like a Christmas walk around the town, it would be nice to see what the other shops have for display. We could go for a coffee together it would make a really nice outing without much expense."

"That's an idea Emma, I agree it would suit me I am not much for going out or going to shows or Pantomimes but an outing with my girls to town would certainly fit the bill, what about you Ruby and Annie, does it appeal to you?"

"Oh! Yes it would be lovely, they chorused, when can we go?" Aunt replied,

"Sometime next week before it gets too busy there won't be as many people around we will get in the tea shops easier. We won't be in the Christmas rush and we will be ready for the final rush in our own shops. We need something to wear, something festive looking, at least in the colour of the season, we want to be in vogue, ha, ha."

Settling down for the evening, this bright thought in mind Emma began to feel better. How could she let Jim put her down at this time of year especially? Not allowing her thoughts to stay on Jim her mind wandered to the coming season. I must ask the girls what they are going to buy Aunt Polly. Perhaps we could put our money together to buy her something really special. I will talk to them tomorrow.

Neil came in the shop, Emma told him of their town trip.

"I would love to come with you, it would be an honour and I would pay for the tea room goodies. A Christmas treat to escort four lovely ladies through the town would be my eyes delight. You wouldn't find me a drag; on the contrary, I would never lose the smile on my face. Aunt has told me about you falling and not being well, I could be your escort it would be a good idea for me to step along with you, I am not asking any personal favour I would be with all of you not just one of you."

He was so kind Emma was over-whelmed thinking Jim should have been offering himself not Neil. Here was Neil wanting nothing other than to be their protector. Of course Neil didn't know about Jim why should he? Emma only chatted in the shop to Neil about things in general, telling personal things to no-one. Neil was obviously troubled about Emma not being well, so kind and undemanding. Emma began to compare him to Jim, what a strange thing to do. Jim was her man she intended to marry Jim. Didn't she?

Neil bought his goods and left. Emma promised to ask her Aunt also Ruby and Annie if Neil could join them on their trip to town Not seeing a problem, why shouldn't he?

A happiness she had not known for a while settled over Emma tomorrow she would help Aunt make the Christmas cake always a special day even at home with Mum, the aroma of the baking cake filled the air, the mood was buoyant they all had a stir and made a wish. It took hours in the oven so all day and the next would have the glow of Christmas and the pungent aroma of the baking. When the cake was brought out of the oven it was turned on to a cooling tray in its pride of place before it went into a sealed cake box. Special things are worth keeping a firm hold of, they never let you down. When the cake reached the table, it was the King and had pride of place. All who came at Christmas had a slice with a bit to take home, never was there a crumb wasted. There is a type of peace when family traditions are upheld, the unspoken word.

Seeing her Sisters with Aunt together Emma took the chance of asking if Neil could come with them on their festive night out Aunt

Polly answered,
"That would be lovely, a man in the company is always welcome he will look after us see that no-one tries to steal one of you away. I would have had my eye on you but Neil will be better he will act as a deterrent, to keep the wrong sort away what do you say you girls?"
Ruby and Annie said,
"It is fine with us we like Neil, especially as he has offered to pay at the tea shop, it would be rude to refuse."
Ruby looked at Annie, they each knew what the other was thinking oneness that took a bit of understanding Emma knew of it. At times, she would count herself out of the conversation merely because the Twins were using telepathy.

Emma seeing Jim again told him of their plan, even asking if he would like to come as well as Neil?
"Me, come looking in shop windows, not likely. My evenings are all spoke for I think it is a daft idea not worth the shoe leather in my opinion. You come here, he pulled her towards him, make my date worthwhile, stop asking silly questions it is you I want not half the town." He slipped his arm around her, again she succumbed to his needs, for her the thrill was thin, she didn't know how to say it,

but must it be every time he saw her? Still not feeling very well she was glad to get back in the warm. Emma was as good as married without the ring and ceremony, this fact she had worked out for herself. He would marry her she was going to see to that and he couldn't have it all his way. Why? Came into her thoughts so many times, she was beginning to wonder if she could trust Jim. "Stop," she spoke the word aloud telling herself not to go down that road. She finished her little soliloquy, telling herself she loved Jim; he would be there for her if she needed him.

Chapter 34

Off to see the town lights they all had a green or red touch in their dress. Emma's red scarf that Aunt had bought her years ago came in just right. The mood was happy and light Emma saw to it that all was locked up safe so they were ready to go. Neil would tap the back door when he arrived.
"Yes, here he is now good timing. Come in for a minute Neil, we are just getting our hats, scarves and gloves on, won't be long."
Neil went in saying as he looked at the girls,
"Well! My oh my, you make a fellow proud, look at your festive colouring, individual too, no one the same but all in the same blend of colours, you look perfect. Come on my dears let us go and have fun."
Emma thought fun, what is that? It was so long since she had fun. Neil was full of enthusiasm his eyes bright his face alive and his manners perfect. Stepping out of the door Neil said looking up at the sky,
"Well how about that! The powers that be are perfecting the scene"
It was lightly snowing! Not enough to be bothered about just a fairy sprinkle that

showed up against the blackness of the night sky. Starting to walk towards town Neil took the arms of Annie and Ruby one each side of him, Aunt Polly with Emma walked behind. Jolly and jogging happily along the girls started to sing a Christmas carol,

"Away in a manger, no crib for a bed, the little Lord Jesus lay down his sweet head." To Emma's amazement Neil joined in, he wasn't as stuffy as Emma had thought he would be. Why couldn't Jim be more like that? Jim was Jim that was an end to it, set in his ways woe betides anyone who tried to change him.

"Hey, don't walk too fast I can't keep up, I was forgetting how far the town centre is." Aunt was out of breath. Arriving at the outskirts of the shops they all slowed down. The shops were dressed beautifully each had a different scene that had been arranged to delight the eye, lovely it was hard to say which was the best because they all looked as though they could win a prize. Each was appealing with sleighs, Santa's and cotton wool snow. The one that had a mountain scene had toboggans coming down the lower slopes. The red abundant on the white, reindeer with shiny harnesses, getting ready to pull Santa in his sleigh, like children Aunt Polly's girls were enchanted. Neil thrilled

because they were thrilled, it was a beautiful evening. The snow had now almost stopped but it left a scene behind it. The night stars began to appear. Neil spotted a nice looking teashop saying,
"This looks about what we wanted doesn't it?"
They slowed down their walk and stopped to look, peering into one of the tearoom display cabinets that stood in the window It had cakes, mince pies, plaited bread with sultanas, fruit cake, assorted sandwiches, accompanied inside by a delightful display of red table cloths with green napkins, they went in.
"Now, said Neil what can I order for you? On the other hand I will order you can choose from the table." He ordered a bit of everything, getting a table for five and a waitress to look after their needs. All of the ladies ate pastries, cakes, sausage rolls and ham sandwiches. Faces alight with the attention Neil was giving them, a magical night to be remembered always, feeling special. Emma thought she would be thinking of Jim all night but apart from just the once earlier on he had dropped out of her mind all together. She was relaxed enjoying the company that held her in the magic of the

moment. Now it had stopped snowing altogether leaving just a white glow over the rooftops and trees. The stars now fully shone out, the sky that hue of midnight blue/ black as their background. People called "Merry Christmas" to their friends, some carrying trees to dress at home. All had parcels tucked under their arms tied with satin ribbon. Many shops had stayed open late to serve. Spirits were high, laughter abundant, choosing gifts from displays in the window discussing who would like what, carefree, light- hearted, as is the spirit of the season. It was as though it rubbed off from one to the other, atmosphere almost as though you could touch or pick up this wondrous feeling, Christmas in all its glory!

Tired now and ready to go home Neil was carrying as many parcels as he could the girls also had their arms full. It had been a bonus the shops being open, thinking when they set out that the shops would be shut. Late Christmas shopping of course! It had been a huge success. Neil thanked them for the time he had spent with them. When they got to Aunt Polly's they thanked him again for being a delightful chaperone. Off he went home a very happy man.

"Tomorrow, you will have to complete your

Christmas windows girls; ours will look just as good as those in the town." Ruby said,
"Of course they will Aunt; we will make sure they do."
"Have you enjoyed it Emma?"
"Yes Aunt, it has been a wonderful night I think we all will remember it. I must say though I for one am ready for bed. Stretching and yawning she picked up her own parcels said goodnight and headed for the stairs.
"Oh! Dear what is that?" Aunt had heard tumbling.
Running to the hall stairway the girls and Aunt Polly hurried enough to see Emma fall. Down she tumbled parcels and all.
"My dear, what on earth is the matter, did you trip?"
Dazed not knowing what had made her fall Emma tried to reply,
"I don't really know, I don't think I am seriously hurt, but I do feel a bit dippy, I will be all right when I get into bed, sorry, I didn't want to spoil anything."
"Are you going to be all right on your own?" asked Aunt
"Yes, of course I will, please don't make a fuss."
"Not a fuss Emma but I am concerned about you. To the Doctor I think to see what is

going on, I am sure these falls one after the other cannot be completely dismissed."

"Yes Aunt, just let me go to lie down now. I will be in the shop tomorrow, so don't worry."

Emma was in the shop in the morning although she didn't feel too good. I'd better not tell Aunt I don't feel well, or else, she will have a Doctor here quick. I don't want a Doctor just a little recovery time. Neil came in later on, of course Aunt had to tell him about Emma.

"That girl is not well Neil I want her to see the Doctor she keeps putting me off."

"Would it help if I had a word with her, I think a lot about Emma I will never rest leaving her not well. Where is she now?"

"Who wants me? Here I am Oh, hello Neil, is Aunt bothering you with my silly mishap"? Neil was worried,

"She has told me of your fall if that is what you mean, you are lucky you haven't broken anything. Aunt tells me you have had several falls just lately, is that right?"

"Well I suppose so, I think they could all be explained away very easily there is nothing wrong with me and maybe I am just clumsy, I must be more careful."

"I have told Aunt if it happens again I will

take you to see my Doctor, he is a caring man and he will soon put your mind at rest. There would be no cost we keep a fee paid to him every week, then when we need him he is there."

"Ganging up on me are you," Emma smiled, Neil standing before her in her hour of need, touched her; it wasn't anything to do with him yet he was worried, he said,

"Promise me Emma, you will get in touch immediately if you need me."

"Yes Neil I will, what on earth do you think is going to happen to me? Nothing you'll see." With her reassurance, he left not wanting to be a pain yet caring very much.

Annie and Ruby would be the next to come worrying. Emma thought I am getting a muddled head, they must leave me alone, I know what will sooth me, finishing the Christmas window off, I can use all my concentration on that, it will be another job done, that is unless I get busy with customers." As expected, Ruby and Annie came in,

"Are you well again now? Do you know how you slipped last night?" Another barrage of questions!

"Yes, I have told everyone now I am alright and I want to get on with my window. I want

it finished today, seeing all the lovely windows in town, has made me want ours special. Have you completed your window yet?"

"Yes almost just a touch here and there."

"Well there are two of you, I have to do mine alone, so go and let me get on with it." Her tone wasn't harsh just definite.

Seeing Jim again, she thought she had better say about her third fall. She didn't want him to give her a hard time, telling him about it all he didn't seem very bothered

"Going gallivanting when you should be resting, that's what it is. It's your own fault; don't come to me griping about it. Get into that entry it is getting cold out here."

Why didn't she run, giving him a whole lot of dialogue he didn't want to hear? She felt like it. All she could bring about to say was,

"I won't come another week, if you think so little of me." She spluttered the words out. At the back of her mind she was thinking, he might hit me, his face is evil.

"Don't speak to me like that woman. Get up that entry do as I say else it will be me who doesn't turn up next week. You want me you know you do, you are no better than me." He roughly kissed her, she felt blood on her mouth from the pressure of his lips, she had

to comply and she had no choice, as he manhandled her into giving way to his needs. No joy filled her heart, she might as well have been a piece of wood for all the feeling he gave her. She felt numb, disillusioned and cold, was he the man she wanted to marry?

He had taken her, shaped her to his will, he owned her body, he would do with it what he will. She was soiled for any other man there wasn't a place to escape. Her Jim, what really should have been said was his Emma, as she was his Emma. Marriage was just a duty now, something you did to show society that things were in correct proportion, that you were not a street girl. Marriage would give her a status anyway. May the dear Lord protect her she had never felt so alone in all her life.

The quicker she could get away from him tonight, the better she would like it. As she left that desolate entry tears streamed down her face, a future of misery, married to Jim.

Chapter 35

At her job in the shop she became very quiet, seeing other couples coming in to buy boxes of chocolates as gifts, finding a suitable gift card, helping them with the wording. The happiness in their eyes holding hands loving each other it was almost too much to bare go on she must, keeping Annie Ruby and Aunt all in the dark about her position. They would want to kill Jim. I mustn't ruin their lives it would if they were told. Thoughts crowded her mind.

Neil was coming in regularly just to see if she was alright, kind thoughtful Neil.
I missed my chance what a fool I was, pretending I knew the way of the world when in reality I knew nothing. Even now, I know nothing... Not being told or shown anything how could she? In her quarter of the woods people had their own code of behaviour it was straight forward, to the point, they married at a certain age had children and made a home for themselves. Standing together in both low and high moments there was no need for tuition it was the natural way. How she wished there would be a time for her in the same respect, no, she had played her trump card when Jim took her virginity. She, so in love with him trusted him with her life, what went wrong? She was sure he would still marry her then all would correct its balance, time would tell. Please let the dear Lord, show me the way, tears filled her eyes. Aunt had come in to disturb Emma, thinking it was the best way to show that help was very near, at hand she said,
"Have you been busy Emma?
"No, not too many folk about today, I am finishing my window while I have chance, any day now the bedlam will start everyone will want serving at once."Emma could hide

her sullen face by doing the window. Feeling she couldn't face anyone today it was early bed for her, hiding from the people who loved her in case she hurt them. Never would she want to do that. Tomorrow she may be feeling a little better, her smile would return, "if only" she thought.

Neil was coming in to see her almost daily she found she was looking forward to his visits he made her feel more secure and he was coming tomorrow. Emma took the plunge saying to Aunt,
"I would like to ask Neil if I can see his family Doctor, he has asked me if I would like to. I haven't had any more falls but apart from the things you keep reminding me of I must admit to feeling giddy, perhaps you are right and I do need a tonic." Aunt seemed pleased and replied,
"I am sure it would be the best for you Emma dear." Late afternoon Neil came, they chatted he asked,
"Are you feeling better Emma?"
"A bit, I think I would like to take you up on your kind offer to see your family Doctor, I have never had a reason to talk to a Doctor, you tell me the one you consult is easy to talk to, is he?" Neil said,

"Straight to the point Emma, he will put you right in no time at all."

"When would it be convenient for me to go?"

"I will pop in to make an appointment on my way home tonight. Don't worry I will pick you up in a small carriage, the arrangement of two-seater with horse is very convenient for small trips like this one, it also keeps everything private. I will let you know in the morning what time the appointment is."

"I would be very obliged Neil, thank you so much." *He left leaving a smile on Emma's face. Emma decided Neil must work in an office he seems to have time to do the things he wants to, perhaps his Father's office? This was all romancing at the moment trying to understand Neil a little better. Next day true to his word, he turned up.*

"Right, we are going to see Doctor Pen at 5pm, let your Aunt know, or she will wonder where you have gone."

"I will be ready I already feel better knowing I am going to be examined. I haven't been happy with myself for months, just couldn't bring myself to decide about seeing a Doctor."

"That's alright Emma but I must run now, I want to get my jobs done so that I am on time for you tonight, don't worry everything will

be fine."

All day long, she fretted, what would the Doctor do? What should I tell him so that he knows my symptoms? Should I have a bath before going? What shall I wear so it can be taken off and put back on easily? What part of my body will be looked over? There seemed a million questions. Doctor Penn would take charge finally. Emma came to the right decision. Here was Neil in the buggy as promised, Emma tripped out to be helped up into the cab.

"This is nice, pity we are not going on a more pleasant ride Emma."

Neil looked at her. A brave smile on her lips she looked both fragile and beautiful.

The clip clop of the fine small horse pulling the cab was getting rhythmic like soothing music. It didn't take long to get to Doctor Pen's surgery, now her heart raced.

"Good evening Emma, is it?"

Neil had gone in with her.

"I told you Doctor Pen of Emma and her falls, we are hoping you can help."

"Rest assured I will if I can. Now I think young man you can wait outside, send the Nurse in." First, Doctor asked Emma to strip to the waist and then examined her chest and lungs.

"Em, em" he murmured. Put the top clothes back on now take off all but the pantaloons. Nurse will you help take Emma's clothes off her?" The nurse obliged.

"Did you bring a water sample?" Doctor Penn enquired,

"Yes, I wasn't too sure what quantity, so I just bought this medicine bottle."

She could see her own hand shaking as she passed it to him.

"Nurse, can you test that for me please." Emma lay on the examination couch feeling very vulnerable. Pressing her middle, moving his hands over her stomach, pushing, prodding he took the water sample from the Nurse.

"It looks like we have found something here. You have a kidney infection for a start, nothing serious. We can clear that up for you with some medication it would have given you the bouts of giddiness you have described."

"I have been so scared to come to see you Doctor, I feel jubilant now it is something you can treat, thank you so much."

She wanted to drop a kiss on his balding forehead she was so new to him so she thought better of it. Doctor Pen continued to examine, murmuring at each consideration as he went.

"There is another thing I have to tell you it is in the order of Congratulations. I shall want you to pay me a visit every month until the baby is born. I can't tell the exact date I think about April the size indicates you are about four months pregnant."

"I can't be Doctor I have been seeing my monthly period."

"No Emma, what you have mistaken for your monthly is a discharge coming from your kidney infection, it often has streaks of blood in it. As I said we will deal with that, aren't you pleased?"

"Of course I am, she lied it is just the shock. I would have thought I would have an inner instinct if anything like that had occurred, I have felt nothing." Doctor said

"Your baby is small, it is your first, it is not odd that you haven't felt it yet, you most probably soon will he smiled. He went on to say. Now there is something to tell Neil! I know you are not married but that is a mere detail. I should say the sooner the better now, so get those Wedding Banns read let's have knees up, ha, ha. I always celebrate with the "Nolan's" I have tended the family for many years. Get you dressed, tidy your hair, you don't want to look like a Rag a Muffin delivering your very special good news do

you."

Not me! Was her first thought as she got herself dressed tidying her hair, she pulled on her boots, fiddled with the buttons, they wouldn't do up she felt all the despair that goes with living a lie. This is where she had arrived in the middle of nowhere. Doctor Pen thought Neil was the Father, so Congratulations! Doctor had said., Emma was trembling all over trying to let this news sink in. What on earth am I going to say to Neil and my Aunt Polly, let alone Jim? I don't know how to tell these people; of course, Jim will have to be told, will he be pleased? I never know with Jim, I have to see him tomorrow, he must give me chance to talk to him, perhaps he will want to get married straight away we have a reason now. This will alter the pattern. Indeed there is Neil waiting for me outside I am not going to tell him tonight. I will say about the kidney infection and let it be. Neil at the ready with a smile said,

"Here you are then, all well and done I hope, what did he say?"

Neil's eager eyes looked down into hers, she looked as though she had been crying.

"There is nothing so wrong is there?" There was anxiety in his voice.

"Well yes and no. I have a kidney infection, it does have to be treated Doctor says the medication will cure it."

"That's not so bad is it? I can be beside you there is nothing to worry about."

He linked her arm through his patting her hand as he did so.

Emma wasn't used to such considered treatment it brought tears to her eyes.

"Shall we go home in the buggy or would you like to walk on this fine evening."

"I think the walk would clear my head Neil, if that is alright with you."

They walked along Neil was enjoying having Emma beside him where in his eyes she should be. He had waited a long time for this opportunity he didn't want to miss his chance. Turning his glance towards Emma he said,

"Emma, when the Doctor came out of his consulting room"… Emma braced herself
thinking her heart would jump out of her chest. Should I tell him? It will be an avenue of lies if I don't. I don't want to hurt him. Neil carried on

"He said to me Congratulations do you know what he meant?"

What shall I say? However I tell him it is not good news for him. Emma made her decision

and said,
"Neil, I have to be straight with you, I have to tell you I am expecting a baby. I am so sorry I know it is not what you wanted to hear, walking here beside you telling you such news is not what I want either, but I don't want to lie to you."
"Emma my dear I knew there was something, for months I have known deep inside of me."
Quietly now they walked, then Neil said,
"Calling in the shop as I did was on purpose hoping you would get to know me better, after you refused to come to meet Mum I had doubts about how you felt but my feeling is real Emma, I love you. It is my sad duty to leave you to tell the Father. That is what Doctor meant then, he thinks it is mine I can only be sad that it is not the case. Please Emma, let me be by your side while you get on even keel and know what you are going to do. Will you tell Aunt or the girls?"
"Neil, the first I knew of it was at the surgery tonight, I am in shock, I had to tell you or lie. I didn't want to lie I know I must go through the motions, but if you will keep it as our secret for the time being I would be more than grateful, I have to tell Jim first." Neil felt as though a physical blow had been delivered in the middle of his stomach, he

said
"Has Jim been your beau then?"
His voice sad his head down, they walked and talked.
Here he was talking about another Man's child to the girl he so deeply loved and not being able to do a thing about it. They arrived home.
Neil kissed her cheek, and said,
"I will do as you say, not breath a word until you have sorted yourself out, and remember I love you."
How could Emma forget, "I love you" is what he had said. Why didn't I realise that before. I thought he was stodgy, being older than me with a posh family put me off and I have been so silly. Would that she could put the clock back, she couldn't. She would see Jim tomorrow. Aunt Polly was waiting for news.
"How have you got on Emma dear?"
Emma thought I am not going to tell Aunt about the baby, here she is looking all doe eyed, filled with worry over me. I just can't until I have settled things in my own mind. Emma replied to Aunt,
"I did see the Doctor. He advised me to take a course of medication that will clear up a kidney infection he has discovered."
There she hadn't told a lie, it was a fact, it

would have to suffice for now.
"I am going in to tell Ruby and Annie, where are they?"
"Up in their room, Aunt nodded to the stairs, stitching I wouldn't be surprised."
Emma went up. Knocking she entered, yes they were stitching.
"What are you making now, you don't have to work at night you know, I have never known anyone to be as dedicated in making things, the embroidery as well, you two put me to shame. Put it down for a minute while I talk to you."
"Yes Emma, have you been to the Doctors? Was it awful? What did he say? Did you have to remove your clothes? Questions were bombarded from the two of them. Emma was used to it. She settled them down, before telling them the story saying,
"I was all right a bit shaky maybe, he is a nice man I didn't have to say much he did all the talking I have a kidney infection."
She went on to tell them in detail all about taking off her clothes and the medication prescribed for her. Annie and Ruby sat with eyes wide open they never wanted to have to go to see a Doctor. There was never going to be anything wrong with them or so they believed. Cleverly, Emma changed the

subject.

"Let's have a look at what you are doing hmm very elaborate. Is this Lady Faversham's coat she will be pleased. You have the colouring just right, the way the silks fade and then bringing the deeper silks in gradually for the head of the rose, it is perfect. Have you still more to do?"

"No, we have finished the Gardenia on the other coat do you want to see that?"

Oh! That is exquisite, you are going to liven up the world of embroidering you will have this shop famous in no time"

"We can show you how to do it if you would like to Emma."

"I think I have enough to keep me busy with the sweet shop there is always something I have left to do and promise to catch up, one day maybe." Saying goodnight Emma went to her room. Undressed lying in her soft bed, things that had been said ran through her mind. I am going to have a baby, I am not thinking about anyone else. In here, (she ran her hands over her stomach) there is a tiny baby it will be part of my life, I will care and love it with all my heart .I no longer care what Jim is going to say, he can go jump in the river for all I care. If he wants the baby he will ask me to marry him I suppose, I must

it is his child too. Certainly, I will be glad when I have told him the news, I don't know if he will be glad, there is no telling with Jim. She slept.

Chapter 36

Standing in the same old place was Jim, cigarette in his mouth leaning on the wall. As she approached, he greeted her saying,
"Your late again, I have told you I will not stand here waiting, where have you been?"
"Just closing the shop seeing everything is safe. Anyway I am here now; I have something to tell you."
"I don't want to know, it will be something you have said before, digging up the nitty-gritty I expect." He moved to go to the shelter they had been using for the past few weeks. Emma thought, I will follow him, I need the shelter to stand to talk to him and as for anything else it is a "no."
"Blimey! Your taking your time tonight, come on first late then slow, you are asking for it my girl. I will give you what for in a minute"
"Jim, stop that silly talk and listen. I went to see the Doctor last evening, I have a kidney infection."
"Well so what, lots of people have kidney infections, it will be got over it's nothing."
"There is something else Jim."

"Oh! For cripes sake what now? There was anger in his voice.

"I am having a baby; it is due sometime in April."

He turned on her, his look vicious.

"Who have you been with you dirty slut it is not mine, I've a good mind to give you a swipe or two, get out of my way." He gave her a mighty push.

"Jim! Jim! It is your baby I have never ever been with anyone else. It is time for us to Marry."

"Marry, what bloke would marry you with a bun in the oven. You're not fit to be a Mother. Marry you! The biggest joke ever, we have been pleasing the mood with sexual instincts. You got as much out of it as me, you're a tart and again I say that baby has as much to do with me as the man in the moon. You are a laugh a minute, you are asking me if my intentions are honourable ha, ha, well they are not, does that answer your question?" Again, she tried.

"Jim I have never been with any other man, I thought we were just biding our time, then you would ask me to marry you sometime soon. How can you accuse me, I have been utterly faithful." His face and his attitude were a picture he growled

"More fool you then."

His hands started to fumble at her dress he still wanted whatever she would give him. "Come on love, you know the score, you know you want it. Having a baby in there means we can have a good time without bother, you'll get over the fuss, someone will adopt the baby and bobs your uncle! I will see you each week as now."

"You will not Jim. I will never ever have intercourse with you from this moment on. Despicable you are to me and I don't know what I ever saw in you. I wish I had been with another man then I wouldn't be as positive as I am that this is your child, I wish to my Lord in heaven it wasn't." Pulling away from him, she moved as fast as she could away from his filthy mouth, tears running down her careworn face dripping off her chin. This was her Jim, the Jim she had idolised, he was a devil may care vile being, never in a million years could she have recognised the man within, face value is what she had estimated him on. What a stupid fool I have made of myself she uttered as she ran, being glad it was almost dark so no one would see her crying. How could Jim say those awful things to her? Shock, her head in a whirl and bowed down from the wind, she

longed to be on solid ground. Seeing Aunt Polly's house in the distance bought a surge of warm relief, I still have a lot of explaining to do, but love will be around me. Jim's voice I never want to hear for the rest of my life. I feel dirty, dirt that no amount of washing will remove. I wish Jim in hell he has abused me. I must forgive myself and love the baby, it is not baby's fault and I will bring him or her up the same as I was brought up with love and care even if I do it alone, I am never going to set eyes on Jim again. She wept realising all the many times Jim had taken her, there had been no love involved. Shameful giving her most precious gift of virginity to a man that didn't care for her in any respect. For the baby's sake I must go on... She was as innocent as a child and had allowed Jim to take her virginity only because she loved him, thinking he loved her and in a matter of time would marry her. He had led her merry dance, never again, his handsome face his strong body had completely fooled her. Getting him out of her mind was a large undertaking; he had hurt every core of her being.

Neil called next day, to see if she was all right he wanted to know how he stood; praying Emma wasn't going to marry Jim. In his silent prayer he asked,

"Dear Lord please give me a chance, I love Emma for all the right reasons to take care of her would be my ideal world I have to convince her that this is so."

Words whirling around Neil's head, words yet unspoken, he had to have the right moment. The first thing he needed to know was how Jim had taken the news of the baby. Maybe Emma was going to marry Jim? No, I love Emma too much to let her go. Where could I take her tonight or tomorrow night for complete privacy, so that both of us can say exactly the right words? Emma my love, I need you. Emma appeared in the shop.

"Hello Neil, nice of you to call, I must say this to you, quietly though. I haven't told anyone here about my baby, so please don't ask me any leading questions."

"I understand Emma, I have been trying to think of somewhere I could meet you to have a private conversation, can you suggest anywhere?"

"Indoors would be best, in the Park in one of those closed huts would do, there are benches in there to sit, you don't have to worry about me Neil this is not your problem." Aunt Polly drifted in,

"Hello Neil, I was glad to see Emma back

from the Doctors. I will see she takes all her tablets, it was bad enough, it could have been worse. I knew very well, there was something wrong, we are in your debt for taking her to see the Doctor, let's hope it doesn't occur again, once the infection has cleared up that is." Aunt had a funny way of expressing herself one of her own in fact. Neil knew just what she meant. Aunt left them. Neil spoke to Emma once more saying,

"Could you bring yourself to come to visit me privately? I don't like places in the Park, too many use them for the wrong reason. I have my own study no one would disturb us and I will be very well behaved." he said with a grin. Emma had no worries about Neil or his behaviour, she agreed after work the next evening he would pick her up in the cabby to go on to his home, then they could talk in the right place where it would be private and safe. Next evening Emma called to her Aunt,

"I am shutting the shop Auntie Polly, I am going out, won't be late back. I feel all right, yes I have taken my medication" Aunt still didn't like the look of Emma thinking the colour in her face was yellow and pale. Aunt walked away muttering

"I mustn't expect too much too soon," she told herself, and then followed Emma to

make sure the shop was locked and the catch firm on the shop door.

The buggy drew up; Neil got out assisting Emma up onto the footplate of the cab. Picking her skirt up to get in she showed off her high button boots and delicate ankle. Neil noticed, so passed a compliment.

"Thank you Neil I dress as well as I can, of course Ruby and Annie help me to make some of my clothes."

"They are a blessing to you aren't they? It is wonderful to see three Sisters who get along so well. Oh yes I have seen you together enough to know."

Pulling up at an ornamental gate the buggy stopped. Neil got down going around the other side to help Emma down, seeing that her foot was firmly on the footplate. Never had Emma known anyone so attentive.

"Did you bring a handbag Emma, oh yes you have it in your hand is there anything else that might be left behind, no? All right then." Turning to the cabby driver Neil said,

"You can go now pick us up at 10pm. please." The horse went at a trot; they were left standing to go through the gate. The house wasn't as large as Emma had imagined, but it was a warm inviting looking house.

"Have you lived here all your life Neil?"

"Yes, I look on it fondly; I have my own quarter with a study that is where we will sit tonight, as long as you agree, and don't be alarmed I shall briefly introduce you to my Mother I am afraid my Father died a few years ago."

"Oh! Neil, are you sure about introducing me? You know the condition I am in will she suspect?"

"In my eyes it doesn't matter you are beautiful as you are, in any case there is nothing showing you are as slim and elegant as always. Come this way dear." Showing her the way to the sitting room for the first time Emma saw Neil's Mother, with a delicate smile on her face as Emma walked towards her.

"Hello Emma my dear, Neil told me he was bringing you, I am very happy to meet you, will you sit for a while." Neil said,

"No Mother, we have some things we want to discuss in private, we need the time.

I will bring Emma another day then you two can get to know each other."

"All right Son, I will look forward to another day with time to talk with Emma."

With that, Neil took Emma along the hall into a private study.

"Sit by the fire; we will get warm and cosy before we say anything." Two chairs were placed either side of the fire and looked welcoming Emma sat on the nearest one. Her eyes wandering round the room she saw it was pleasant, with a desk, writing paper and ink ready for business The carpet was in a deep rich blue, the furniture complementing in dark oak. Emma had her mind working, thinking the right words must be said, and what is Neil going to say to me? I am in such a state of indecision I am relying on him to be positive. Neil poured a small glass of wine and offered it to Emma as he pulled a wine table close to her chair, Emma made an effort to relax. "Have this wine and be prepared for what I am going to say to you, and don't be afraid, everything is fine" Emma did as he asked, wondering all the time how all this was going to turn out. There was an atmosphere in the room; Neil thought he hadn't better be too long before talking to Emma. He was ready to begin.

"I don't want you to say anything until I have finished Emma, a lot depends on what you say in reply, everything tonight must be the truth, I can't build on lies." He went quiet for a moment....

"Darling Emma, loving you is all I want in

life, I have loved you from the very start, remember the time you wouldn't come to tea, to meet Mother? Well, even before that. You have been part of my daily thoughts, there is no-one else for me and I am asking you to marry me. Emma began to protest.

"Hear me out, I know there is a baby to consider, that is YOUR baby and I would welcome it with open arms my love. To have you beside me the rest of our lives this is of paramount importance to me. Your baby would be my baby we need not even tell anyone anything different, look at Doctor Pen he is already Congratulating me.

You must tell me of any other person that you may have spoken to, we could make this work. Now, what did Jim say last night?"

Her eyes were glassy with tears, somehow, she must tell him of the horrific confrontation she had been through with Jim.

"First of all Neil, he does not want to marry me, calling me a slut and many other names, saying I have been seeing other men. That this is not his child I can assure you I have never been with any other man although perhaps now I wish I had because I do not want Jim to be the Father. He had me completely fooled. I thought it was only a

matter of time before he married me, I should have known better by his attitude towards me. I was trapped and had to keep seeing him, I became frightened of what he might do if I didn't turn up. I had visions of him tracking me down he was ruthless. I am never going to see him again does that answer your question Neil? As for anyone knowing no, no one knows, not Aunt, or the girls, I needed some time to be sure of my ground before it all came out. Of course Jim knows, but he is in denial he is a vile man. I have been unhappy for so long, but I thought I had to follow the natural pattern of things, I had sorted my own destiny badly, just had to go through with it. I think that is all I can tell you, it is with complete honesty."

"Then think about what I have said, I love you with all my heart, so you made a mistake no- one need to know but you and me."

"He pulled her up from the chair pulling her ever closer. He whispered,

"Say you will marry me Emma make my dream come true, I don't care what people think it is you and me that are important and of course the little one, our families would be delighted. You still have your figure so if we married very soon you need not tell anyone. This could be between you, Doctor Pen and

me. It would save heartache plus explanation for everyone. I am your devoted servant I would be beside you in everything you do. Your life would be my life and I would be the happiest man alive."

His arms tightened around her, he wanted her to feel protected and dearly loved he looked fondly at her lips, gently pressing a kiss on them, she didn't pull away, this is what love should be like gentle and undemanding until she offered herself to love him as he loved her.

Chapter 37

They stayed in each other's arms for a while Neil never wanting to let her go.
"I cannot give you my answer tonight Neil. All you have said is going to benefit me, but what about you taking a wife carrying a child that is not yours it is a big commitment. I wouldn't want you to feel I had manoeuvred you in any way. What I can tell you right now is I have no love for Jim. I never want to set

eyes on him again. He is every woman's nightmare he ought to be on a chain, yes, that is how I think of Jim. It will take a little time to get the horror out of my mind. I will dearly think of your offer and it won't take that long before I give you my decision, you have always been a very good friend and now I feel far more than that is between us. I am just so confused and I need a little time."

"You can have all the time in the world I wanted you to love me as well as being in love with me, see I am thinking of myself now, obviously you won't be out of my mind for one second you are so very dear to me."

Hearing the plea in his voice entered Emma's mind pattern, could a man love her so much, give her so much when she had very little to offer? The feeling of doing something right with honesty did Emma a power of good, slut she had been called only a day ago. Now here was Neil, loving her asking her to be his wife. With Neil she could face the future, she could go to bed tonight to sleep not cry. Thinking all of the times Neil had been in the shop just to get Mother's sweets he had told her, she knew now it had been to chat he had been in love with her, had she known and ignored? Yes, she had, the other lover was Jim he had looks and physique, mystery and it had tempted her. Neil had looks he was a tall man, but in a more dignified manner, with Jim, the devil tempted and she had fallen. It was as her Aunt Polly had said when she asked Emma, "Do you know the ways of men?" Emma had said she did, but she was not telling the truth. She had learned the hard way; her journey was not yet over. Still she was frightened of Jim and what he could do when he found out she was marrying Neil. Would he let her go that easily? Emma said goodnight to Neil's Mother. Neil took her home in the cab that had been arranged for 10pm. arriving at Aunt's shop he kissed her once more and used the key in the lock to open the door. Neither Emma nor Neil wanted to bump into the family they had things to think about privately. Neil wouldn't leave her alone now she had confessed her fear, he would be there to protect her. Every day Neil called in the shop to see that Emma was safe and feeling better. They had decided to give Neil's proposal a week to settle so that both of them had the time to decide finally. Neither Emma nor Neil wanted to leave it long. There was the baby to consider. Looking for Neil every day enjoying his company made Emma a lot less worried, in fact there was a fire kindling inside her, getting bigger each time she saw Neil's loving face. Jim, hadn't shown his face, Emma knew he had something to hide; she wanted no part of him wishing she had never met him.

"Hello Emma my love, yes here I am again, this is the best time of the day because I see you, hope you feel the same."

"Yes Neil I too look forward to seeing you, I have felt far more at ease since you have taken me into your world. I will be glad when our week of waiting is over we can then let the world know about our plans, Aunt, well! I can't wait to see the look on her face." Neil replied,

"It will be a surprise to a few I would think a happy one at that. I just am finding it hard to wait. I want you in my arms Emma darling to hold you and never let you go. Yes Emma I love you as much as all that." He went behind the counter and gave her a quick squeeze and brushed a kiss on her lips. It was difficult to show any real caress, this after all was a shop. He stayed and chatted for a little while and then left, sighing relief because Emma was not pushing him away.

It was on his leaving that Emma noticed a Lady standing looking into the shop window. Paying little attention, she went on with her

work. Glancing up after a while noticing she was still there, Emma looked more closely and thought no, I don't know her, but she seems to be looking for someone. The shop was slack, so she went into the girls' fashion shop saying,
"There is a Lady standing outside my window, she has been there some time now, I don't know her. I wish you would come to see if you recognise her." The girls followed Emma. Ruby looked and said,
"No, it is not one of our Customers, have you seen her before Annie?
"No I haven't she is perhaps just window shopping. I bet she's looking at your famous Christmas display Emma. She gave Ruby a little dig smiling.
"We don't know her Emma it isn't anything to do with us." Off they walked back into their own sewing domain whispering as they went,
"Emma is looking for something that isn't there Ruby, she has been quite peculiar lately, it is since she went to see Doctor Pen. Perhaps it is the medication affecting her, we will have to keep an eye on her and I know Aunt is doing just that. Emma will be her old self soon, I hope."
They were all now looking after the two

shops. Emma dusting the jars of sweets then going to the window to make sure things were pristinely polished. Again, the Lady appeared looking as though she was trying to see inside the shop, walking up and down in front of the shop she was peering in almost rudely. Emma scrutinised her once more, no, she was sure she didn't know her. The shop doorbell announcing a customer rang sharply. Emma turned her head to see who had come into the shop with such bluster she said,

"Good afternoon Madam, can I help you?"

"Don't Madam me young lady, it is you who in all truth are the "Madam." I have seen you walking twice with my brother Jim. I have wanted to come over to you to give you a piece of my mind, yes even in the street, I promised myself if it happened again I would come and see you, so here I am."

"Just a minute, Emma defended herself, what has it got to do with you? Maybe you are Jim's Sister but that doesn't give you the right to dictate to me about what I should or shouldn't do with your brother. We are both adults and should be able to choose who we walk out with."

"You would walk out with a married man, without a second thought?" Emma was aghast and said,

"Married, Jim isn't married."

"Yes he has been married for years he has two sons with his wife. I see you as a threat, my Sister-in-law is a lovely lady and I am seeing that nothing untoward happens to spoil her life with our Jim. He is a character I have had to step in before and it is ladies like you that tempt our Jim. I think I have said all I came to say. Just you take heed." As fast, as she had come into the shop, walking with a distinctive wobble banging the shop door, the bell clanged as if it would come off its fitting Jim's Sister left. It had shaken Emma to her roots, Jim all the time he had been dating her had been married with two sons it couldn't be possible. He couldn't have married her even if he had wanted to, he had taken her virginity her body and her mind, all without a second thought towards her welfare, the baby she now carried was his and he had denied it. How many other children were there about that he had denied? Shuddering as she sat down the answer riddled her head, and her thoughts turned to Neil. Oh! Neil, dear Neil, you have offered to be my rock, I will never give you cause to regret your decision, I never ever want to see Jim again; he is as the dirt beneath my feet, loving you the rest of my life is all I want to do. I was so silly I can't even

stand the thoughts in my mind, giving all I had to give, Jim all the time knowing I was only "a bit on the side." If I had the strength, I would strangle him. Right from this very minute I am going to tell Ruby and Annie I am finished with Jim. I don't want to associate my name with his one moment longer. To think, he wouldn't let me put my arm through his while walking, he took me round the back allies of everywhere we went, he wouldn't take me into a teashop, or walk with me through town, now I know why, I am revolted by his behaviour Why didn't I not recognise the signs? Now it is laid out before me it is perfectly clear. It has destroyed any tiny resemblance of love I had for him. I am so lucky to have you Neil, you have been here all along for me and I was star struck, beguiled, not knowing what real love was all about, Jim had me at my tender age for his pleasure doing with me what he will; laughing at the faith and dotage I laid at his feet. I thought after he took me I must marry him it was the only thing in my head that made any sense. Now I know better. I shall tell Annie and Ruby, I must think a little longer before I tell my Aunt I must discuss it with you dear Neil hoping you can find forgiveness for my stupidity. Emma stood, her eyes closed as this soliloquy came tumbling out, trying to justify her position, wanting Neil to be by her side, her world had been rocked and she must get it back together. The shops were closed Emma went through to the girls so she could catch them together without Aunt. While they were lingering leaving things tidy before leaving Emma said,

"I want to speak to you privately before we go in to tea. I want to share this experience with you before you get any older, in case you walk into the same trap as I have." What, on earth did Emma mean? Ruby and Annie went back to Auntie Polly's tea tables and sat down.

"Come and sit over here with us Emma we can talk privately, what is so important then, you are not going to tell us Doctor Pen has found something more wrong with you? Dear Emma, you can't be ill we love you. Things would not be the same without you."

"Don't distress yourselves, I am going to tell you everything, you must keep it to yourselves. I will be relying on your discretion." Enough to take in all in one go, Emma had reached the part where the baby came in to the reckoning, and should she confide to Ruby and Annie? Neil had said not, he wanted everyone to think it was his

child. Emma held herself although she hardly knew how and kept that secret.

"So Jim is no longer your boyfriend, don't you see him at all?"

"No, I don't, never again will I want to and he completely fooled me. That is why I am telling you, so you don't make the same mistake."

"Did Neil take you to see the Doctor again?"

"Yes he did, I am seeing him now, Neil is kindness itself and I don't know why I didn't see that before, I was blinded by my own importance, thought I could deal with Jim, I obviously couldn't. He was handsome, his body alluring, I thought this was love, it has been nothing like love and looking back I see I didn't know the first thing about love. It is with regret I think of Jim, I hope I never see him again, he is a part of the past I want to forget."

"Your secret is safe with us Emma, it would only make Aunt uncertain and poorly we don't want that do we"?

"Exactly it would be brought up at every given occasion. I would never be able to live it down and Aunt would think she was doing me good; I can honestly say that would not be so. Not only that, the fact that Jim is married would put Aunt into a flap, in her world,

these things just don't happen. Be quiet now I can hear Aunt Polly coming."

"Where are you girls, sitting talking at your leisure while your cup of tea gets cold, enough now, put off the lights come to the table in the kitchen, we have hot pot tonight it does keep hot that is why I have left you talking so long, goodness me what do you find to talk about. It will soon be bedtime at this rate."

"You should know us girls by now Auntie Polly we always have a lot to say." Ruby was trying to lighten the situation; it had worked itself into getting very deep. Aunt was quick to pick up the feeling in the room; they had to side track her. They followed Aunt into the kitchen and sat down while Aunt served the hotpot.

"This hot pot is lovely, what meat did you use?"

"It is just shin of beef; it always has a lovely flavour although I have to take out the fatty bits." Talk to Aunt about cooking she is yours, priding herself in the little know how that she had. She was delighted when it was received with zest and the plates were left clean. Learning a lot from the girls (as they had been taught by their Mum) Aunt was only too pleased when the meal was prepared

well and looking good.

"Don't forget to take your medication Emma, before you go to bed, are you feeling any better? At least you haven't fallen over since you went to see Doctor Pen. Something is doing you good. I noticed you are seeing a lot more of Neil these days, where has Jim got to?"

"I don't see Jim any more Aunt, we parted a while ago."

This was a white lie; Emma paving her way to being with Neil and settling with him. Aunt knew Neil had been calling regularly it would be a natural thing for him to come into the picture, he and Emma as a couple would be very acceptable in Aunt's eyes, Aunt thought highly of Neil and was glad Jim was off the scene. Emma thought, this is the right way to go forward, without hurting people that I love. I must talk to Neil again tell him how I am progressing, including him in any final picture I have in mind. I know he will be pleased I will be glad when all turns into reality. A magic web you weave, when you practice to deceive." Emma knew this was true and wished white lies were not a part of the outcome.

Neil was agreeable about Emma telling Ruby and Annie about Jim. He was pleased she hadn't told them about the baby, in his mind the baby was already his, it was part of Emma and he loved Emma with all his heart. He would love the baby also there was no mystery about that. There was no hesitation he and Emma would be married. That made him the luckiest fellow on earth, what Emma had done with Jim had passed. He looked into himself and knew he was Emma's future.

Emma had not yet told Neil, about Jim's Sister visiting the shop. Should I tell him, or not Emma thought? I don't want to upset Neil he has enough to put up with as it is. Yet if I don't tell him, it will be one more secret to hide I don't want any more secrets between us. I will tell him at the end of the week when I see him in private. We will decide a few things and I will be in a positive position, by then I will be sure of myself. I know that Neil too will know where we stand. I can't wait for security with his love to be with me, it is a fine thing that Neil is going to do, we both know it is not his baby and he loves me just the same. I'm beginning to love him, my heart has been broken in so many ways and I must give it time to mend. Another thing I should tell Neil is I still keep getting dizzy spells, I feel quite ill. What is wrong with me

I should feel jubilant now that Neil is looking after me, I think a lot about him too and positively look forward to seeing him it is the headaches I still have, also the shivering; perhaps it is all to do with the kidney infection. I suppose when I see Doctor Pen he will want to know, until then I must put up with it, as long as it doesn't get any worse. I never thought of being a trouble to anyone, I always have been positive about things I wanted to do, now I am floundering and find I do need help.

Chapter 38

Neil had called in the shop to make sure that Emma was going to keep her Saturday date. He was reassured and arranged to pick Emma up with a cab at 7pm. He being spot on time showed again that he cared. It was a foggy night and cold, Neil helped Emma into the cab she sat down and shivered, Neil drew a tartan travel rug over her knees, he wanted to put his arms around her, he would bide his time he could wait. Arriving at Neil's home Emma didn't feel so out of place as she had been doing; it seemed very natural to follow Neil to the study, there to greet them was a cosy fire.

"It's a lovely fire Neil, ooh it is snug and warm in here."

Coming in from the frost and fog made the room a haven, the chairs still either side of the fire as before, lovely logs had been built up burning with a twirl of flame, it crackled, sent sparks. She felt better at ease now; she had visited before so it wasn't so new to her. Neil said,

"Yes, I wanted you to feel relaxed; the fire on such a night as this is very welcome isn't it?"

Emma wanted to get straight on to the crux of the matter in hand saying,

"I think I am ready to set wheels in motion Neil, I have considered all week as you asked me to, when I have told you what has happened during this week we can begin to make plans."His smile broadened saying,

"That's my girl; I was hoping you would say that dear Emma, you don't know how I have thought about you every minute of every hour. No one will ever love you as I love you. Now it seems we are going to belong together,

it brings a warm glow all over even to contemplate the idea." He kissed the top of her head as he passed her chair.

"Will you have a small glass of wine? It will warm your insides through."

"Funny you should say that Neil I have been shivering a lot lately, a headache too, when I go to see Doctor Pen I think I should tell him."

"Of course you must, perhaps the medication is not working. He will want to know any symptoms you might have, he has to keep an eye open for babies' sake as well as yours. I hope it is not something that will affect the baby, now you have me worried."

"Don't be silly I am only trying to put your mind at ease, not worry you."

"I must tell you, this is not nice Neil but Jim's Sister came into the shop in the week threatening me to lay off Jim, calling me a slut and a few other fancy names, it made me ill. I told her I never want to set eyes on Jim again. Here is the thing Neil, Jim is already married and has two sons I was in shock, all the time I spent with him led me to believe soon he would marry me, I never gave a thought to any other outcome. I understood that the demands he made on me all led up to that one thing. How wrong was I, I am so

sorry Neil if I could put the clock back I would. All I can say is the man is despicable, he knew what he was doing, went on with no conscience at all. I am ashamed of myself and can't find the words to describe Jim's part in this matter. I never want his face to be before mine ever. There is nothing to say in my defence. I just want to forget, for weeks I have been trying to stop it all, he is an evil man never taking a bit of notice. Here I am and here I am going to stay I won't give him one more thought. Neil said,

"There are things I would like to do to him, but I would swing for it! Let us both put him and his trials on the back burner eh?" Neil and Emma went very quiet. Neil went over to Emma and stood before her, he was now very serious saying,

"I have something I want to say to you tonight. He looked at her with devotion, he came from the standing position and kneeled before his love, his eyes never leaving Emma's eyes there was an aura of love around them as he said,

"May I ask you Emma, the big question that has been constantly on my mind ever since, I can't remember when. Darling Emma, will you be my wife, I love you with all my heart I will cherish you until the day I die, you are a

very dear person to me, please do say yes. The past week of waiting has been never ending my darling Emma and you are my whole world. Emma's reply was sincere,

"You are everything to me Neil, a lovely man, I don't deserve you, and yes I will marry you, I too will love you all of my life." Emma had consented to be his wife.

They lay on the rug before the fire arms entwined, safe, content, nothing now stood between them. Neil broke the silence saying,

"We have each other now I will never let you go. The fire is burning brightly and I have you in my arms, forget all but us two, we can make our wedding plans now nothing is going to get in the way I promise you in fact. He leaned over her and scooped her up in his arms, her head fell back and her hair tumbled down he kissed her. No matter how this had been brought about, no matter all it entailed, this was going to be, the future was theirs.

Emma saw Neil on Sunday again when they went to Church to hear the first of the Wedding Banns read it was a happy occasion, eyes gleaming, shining too with the tears of joy. Holding hands on the way out of Church, they had many Congratulations.

"Neil, it has been a lovely morning, but I am

afraid I must ask you to take me home, Neil thought that a bit odd and said,

"I had planned to go back to Mother's she is getting dinner, it will be a disappointment if we don't arrive. Is something the matter dear?"

"Yes, I don't feel well, it may be all the excitement getting to me, perhaps I could come with you for dinner, but after I must get home to rest."

"That's what we'll do then, I am sorry darling that you don't feel stronger by now. Will you go and see Doctor Pen once more in the morning? I would be happier if you did." Emma was unsure of the feeling, she felt really ill and wanting to be home in her own bed. Looking at Neil she said,

"I may be over this feeling by morning but if it is still the same, yes I will see the Doctor."

Neil's Mum had prepared a very nice meal, welcoming Emma to her home. There were many questions to be asked and answered. Mum hadn't had time to get to know Emma, now she was going to be her Daughter in Law that would make a difference in their conversation. One seemed pleased with the other, so all went well. Neil excused Emma not staying long and told his Mother he was going to take Emma home. Mother didn't seem to mind the early departure. Neil tucked the blanket around Emma seeing that she was comfortable. The cabby trotted his horse by now he knew where to go. Neil put his arm around Emma protectively. He could feel the heat in her body, feverish he thought. Just as well to be safe tucked up in her own bedroom, he couldn't let anything happen to her now. Arriving, Neil told Aunt Polly Emma had not been feeling too well saying,

"Emma and I have decided to give it a day or two to see if things are better by Tuesday if not Doctor Pen will have to advise do you think that is the right thing to do Aunt? Aunt said,

"Yes, you can't be too careful she has been off colour for ages now." Emma said,

"Don't fuss Aunty I will be perfectly all right, just need to rest. Neil and I have heard the Wedding Banns being read this morning, no we are not rushing things we want to organise as much as we can so we will have a Spring Wedding."

"Why! Dear girl, you have only just got engaged; I don't want to lose you."

"You won't lose me Aunty, I will still come and look after my sweet shop, yes I have discussed it with Neil, he is perfectly happy for me to do that, aren't you dear"? She

looked up at Neil her eyes trusting, loving wanting to please him, their secret still between the two of them.

Monday at breakfast, Emma declared she was all right to do her shop work.

"There is no need for me to do any real work Aunt I just have to be there to serve the odd Customer, there are never very many shoppers on Monday and it is usually a quiet day."

"Are you sure, I will close the shop if you would like me to, your health comes first, how do you feel this morning any better?"

"Not too bad I slept well, there can't be that much wrong with me. I will come in to tell you if I feel the need to stop."

"We'll leave it at that then and wait to see how you are later on."

Emma wasn't telling the whole truth, there was something wrong. She couldn't decide how to deal with it this dizzy feeling, the headaches, her legs felt weak and she thought working through it might be the best way to go. Standing behind the counter, with her back to the door, the shop bell rang she turned to see who it was. Thinking the floor was going to come up and hit her, she clung on to the counter, at a loss for words as she faced Jim! What, on earth is he doing here?

Emma had so many thoughts driving through her head, trying to keep calm was taking quite an effort I must keep my wits about me; this is like a bad dream. Jim is the last person I want to see, I must keep calm, I must keep calm…..

Chapter 39

"Hello Emma, I have missed you this was the only place I was sure you would be, so here I am. Say hello to your "Jimsy." You look flushed you needn't blush on my account. We'll soon pick up where we left off." Emma's breath coming in gasps, she said,
"Pick up, oh no, there will be no picking up with me." Jim's eyes were full of awe.
"Don't be silly, we are a pair, I want to see you again."
"Well I don't want to see you I am not your girl any more, never will be. You never told me you were married and have two boys."
"Who's been telling you tales? Even if I have we could still have a good time, meeting once a week was ideal, nobody needs to get hurt you carrying the baby would make a difference, I wouldn't have to be on the alert all the time. Come on Emma, you know you still want me."
"Certainly I do not want you, you are despicable and you are everything I hate in a man. Meet you again, no, no, no, the likes of you should have a tattoo on his forehead so

that girls like me cross the road so as not to meet and get so cruelly hurt." His face was full of anger, thinking Emma, would be a pushover not preparing himself for this onslaught, Emma was very glad the counter was between them.

"All right then slut, have it your way, you'll be begging me before long. Don't ask me to buy a pram or anything else for that matter, that little beggar that you are carrying isn't mine, or have I mentioned that before, girls like you are ten a penny. I'm off."

Emma didn't know how to stop from fainting, as far as feeling better she knew she was worse, perching on the stool behind the counter needing to be still, the room swirled around her. At this moment, thinking she would like to live a million miles away, where Jim couldn't find her. Hate was not a strong enough word. Trying to keep stable Emma felt the floor come up as she went down in another fall.

"What is the commotion in here?" Aunt found Emma on the floor rushing over and seeing the state of things called,

"Annie, Ruby come here. Go to fetch Neil Ruby, Annie fetch a warm blanket, be quick." Aunt upset, gave her orders.

Ruby ran as fast as her legs would carry her,

she knew where Neil would be.

Neil contacted Doctor Pen, while telling him the bare facts, he added,

"Please will you not say anything about the baby, I don't want to let Emma down and we had decided to keep it to ourselves a little while longer."

"I will be the soul of discretion, don't worry let us both get over there to see what is going on." Doctor Pen, went with Neil in Neil's own two-seater carriage, they hurried to Aunt Polly's.

"She is just coming round Doctor, I am not at all happy about these falls, she is getting no better."

"Stand well back give her some air. Now Emma, let's see what we can do for you."

He took her wrist timed her pulse he looked at the gleaming sweat on her forehead and her pale face.

"We need to get her into Hospital Neil, I will make all the arrangements you stay to keep her calm." Mr Neil Nolan had a private deal with the Hospital so Neil had no problem about Emma being well looked after, she would be getting the best of attention. Neil didn't need a reason to stay, he would be right at Emma's side holding her trembling hand telling her everything was going to be

all right hoping all would be well this was just minor setback.

Emma had never been in Hospital before it all seemed like a bad dream. The Nurses had her ready for examination. Doctor Pen, with two other Doctors were pulling on surgical gloves to proceed, It didn't take long, as they all came to the same conclusion, this was poison from her Kidney infection gone into the blood stream. Doctor Penn took Neil to one side and said,

"I am very sorry about this, she will be fighting for her life and it is likely she will lose the child. I must have her under strict rest and see the outcome daily. Of course, you will be told if there is any change for better or worse. You may sit with her if you wish, but don't disturb her sleep it is of paramount importance, we will do our utmost to get her well, be assured about that." Neil was devastated, not Emma his own only true love, he didn't know what to think about the baby, he had come to accept it as his own he had to satisfy himself with the thought of all being well again, if one of them was to survive it had to be Emma. He looked at her pale face perspiration on the brow, the uneasy heavy look around the eyes. He had seen it several days ago he just thought it was the kidney

infection that was troubling her not realising the depth of the problem, he remembered taking her home early on Sunday after the Banns were read. All little niggling signs, he had taken no notice he would watch over her now until she got better, she must get better they had a Wedding to attend.

The days passed, Ruby and Annie visited they didn't know what to think. It was out of the question that Emma might die she was their Sister, so young. Aunt Polly kept enquiring taking small amounts of delicious food in to entice Emma to eat. Emma still in a fever was eating very little, that which she did get down sometimes came back. Doctor Pen kept reassuring the family that the best of treatment was being given. He pulled Neil to one side as he was leaving.

"A quiet word dear boy, you know Emma is having a struggle don't you. She has had some blood loss from the womb the baby is hanging on a thread it is my opinion she will go into a repulsive phase, so the baby will be dispelled. I am only telling you this so that it won't come as a big shock, I am so sorry. Do you want me to tell her Aunt and Sisters?

"No I think not, we were hurrying the wedding as you realise, if the baby is lost I see no advantage in leaving Emma with the many

explanations she would have to face. Of course when Emma has recovered the wedding date will be set again, we do intend to marry baby or no baby. I love Emma dearly; all I can hope is that she will recover. In fact, I can't see any other outcome. My eyes are blinded with tears and please Doctor Pen help her all you can."

"I certainly will Neil, if she aborts the baby, she will have a better chance, but that is up to Mother Nature, I can only stand by to help. She will be weak for a while, when this is all over, you I know will see that she is looked after."

"Thank you Doctor, I am going back in now before I leave, I feel I am leaving her in the best of care." Ruby and Annie ended their visit and went into the waiting area leaving Aunt Polly to say her goodbyes. Emma was lying in a pool of sweat not really knowing who was with her. She felt a kiss on her cheek she took this in and knew it was good to have someone with her. Aunt looked haggard, how was she going to tell Ada and Albert that their dear Emma was so ill she said,

"Have you spoken to Doctor Pen Neil?"

"Yes, Aunt he has assured me that all that can be done is being done."

"We can only wait then, is that the case?"

"It is Aunt, it is. I am going to sit with her a little while longer. When I go rest assured I will be back at any sign of change, my Mother is also worried, she will be glad of my news when I get back tonight. We are at a cross road, soon the fever may abate, once she can get normal sleep things should improve see you tomorrow then, goodnight."

Neil went back in to Emma, he picked up her limp hand caressing it as he did so, he took it up to his lips gently kissing it. How lovely it would be to see her back in her sweet shop, eyes smiling serving the customers with her usual personal attention. When things change, they change so quickly. It was like blinking an eye, the surge comes and then it carries you along, after you are left with the debris to clear so that life can go on. Doctor Penn had spoken to Neil and told him the baby had been aborted, at the same time reassuring Neil that Emma now had a much better chance of surviving this ordeal.

Neil now knew that Emma had lost the baby she was carrying he was both sorry and glad. He was sorry for poor little mite, but glad that Emma would not have Jim's child. It meant that he beside Emma could have a child of their own the thought pleased him that is unless the illness had stopped Emma from having children and only time would tell that. For the moment he had to be satisfied that Emma was making a slow recovery, now she was recognising him and her family, it had been very awkward for Aunt to understand, as the baby and losing it had not been brought into the equation, there being more wrong with Emma than Aunt or the family knew. There now wasn't a need for them to ever know, the same being said for Emma's Mum and Dad. Serving no purpose and it being the best way to go Neil told Emma, as quietly as he could what had been decided between himself and Doctor Pen so that she also could keep this a secret.

"Emma darling, it is the best for all concerned it happened naturally you have nothing to blame yourself for, all being well we can have children of our own, a fresh start leaving the past behind. We will fix a later date for our wedding. All will be well I promise you."

Emma had listened to his every word replying with a squeeze of her hand a look in her eyes, he had taken all the upset in his stride. He was a tower of strength to her.

Her voice being low Neil had to bend over the bed to hear what she wanted to tell him.

"Dear Neil, thank you for all you have done I realise your way is the right way for us both, I love you" Her talking had taken all her strength for the moment. He put his finger to her lips and shushed her. She had said, "I love you." She loved him how long he had been waiting to hear those words the warm feeling of joy, unexplained depth of contentment filled his very being. Nothing could stop them now. Closing her eyes Neil could see he had tired her he let her go to sleep knowing that it was the best medicine for her; he hoped he would be in her dreams. Tucking the covers around her so that she could feel the love and protection he would leave behind he went quietly away knowing he had done all he could for her leaving part of himself behind for she was part of him.

Chapter 40

Christmas was spent mainly in the Hospital, not only for Emma, all the family visited, in fact the Nurses shoo shooed some of them from the bed being too many around at one time. Emma on her way to recovery had never had so much attention in her life. Neil constantly there carrying fresh flowers, some of her very own favourite sweets and chocolates.

"You must not keep bringing me these things to eat, they are all very nice but I have to look good for my wedding day, what about my figure?" They all laughed because Emma had lost a lot of weight, she was too thin and needed to fill out a little.

This was a Christmas, that wouldn't be forgotten. Emma was so delighted at the attention that had been lavished upon her. Now and again though Jim would creep into her thoughts, she didn't want any contact with him so hoping, praying he never ever turned up unannounced. There was no way to deal with him; even the baby was of no consequence being that there was no baby now. Emma lay and thought about that, had she been lucky or had she lost someone that would have been close to her the rest of her life? The dye had been cast there was no way to return. Acceptance must be the way to go. Alongside Neil, always depending on him, he being solid there was no hesitation in her mind "if only" again these two words occurred many times as her thought stream went beyond all reality. What was life all about? Why hadn't she seen Neil in the light that now she found him? I must have loved him all along as I love him now; it was the pull of Nature her enquiring body longing to know, Jim had made her feel the awakening of her own sexuality. Jim's devil may care attitude enticing, they had been her pitfalls, so young so wanting to be grown up without the interference of Aunt Polly, knowing absolutely nothing about sex, walking into the trap so willingly thinking she had found love, infatuation had swept her off her feet. Believing and being so sure of mind that when a man has known you in that intense way you had to marry, how wrong she had been. The love she now felt for Neil had no resemblance to the love she had felt for Jim. One demanding occasion each week did not register as love, a lesson she had learned the hard way.

"Neil, Neil! An excited Emma said, as Neil sat down beside her in the ward, I am coming home! Doctor Pen came and told me this morning. I will have to take things easy for a while, I don't care about that. I will be in my own bed in my own room." Neil looked fondly at her excitement saying,

"That is wonderful news, I will be able to spoil you my darling and you need a bit of spoiling. When you are strong enough we will go for rides with the pony and trap, yes through the Park or any other place you want to go, we now have a future and I want you by my side for always." He bent over and warmly kissed her lips. Emma's mind began to work, if on these rides Neil wanted to go to see her Mum and Dad's house what would she say? It was a humble abode, perhaps Neil was thinking it was like Auntie Polly's well it wasn't. There wasn't a grand staircase in Mum's house there were no carpets on the floors no inside toilet, the bath hung on a nail outside the kitchen door, a black lead grate gave the warmth and did the cooking, How could she possibly take him to her former home? There was barely a decent chair to sit on. She tried to recall what she had told him about her home, but couldn't remember saying much at all. Neil interrupted her quiet

moment saying,

"You have suddenly gone very quiet Emma, is anything wrong?"

"No everything is fine, just thinking about getting home, everything will be all right won't it Neil?"

"Of course, we will plan our wedding, get Ruby and Annie to make your dress and their own dresses as they of course will be your bridesmaids."

"I have thought about that Neil, I think they will have to have the title "Maids Of Honour" they are too grown up to be bridesmaids"

Neil smiled, as she had answered with thought. It assured him she was on the way to health again he said,

"Colour yes we will choose for you and for the girls, I expect you to have white, with lace and a veil, looking more beautiful than ever, you will make all the decisions. I will approve does that sound about right?" In a glow of togetherness, both smiling, Emma knew nothing could go wrong, she wouldn't let it and her childhood dream of getting married in white was going to come true.

"Where will we live Neil?"

"We will find the right place for us it depends on you, where would you be most happy? A Town house or a Country Cottage I know you

will want to be as close to Aunt as possible do you think you will keep your sweet shop in business?" Aunt Polly, Ruby and Annie too knew that Neil would fit in with this arrangement; he was good at fitting in, and of course Emma would carry on in the sweet shop.

"What can I bring you when I come tomorrow? Will the girls know what clothes you would like to wear? It will be strange you getting dressed won't it? Strange, but pleasant hey, bet you can't wait. 10am I will be here, by lunchtime you will be home. There will be no rush just take your time you may be a little wobbly on your legs, you have been in bed for many weeks, so don't count on going it alone, I want to be with you to see you safely home. I also want to give your family a word or two, so that they won't expect too much of you, I just don't want anything to go wrong, tomorrow will be an important day for both of us." He kissed her and left, things were going well.

Home, here at last Neil had warned her that still being weak she would have a job on her hands just to walk from the cabby to Aunt's door, it was so tiring. Everything seemed strange, looking at familiar things in an unfamiliar way, her shop was arranged differently, thinking the girls had done that and she would soon put it back to the way she liked it.

"Lovely to have you home Emma," Aunt Polly was ushering her in. There was the smell of, what? It was Aunt's shin of beef pie; to Emma it smelled like a feast, the aroma permeating through, it made her mouth water.

"I can smell your pie Aunt, it smells lovely and I have been saving a corner just so I can enjoy some with you."

"We will soon get some meat on those bones, wont we girls?"

Ruby and Annie, agreed saying,

"To be together again and not having to worry about you is what we all are hoping for. There are lots of things to tell you as you get stronger, how do you think you got the infection Emma?"

"Hey come on, I have hardly sat down you want to know everything all at once, I will tell all in good time. We have catching up to do just at this moment I feel strange, need to get on solid ground again, we will be talking for days once I get going."

"This is what I warned you against Emma," Neil stepped into the conversation understanding but firm he told the girls to

give Emma some space. The girls didn't take offence, to the contrary, they were glad to see Neil looking after Emma's best interests; they had wondered once or twice, what had happened to Jim. Emma never mentioned him, obviously he wasn't on the scene any more. Neil in command, Jim a ghost from the past he was not likely to be spoken of ever again, Emma doted on Neil.

Emma joined them at the table for dinner and devoured every mouthful, she was so happy to be back at Aunt's, Neil sitting opposite seemed very natural, he after all was going to be part of Emma's life. After the meal Neil took Emma upstairs to her own bedroom. Emma remembered how it looked to her when Aunt had shown her for the first time. She saw it again through those eyes, so very glad to be home. Going over to her bed, she saw her reflection in the mirrors. Now she knew what Neil had been saying, she was still very thin and she still had that vague yellow pallor in her face. Knowing she had to build back her strength, this was not going to be easy, after all the family knew nothing about her losing the baby, of course they didn't know she was ever having a baby, it being best left that way. I have to build myself up, I see that now, it has come to mind seeing

Ruby and Annie and how well they look I will get there soon. Neil won't want to start a family straight away I know he will wait until I am ready. I will do my utmost to get well and fulfil some of Neil's dreams. I am very lucky to be loved also very lucky not to have to explain my baby to Aunt and the family. How I wish? Wishes very rarely came true so the wish was left unsaid."

A couple of weeks later Aunt asked,

"When do you think Emma you will be ready to start in the shop again? You have made good recovery, I think a couple of hours a day might even do you good, get you into the swing of things again." Aunt considered how to treat Emma, she knew she wasn't herself yet, it was difficult to judge whether or not to encourage Emma back to normal so soon she still looked a bit off and unsteady, a bit at a time Aunt thought no real work. Aunt would encourage Emma to go into the shop each day just to get her idea of routine again.

"I am sure Aunt it won't be very long now; I would like to leave it until I have seen Doctor Pen at the Hospital again I will talk to him about it, see what he says."

"That is good, I am not pushing you dear I want the best for you, what day do you go?"

"Wednesday at 10am it is a check-up. I will

feel a lot surer of myself after that. Neil is taking me, I am glad to say, he is a dear, he is always doing something for me I don't know how I will repay all the kindness he has shown me. I know he loves me, but the effort he puts into showing me is of great importance I love him all the more for it."

"Yes you would go a long way to find such as Neil, I think you are in for a very happy life with him not like that Jim, he was a rough character if you ask me I was so glad when you finished with him."

"Don't talk about him Aunt he is not worth the breath. I learned a lesson I will never forget." Emma cut herself short there thinking she might slip up and say something about the baby. Instead she said,

"I am going to have a little while with Annie and Ruby."

Emma left thinking how on guard she had to be with her talk when it was anything about Jim. She could do it, after a time it wouldn't be something she had to forget, it would be something that had never occurred in the first place. Deception wasn't a part of what Emma was made up of it was difficult.

"Hello you two," Annie and Ruby sat stitching, what are you stitching now?"

"We get lots of orders for embroidery on all

sorts of things, coats, dresses, nightdress cases chair backs, even the very posh upper class maids aprons. The general upper classes love nothing more than being individual, each one trying to outdo the other. We are never short of work it is a good job we both like our work isn't it?"

"Soon you will have to make space for my wedding dress, also your own dresses. Have you decided on a colour? I know it was pink are you still going to have pink?

"The wedding won't be for a while will it Emma?"

"I can't keep Neil waiting for long he has done all he can to get me well so sharpen your wits and come up with a special design for me, you don't want a rush job on your hands do you?"

"We won't it is a time we have been waiting for. The dresses will be made with all our love to send you off. Ruby we must get our heads together to finalise colour. You Emma, could let us know what style you would like perhaps we could get some ideas, we will start looking at wedding photos in the papers and then we can all discuss design, materials too, we will get some samples when we go to get stock."

"That will be just as I would want it, we think alike us three." The talk was over Emma

went back to rest a little lighter at heart a smile lighting her face.

Chapter 41

Ada sat opposite Albert, her mug of tea in her hand.
"We have had a letter from Emma, it has worried me."
"Why is there anything gone amiss with Emma?"
"No it is just that Emma wants to bring Neil to see us."
"What's wrong with that Ada?"
"Nothing really, he has such a posh home, our Polly's is posh too, he will expect us to be something we are not."

"Don't be daft, he will take us as he finds us, it is Emma he is marrying not the family." Ada said,

"Everything is so very different here I think there are only him and his Mother in that beautiful house. He has a study, a place of his own to take any guest to. Our, Emma hasn't anywhere of her own, not even her own bedroom here." Albert stood up and went across to Ada, he put his arm around her saying,

"Come on old girl, don't be worried, our Emma wouldn't want that, what we have got, has been earned by fair means, you have been a good Mother to all our children I am proud to say. It doesn't take riches to be well mannered and clean. Love, that is the key, ours certainly have been loved."

"I don't cook the sort of food he will want, in fact I haven't a clue as to what he likes, I suppose they will want one meal with us, dinner maybe, what on earth can I get?"

"No worries there Ada, a meal that you cook for dinner probably will be the best meal he has ever had, even if he has been served by cooks, I would put your meal to the fore of anything a cook could bring to the table."

"Thank you Albert, will you help me plan a menu?"

"I could do that in two minutes flat. Do you want me to?"

"It would take a weight off my mind if you would."

"Right, we will have oxtail soup the butcher had some really nice oxtails fresh, they would make good stock. That is when I went in yesterday. As a main course shin of beef pie with some vegetables from Tom's allotment. He grows lovely stuff.

"Oh! But Albert, Polly does that."

"Not like yours Ada, her pastry is heavy. Yours is crisp and flaky and it would be an offer he couldn't refuse. Then to finish the meal one of those apple pies with the open top served with custard. There you are mouth-watering food fit for anyone, has that helped?"

"If you say that is what to get then I will, it will certainly be better than trying to concoct a speciality dish that I don't really know how to get together. I will black lead the grate, find a table cloth they should be in the upstairs drawers, scrub the kitchen floor and clean the windows, that is all I can do, I hope it is enough."

"Enough! I should say so, couldn't do more if the King was coming!"

Emma feeling much better now she was

tending her shop, not doing full days just 9am till 4pm suiting her very well. The odd hour she would go to talk to Annie and Ruby. They had given her a tablecloth with an embossed pattern to embroider for her bottom drawer. Each corner had a different cottage with garden, so deciding on the colour and playing with the coloured silks each corner had a different hue. Emma had been delighted, not being the favourite of her things to do, but this had its own appeal, she would go from her shop to get a cup of tea for them all at four, then close the sweet shop and sit talking with Ruby and Annie until closing time, doing a bit of her cloth each day, they sewing a favourite piece too. Emma thought she would miss that part of the day when it came time to do her full hours. Emma said,
"You haven't brought me any samples of cloth for my wedding dress yet you did say you would? Annie replied,
"We will, Ruby only mentioned it yesterday, we thought it was a bit too soon, we didn't know how you felt."
"I am ready, I needn't make a final decision I can look at the cloth several times. I will know then I will choose the right one. Neil has asked me also about the colour you have chosen, do you know yet?"

"We keep changing our minds we both have to agree, of course we usually do and I think it is because we have been waiting for you to tell us you are ready, now that you have we will think more on positive lines."

"Ruby did you know Emma is going to take Neil over to the Ford to see Mum and Dad? Ruby replied

"I had heard something of the sort from Aunt, but you know how she bustles about these days tells you a story, you get the rest next day"

"Annie, don't say that about Aunt she has been so good to all of us. I don't know where we would be without her." Emma soon stood up for Aunt Polly, she had a great deal to say thank you for. She had just turned her head and there was Aunt coming to tell them tea was ready to be served, oh! Yes, where would they be without Aunt Polly?

"What have we got tonight for tea?" Annie asked

"Poached smoked haddock with tomatoes. The bread is freshly made so you can eat a slice with it delicious, and I love rice pudding for afters."

Sitting, around the table, they always had light conversations with each other.

"How are you getting on with your table cloth

Emma," Aunt asked.

"I am happy to say it is coming along nicely, I am on the lavender corner now and I finished the pink one yesterday, it will be so nice, I shan't want to use it for meal times. I might have it as an afternoon cloth, it will stay nice for much longer if I do and you know my embroidery pieces are few and far between, so I want to treasure it." Annie and Ruby, smiled and said,

"If you did more of it Emma it would become easier."

"Well I don't, just because you find it easy doesn't mean to say that I have to. Stop tittering or I will come around to box your ears," that only made them laugh more, it was good-humoured banter no one was going to box anyone's ears.

"You girls will be the death of me Aunt looking good humoured with a smile stated. I will pack you all off back to the Ford if you give any more cheek at this table, there'll be no rice pudding if you are not careful."

Neil had been taking Emma to his home each day just for an hour, talking about where they were going to live, Neil said,

"I have always loved the idea of living in a cottage, although we mustn't be too far away because of our work, do you think we could

get around to look at the places available, it has to suit both of us in whereabouts, considering also inside space"

"Yes that is a good idea Neil, practical and pretty with a view. I can't think of a cottage without a garden so plainly that would have to be a consideration. Oh! Neil, we are talking about our first house or cottage, roses around the door, with a riot of colour to run along with the wavy garden path. We could have a wisteria that would drape its way at the front, forget-me-nots and lavender. I can picture it all in my mind's eye, a stable to put the horse in an outbuilding to keep the cab. We would go trip trotting along, you with your arm around me and me dreamily looking at the country side Emma's face was a picture imagining the scene.

"You make it sound heavenly Emma you by my side, me the luckiest man in the world." He bent his head and kissed Emma's forehead. Long gone the thought of Jim. Emma now knew the difference between Jim and Neil she had a future with Neil one that would last forever, it made her cold like ice dropping down her back when Jim momentarily crossed her mind. Try as she might he would not be blocked out altogether, she had been very lucky that circumstance

had given her a loophole, there was just herself, Doctor Pen and Neil who knew anything at all about the baby, it was working. In fact, not carrying the baby for long it's short presence had almost faded from her mind, as though it never was. Emma was ready to start with a clean slate, everything being in order gave her confidence.

"Burr, it is getting chilly in here, shall I put some more wood on the fire, or are you ready to be starting home?"
"I am not going home just yet Neil, I am too cosy here. Yes, build the fire up; we could stay like this forever just you and me darling. The candles make the whole room inviting. Hmmm it's so good to feel you close. I keep thinking "What if." You near to me make all those sorts of thoughts disappear, I do love you Neil."
Now the fire burned brightly again the rug on the hearth glowed from its flame the frost outside gave a sense of a picture postcard scene. The gas street lights making a yellow flare on the frosty cobblestone walkway, a night of magic where dreams come true, reality drifts into the dream, so they become one. Sparkling, majestic you try to hold it in your hand and it slips through the fingers

because it cannot be held. It takes all the sharp and dark feelings away leaving awareness that cannot be explained.

Later lying in her bed Emma went over the evening in her mind, it had been a balm to a troubled soul. Neil had told Emma to forget the past. Now both looking to their future, she was going to give it her very best. Tomorrow I will see if the girls have the wedding material for me to choose from. I am finding the preparation overwhelming and exciting. I don't know how to get things coordinated. I suppose all will come right, Neil is right I do too much worrying. Falling asleep even as she whispered the words to herself her dreams were not troubled she was flying on her own magic carpet. The landscape lay out beneath her, trees that took weird shapes, clouds for her to ride on, her darling Neil waiting for her.

Auntie Polly called upstairs Emma opened her eyes to another day.

"Come on girls not going to stay in bed all day are you?

"We're coming, we all want the bathroom, won't be long."

Down the sweeping stairway they came, all managing at the same time.

"Eggs, is it Aunt?" Aunt must have got up

early because the table was laid and place settings dealt with. It wasn't every morning that there was time, it all looked very welcoming. It was a cold morning, the fire burning already giving the heat they needed. Aunt said,

"Will 9am until 4pm suit you again today Emma?"

"That will be good for me Aunt."

"Have you a lot of work on today Annie?"

"Yes, we have two ladies coming to see how there order is progressing we are not worried about it and the items are already near to being finished. In fact we are glad to show the pieces, they have turned out well I have done one order, Ruby has done the other and you can't tell who has done what being as they are both good, it doesn't matter."

Aunt Polly smiled to herself she now was used to the special place that was held between Ruby and Annie. She was pleased having also contented customers, this made for goodwill and that is always welcomed.

"Right I shall leave you to it then, I will do the washing up and on to some work in the house, then I will be free to see that our ladies get their tea with cakes this afternoon, we all will be busy. Ruby and Annie leave your dresses for washing I noticed they

looked a little soiled good job you made a second dress each, have to keep everything smart our customers are what I call the upper class they enjoy coming here to buy, drink tea and chat, only the best will do. With pretty girls like you they feel at ease, they are always telling me tales about the ladies they are friends with, I find it very interesting, nothing personal, just chit chat you know. Emma your dress was washed and pressed while you didn't have to wear it so should be all right this time."

"Yes, it is Aunt I am going now to open up the sweet shop, we'll have it dinner time before we get anything done at the rate we are on today. Come on Ruby and you Annie we have to serve the public." They got up from their chairs and had a laugh with Emma Ruby saying,

"Oh you Emma, stand behind us with a whip why don't you?" Briskly they all went to their positions ready to get on with the day.

Chapter 42

In the shop Emma looked for what needed doing, not being over her illness it was the smaller duties she was taking care of. Halfway to putting a spring window display in, trying to decide for colour yellow of course the colour of chicks and daffodils having some boxed chocolates with a spring scene on the box was a must. A length of yellow satin pleated all along the bottom of the display and of course the beautiful Easter Eggs. Being pleased with what she was doing she hummed a little tune; she was coming out of her gloom. Deciding to be happy, leaning to the corner of the window she glanced up it shocked her! Jim looking straight at her, her heart did a lurch her face reddened. At once her thoughts were in turmoil. Oh, go away for goodness sake. It had spoiled her moment, she felt her whole self tighten up and there wasn't anything she could do about it so she just acted casual. She gave him a little smile and backed out of the window hoping he would be gone. Of course going back into the shop post haste where she could put a distance between her and Jim, the bell tinkled, oh no! It was Jim; at least now, the counter was between them.

"Good morning Jim, politely addressing him as she would anyone."

"Good morning is it! Is that the only greeting you can give to the Father of your child?"

Emma realising Jim didn't know about the baby being lost felt suddenly guilty, also he must not make conversation to this effect as Aunt, Ruby and Annie had never known there was a baby.

What did he want? How could she get rid of him, No, no, no, this was not happening she felt sick.

"I have been in the shop before, twice in fact, but you haven't been here, I need you Emma I want to see you, we were made to see each other."

She couldn't help herself in her reply,

"Do you recall just what you called me? Disgusting and slut in your eyes is that what I am? What about your wife and your two boys? There was no denial of that fact."

"We can sort that out Emma I can see you as much as possible I really want to see you."

"Well I don't, I am not going to ever see you again Jim. Then he let rip,

"You will see me, I am not taking no for an answer, you little bitch, think you can do as you please, no, you can't. I will not let you. The baby you carry is mine. I am already part of you." His voice had risen he was thumping the counter. Any minute now Emma would have Aunt and the girls coming to see what the commotion was all about, she had to get shut of Jim. The only way she knew was to say she would meet him. Her heart in her

mouth there was only the one way she could do that, she said,
"If it is all that important to you I will see you we will talk things over, now will you leave, this is not a place to argue in I must get on with my work."
"That's more like it, Jim thought he had won, you know it is best for us, so I will see you in the same spot that we met before it is always quiet there." His face relaxed, thinking he had his own way he lit up a cigarette. It was the opportunity she had looked for saying,
"Aunt doesn't like cigarettes smoked in the shop, perhaps, it would be better if you left."
"As I will see you tomorrow I will go, don't be late, you know I can't stand it when you are late, we'll have a great time together it will be like old times."
With that, he left leaving Emma distraught. She would have to tell Aunt that Jim had just called in case she had seen him around. The person she couldn't wait to tell was Neil; they had to work it out somehow, how? She really didn't know how. Aunt came into the shop saying,
"Did I hear someone raise their voice in here? I would have come sooner, but the job I was doing needed my attention, Emma who was it?"

"Jim Aunt Polly, I didn't want to talk to him he was so insistent he raised his voice, don't worry he has gone I shall tell Neil tonight. I must say it has made me feel quite ill him turning up out of the blue. Do you think I could drop the catch on the door and come to sit in the kitchen with you for a while?"

"Of course you can, we will make some tea, don't think we want him around again do we Emma?"

If Aunt had known what Jim had said she would have been far more worried, as it was, she took the fact that Jim had been readily sent off. It was Emma's illness that was making her unsteady, she needed time. Together they went into the kitchen, before long Emma felt more herself again, sitting beside the fire burning in the black leaded grate had a sense of solidarity, home, security, all those things at this time were the tools to bring Emma back to normal.

"Did he say anything specific Emma?"

"No Aunt, you know what he is like; he thinks a lot of himself, wants everyone else to do the same. I don't want anything to do with him ever."

"I am glad to hear that, I always had him down as a rough nut, handsome yes that is where it ends, he has no decorum he needn't

bother in future I will tell him myself if needs be." Emma didn't want Aunt involved, so said,

"There is nothing to worry about, Neil will sort him out."

Neil came to pick Emma up in the buggy still giving her plenty of attention, placing the travel rug around her knees. His arm around her, a comforting sound coming from the horse clip clopping along the cobblestone road. The gaslights lit, the evening air still sharp, winter was reluctant to leave, and the snowdrops glistened in the parks like pools of light Emma snuggled up to Neil.

"How is my favourite girl tonight then," Neil *softly whispered in Emma's ear. Expecting her to say all was well, she didn't.*

"Neil I have been very upset today do you think I could wait to tell you when we arrive and are settled in the study?"

"I shan't want to hear anything has happened to you Neil remarked in a worried tone, I thought you seemed on your way to recovery." They went quiet holding hands to feel close; Neil loved her so much he wanted to protect her from the world, keeping her beside him sharing her innermost thoughts keeping her safe Emma knew this, she would do anything to right the wrong life had dealt

her not wanting to tell him about Jim and his demands. On arrival Emma went in to see Neil's Mother, a thing she very often did if there was time. She didn't want his Mother to think she was stealing Neil away from her. Mother doted on Neil, when he brought Emma in with him she was delighted, mother liked Emma thinking Neil had chosen well, it was good of both of them to include her in their life.

"Hello Emma, come in sit down for a few moments by the fire it is still cold isn't it."

Both Emma and Neil greeted Mother Neil put his arm around his Mother's shoulders dropping a kiss on her head. He knew this gesture would give his Mother a feeling of security he wanted her to feel secure and he loved her.

"Is there anything I could do for you Mother? Have you had your tea?"

"Yes dear boy I have everything I want especially now that I have seen you two you bring light into my days, I will be happy to know when you have fixed a wedding date. I know you want your own home, also I know you will be visiting me, I can come to see for myself you're new home and I get quite excited about it all. Emma will you bring your wedding dress materials to show me, have

you made your choice yet?"

Mother wanted to get all her questions answered, time was as precious as money. It would make her very happy to see these two settled together.

"I have narrowed it down to choose the best from two, yes I will bring them along one evening, I would like you to help my final choice, I will bring Ruby and Annie's choices too we will spend an evening together, Neil can disappear to his study leaving us two to chat. We will talk about the wedding arrangements and the seating at the Church Hall. It will be a very short ride going from the Church to the Church Hall, it won't work the horses too much the horses will be fresh then for the journey to our new home."

"Oh! I see you are arranging it all so well, I know you don't need me, yet I am thrilled at the thought of our evening together choosing colours talking it all over, you are my dear children I love you both, for you and Neil to be happy is all I want to see." She fondled Emma's hand a contact to be enlarged upon in the future days.

"Hey, come on you two, let me get my Emma to myself it will be time to go at this rate." They laughed and went on to the study. Emma wished she did not have to tell Neil

about Jim, she had created such a cosy feeling with his Mother she didn't want to spoil it but tell him she must.

"A small glass of sherry Emma, now you can tell me what has happened, is it bad news?"He hoped it wasn't, so he settled down to listen.

"It's Jim Neil. He has been bothering me at the shop. I was worried to death Aunt would hear him he still thinks I am having his child, he insists on seeing me again. I am frightened of him he lays down the law and is very adamant. I had to make another date with him just to get him out of the shop, I don't know what to do and I fear he will be back."

"I do not like this Jim. I could kill him with my bare hands for what he has put you through in the first place. Don't worry my darling I will think about what to do, if he harasses you again I will get the Police on to him, as far as the date you have made you will not go, I will go to put him in his place. He is the sort that thinks he can take giving nothing in return. I will give him something to think about."

"Please Neil, don't put yourself in danger, he is a strong man, when he gets angry there is no controlling him."

"Are you saying I can't handle Jim? I can handle him all right. He will cower down when he knows he has a man to deal with, I shall not mince, my words. The anger I already have will sustain me I shall finish this once and for all. Despicable fellow, this is one time he won't win." Emma could see Neil taking the load off her shoulders and went on,

"I spoke about his wife and boys it didn't make a scrap of difference he talks about them as a side-line in the back ground. His advances towards me are just the same as before; he really believes he can come into my life again with the same routine. One minute I am a bitch, yes that, is what he calls me, the next minute he is all over me, can't do without me. Being vicious and horribly spiteful, I don't know what he will do next. I am so sorry Neil, I thought I had broken free; I honestly didn't think I would ever see him again; I really don't want anything to do with him, he must stop thinking he can see me, it is you I love and always will." Neil went over to Emma, he put a reassuring arm around her shoulders and then tears began to spill.

"Take this event out of your mind Emma he is going to have no claim on you or liaison with you. If I had my way I would lay him on

the ground step over him as you would with anything vile encountered that is the word for him, vile."

They kissed; he had put her fears at rest, what was the answer? Emma was sure she didn't know. It was all out in the open now she trusted Neil to end it. Very quietly, they sat on the rug before the fire a blemish staining beautiful thoughts about their wedding day.

"Come on Emma," Neil got up and held his hands out to help Emma to her feet; they stood for a moment entwined.

"We have to think about this new development. Jim can't be allowed to cause you any distress."

"I just can't see him Neil. The very thought frightens me."

"Of course it does, you my dear are not going to see him well only momentarily. I have a plan. See what you think of this. I will go at the time you have fixed; I will introduce myself to Jim trying to keep him calm while I tell him of what has happened. Also I will ask Doctor Pen to bring you along; we will go early to find a well-hidden hiding place at a safe distance, so that you and Doctor Pen witness what goes on. You and Doctor Pen will know if or when to step in. Hopefully Jim

will see it is all a losing battle and retire, he never needs to know you have been watching, but if he cuts up rough, you and Doctor Pen can witness with your own judgement and assess if anything is going too far. Doctor Pen knows you lost the baby, there need be no more dealings with Jim."

"It will be wonderful if it works Neil, Jim is a slimy character, I don't know if you would get the chance to explain very much, yes, it is worth a try, with you to talk to Jim, and Doctor Pen to stay hidden with me I will be safe and far away from Jim, with two men to contend with he can hardly attack me. The date is for the day after tomorrow will you be able to contact Doctor Pen in time?"

"I'll go and speak to him. Neil went to contact Doctor Pen by telephone. He came back to Emma with the details of the phone call. I have asked Doctor Pen to be best man at our wedding and he is happy to do so. I outlined the facts about Jim, not telling him the whole truth; he agrees Jim needs a good talking to. He is willing to be a witness protecting you at the same time if Jim gets aggravated. I have told him the destination and the time. We will pick you up in Doctor Pen's carriage. We will leave the carriage tucked out of sight and walk over to the

condemned cottages, you and Doctor Penn will get a good view of the spot where the meeting with Jim will take place, then we will go from there."

"You make it all sound so simple Neil, I really hope it is, Jim is trouble and I want him out of my life."

"No more than I do darling Emma we have lots of things to plan this is a darned irritating added extra, let's hope it will soon be over. I am going to take you home now Emma I don't want to over tax your strength and you need some sleep. I don't mean, lying in bed worrying, I mean sleep. Promise me no more bad thoughts; we are going to get this job done, darling Emma if only you had told me sooner."

Yes if only she hadn't wanted to save Neil the knowledge about how Jim had treated her. Now not wanting to encounter Jim in any way there was no other place to hide her worst fears. This must be settled once and for all.

Chapter 43

They arrived at the determined destination, Thursday at 7pm. having alighted from the carriage a little earlier, they picked their way through the wasteland filled with briar's weeds and mud, found a suitable place to hide, Emma and Doctor Pen, so they could see the spot of the designation clearly. Neil went over to stand there checking that the place was in clear view. He took his

position where Emma was to keep her date, all waiting for Jim to arrive...
Here was Jim; he sauntered up, leaned on a derelict wall looking around for Emma annoyed at the fact that there was another man in the spot he had chosen. Neil went towards him saying,
"I have come inform you Emma is not coming." It was a clipped short statement.
"How do you know Emma isn't coming she told me herself she would be here. She wouldn't dare to stand me up, she would know what she would get if she did!"
"I assure you she is somewhere you will not find her; the message is she does not want to see you ever again." Jim's eyes went to slits; a vicious look crept over his face he growled his reply,
"She'll pay for that."
"No Jim she won't, you are to stop harassing her."
"Who says?"
"I say, Emma is to be my wife."
"That's a laugh she is carrying my child." Smoothly, Neil said,
"Again you are mistaken, Emma has been very ill, during that illness she lost the baby. Being in Hospital at the time and being cared for as she had a kidney infection, she didn't

know much about what was happening, she was in a fever I can assure you there is no child." Jim went red with anger without the child he had no holds on Emma it was his trump card.

"I always knew she was a bitch she has done it to spite me, she doesn't love you it is me she loves. I will send you home looking pretty then she will know what she has got coming." With that he lurched a blow at Neil's face, Neil defended himself and retaliated in the same manor. The fight started, blow for blow, each man being angry, heated over his claim for Emma. Blood began to trickle down Neil's face. Jim spluttered out,

"I will finish you off, you lousy "tup" your own Mother won't recognise you, when I am done." In a complete frenzy, he was punching Neil as hard as he could.

Counteracting, Neil clenched his fist tighter to smack Jim with all his force Wham!!! He hit him hard. Jim's coat flung open he had on a leather belt with a knife and his right hand went down around to the side of him. He pulled the knife from the sheath on the belt it was very sharp. He flung himself into Neil reaching for his face. Neil dodged the knife and the skirmish went on. Now Neil had Jim's arm that held the knife, he grasped

Jim's wrist and with all his power he pressed the knife away from his own face turning the blade towards Jim. He put power into his own two hands to push the knife away it was a battle of strength. Jim's hand swung round, the knife blade turned. The knife in Jim's right hand now had the blade turned towards his own face. There was a contest of power again, as the blade cut down Jim's own left cheek. Jim bellowed with pain the knife dropped to the floor, both of Jim's hands went to his face. The blood ran down, there was no doubt about it Jim had severed his own cheek from the eye down to his chin. He wailed in pain, a pitiful sight. Panic set in, Neil called out loud for Doctor Pen to come and assist. Emma, with Doctor Pen came running towards them to help. Jim fell helpless to the ground saying still with the vicious tone,

"I will get you for this, you and your bitch of a woman I'll make you pay." The pain striking as Jim tried to speak soon quieted him. Neil produced a clean white handkerchief and made it into a pad so that Jim could hold it in place so to stop the bleeding, Doctor Penn went back to his carriage for his medical bag, soon he had Jim's bleeding face somewhat under control.

Doctor Penn said,

"We must hurry Neil, this is a deep cut it needs surgery, help me lift the fellow.

The carriage was brought as near as it could be; they hauled Jim over to it, now he must be treated quickly, never had Neil been so grateful that he had Doctor Pen on hand and that Doctor and Emma had seen this all happen. Jim was a self-opinionated man he had come to this moment via a trail of destruction towards Emma, even so Neil hadn't wanted this to happen it overwhelmed him, Neil was a kind and thoughtful man but Jim just would not listen. Neil knew now what Emma had tried to tell him, of course he was glad it wasn't his own face that had taken the sharp edge of the blade but being the man he was he didn't like to see Jim in pain. Jim had brought it on himself. Emma flung her arms about Neil.

"What can I do Neil, are you hurt?"

"I will live, he said trying his best to smile, let's get this one nodding towards Jim, back to the Hospital, Doctor Pen will stitch his face, what a thing to do he could have killed either of us and no doubt he will think twice before he asks to see you again, so some good will be done. He will have a lot of explaining to do to his wife. Wonder how he will wriggle

out of this one eh? We can only hope the cut will heal well so the scar will be unnoticed, I will see to it that he gets the best of attention, I must admit I am glad it is over." The carriage pulled away, Jim rolled into a ball in the corner of the seat still holding his face. They went as quickly as they could driving the horses to a gallop, soon they would arrive at Doctor Pen's private Hospital all the passengers hoping for the long-term outcome to be all right, shocked, weary and ready to let the anger plus passion go. All Jim could do was hold on to the pad that was soaking the blood from his face.

"Are you all right Neil?" Emma was just becoming herself again after the tussle with the injury, the blood from Jim's face was everywhere, it seemed strange that both Neil and Jim were both in the carriage, everything that had gone on was strange, as was all the very new things she had encountered. Still she hadn't got a grip on the situation, she trembled uncontrollably. Wanting to know, yet not wanting to know Emma struggled with this unusual situation, she said,

"Will Jim's wife have to be informed?"

"Yes, we will contact her as soon as the cut has been stitched, do you know her name?"

"I think it is Nanette, Jim will have to give

you her address as soon as he can he is not in any fit state at the moment, is he? Do you think the Police will need to be informed? Dazed as he was Jim heard the word Police, his words were muttered,
"Don't involve the Police can you hear me? Don't involve the Police, he repeated."
Doctor Pen took control,
"We will get him comfortably in a bed, then he will need the operating room to get the wound stitched he will be all right, the volume of blood is superficial, don't worry any more Emma, you just leave things to me. Jim obviously for his own reasons does not want to get involved with a Police report, I think it is better left as a private matter, which is what we will do. It would do us all good to be calmer. As Doctor Pen said these few words Emma and Neil felt better. Doctor Pen had been a lifesaver throughout these past wearying weeks, both Emma and Neil had much to say thank you for, without him they would have been going to the Police now trying to explain away the incident. As it was they knew Jim was being cared for, Jim's wife would come to take her part in the load that had to be carried. Jim wasn't going to be the same any more, even the scar his cut would leave would render him less attractive

to the ladies. Whether or not he knew it Nanette would be playing a bigger role in his life. He was at the mercy of Doctor Pen who could, or could not make a success of his facial repair?

In his new surroundings Jim began to take stock, how had he managed to get here? This was a Hospital. Someone would have to pay for this bed and he knew by the pain, someone would have to look after his cut, it was his face, as hard a man as Jim was he still wanted his face to look attractive, how would he tell his wife. Jim's thoughts were interrupted when two Nurses with a wheelchair came into the room. Jim was a big man; it would take two Nurses to get him into the chair. A wad of lint was still held to his face as he was taken down to the operating theatre.

"Put him straight on to the table nurse." Doctor Pen took control, first he had to weigh up how deep the knife had cut and then look in case the wound had cut anything more than the flesh on his face, also where the cut started and ended. He examined his patient.

"Hmm, I think you have been lucky Jim it is not as deep as we thought, he wanted to put Jim's mind at rest before he did the job of repair, Doctor Penn always thought of his

patients peace of mind, but in this case he found it hard to do. He gave the Nurses a look that told them he wanted Jim to have an analgesic.

Jim mumbled venom still in his tone.

"I am going to get Neil or Emma for this." He then fell into a sleep.

Doctor Pen immediately pulled on his gloves to get to work. Stitch by stitch with care, clean and clear his hands worked to repair the knife damage, his trained eye knowing exactly what to do. It took a while but now Jim's face was stitched and held into place while nature took its course. It would be weeks in the bandages, which were now covering three quarters of his head. He was taken back to the ward, Doctor Pen went back to have a word with Emma.

"You have had a lucky escape my dear, I don't know how it would be to marry a man like Jim, all I can say is I pity the girls that do. Neil told me he was your former boyfriend, a sorry heap of trouble. Your life with Neil will be serene; you would not have had a life with this other one" he said referring to Jim. Emma was still stunned but knew Doctor Penn's analysis was so right it made her shudder. Emma was ushered away into a small waiting room where she could

talk solemnly to the Nurse, it was Neil that spoke to Doctor Penn,

"Have you been able to make a good job of it?"

"Yes, the cut was clean the knife must have been very sharp, which funnily enough has worked in Jim's favour, a matter of time now, although he will be very sore for quite a while. It has taken twelve stitches to pull the wound together, yes there will be a scar, a small price to pay considering what he intended to do to you or Emma. You must realise that Emma is still in shock, and that Emma has her own battle to survive, she is still in recovery from her own illness. A quiet period must follow all of this you can postpone your wedding until Emma is stronger. Emma in the room with the Nurse didn't want to say anything, so she just nodded at the right moments and hoped that would suffice. Doctor Penn was still talking to Neil and said,

"Neil we will send for his wife Nanette is it, very shortly now, he can conjure up his own excuses, I don't envy him he is a devious character he will come up with something plausible no doubt, he makes a good liar as we know by past experience." Emma now back with Neil nodded, she knew better than

most about Jim's lies.

"I am looking for Jim Enderton Nurse, I have been told to come as he has been injured."

"You are Mrs Enderton then?

"Yes,"

"Wait here for a moment; I will get Doctor Pen to see you."

While Neil and Emma stood together they had heard Nanette arrive. A good chance to see just what Mrs Enderton looked like. Nanette was not at all like Emma had imagined, this lady held herself well. Small boned and pretty, why then did Jim have to play these awful tricks on her with another girls? Was it just to satisfy his desires as a handsome man needing more than one iron in the fire? To think he had two Sons as well. The thought swallowed Emma up she had been as nothing to Jim, a passing fancy, while to her he had been all her dreams come true. How sad, thank goodness, she now knew him for real she again shuddered from top to toe.

"Mrs Enderton?" Doctor Pen announced himself to Jim's wife.

"Yes I am Nanette Enderton"

"Ah, your Husband has had a misadventure. A gang of roughnecks set about him on the

wasteland where he was walking; of course wanting to get his money. Jim wasn't going to tip up, so a fight began. Unfortunately, they noticed the knife in the sheath on Jim's belt, not getting what they wanted by rough treatment, they resorted to stronger persuasion with the knife. I am afraid Jim has been facially damaged he has a deep wound on the left cheek, we have stitched him up he is quiet now and I can let you see him for a few moments I want to keep him quiet he needs to get his balance and to realise what has happened, he is in no further danger."

Nanette's hands went up to her face, full of dismay she tried to take in what Doctor Penn had said. She couldn't believe it. Seeing her dilemma Doctor Penn nodded his head to where Emma and Neil were standing and said,

"This couple witnessed the fight, would you like to speak to them?"

"Yes, I would."

Noticing that Neil's clothes were dishevelled and that Emma looked full of concern Nanette went over to them. Introducing herself she told them what Doctor Pen had said, they went along with the farce what more could they do? The explanation wrapped it all up neatly also giving Neil a get out. He would speak to Doctor Pen later. As regards Jim, this would put matters right, not wanting Nanette to know the truth. Doctor Penn just had a moment to talk to Neil and Emma before Nanette got over to them he had said,

"I know you overheard what I told Mrs. Enderton, I feel enough is enough, let sleeping dogs lie, no good can come out of the truth now. Turning his head to say here is Nanette now, go along with the story, it will ease her burden." Neil was wondering how Doctor Pen had thought up the tale to relate it so easily to Jim and Nanette. Jim knew it wasn't the truth, but the truth would put him down in Nanette's eyes, he now realised he needed Nanette. Emma could go to hell.

Jim lay soliloquising, while coming round he felt the bandage all around his head, he felt the pain when he tried to speak and he was done for. He spoke within his own thoughts very quietly saying,

"I have been stitched up good and proper both mentally and physically, this is going to take a long time to heal. My face my looks, no more pretty girls to hold, to make love to. I can't go to the Police to tell them it was Neil that knifed me, that truth is already history.

According to the Doctor's story Neil had been on the scene to help me, I will have to take the easy way out, I am hurt and I need Nanette more than ever before." Jim's thoughts travelled as he felt pain with disillusion. He drifted back into the never land that is neither sleep nor awakening murmuring,

"I did it, the knife I drew out was meant for Neil. I felt him take control and the knife turned towards my face Neil grasped my wrist to push the knife away from his own face and it then went into the left side of my face what rotten luck my own executioner."Nanette leaning over the side of Jim's bed couldn't tell a thing he was saying. She spoke in a tender caring manner,

"I am right here Jim beside you, I am so very sorry this has happened my darling. Every day is a new day slowly you will get well please don't worry. The boys send their love too, they will come to see you when you can sit up to talk to them, at the moment you need quiet and rest." She stopped speaking as Doctor Pen came towards her.

"I think you should leave him now my dear, he has had a huge shock, apart from the cut he has stitches to deal with, and his whole body will be trying to adjust. You can come

back tomorrow."

"How long will he be in Doctor?"

"I really can't tell you at this early stage, first we have to see that he is on even keel again and then when we change the dressings it is a judgement to be daily assessed. It will be a week to ten days before we can see if the stitches can come out maybe longer, it was a deep cut, just let time do its job, we will take care of him until you can do it yourself. He is a lucky man not to have had further damage." Nanette said,

"I realise Doctor this is a private Hospital, I won't be able to keep up with the cost."

"You are very fortunate the man who helped Jim, Neil is a patient of mine the whole family are. He has told me to put the cost down to good will, he will pay, he can afford to. So there that is another worry off your mind go now get some rest yourself it has been a shock for you too." She went back to Jim she tenderly kissed him noticing he had gone to sleep again. This was good; sleep was the best medicine for a troubled mind. Before she left, she whispered to Jim,

"I am here my love every day I will come to see you. Soon you will be home." Kissing him very gently she left.

At last Emma with Neil arrived home, in

Neil's study they talked about the event.

"What did you think of Doctor Pen's explanation Emma?"

"I thought it could not have been better, very real not like a concoction of lies, a means to an end. I would like to have known what Jim really thought of it; of course, he had to go along with it, to convince his wife of his innocence. I never want to go through anything like that again, as Jim must rest so must you Neil, it has been such a big shock even I feel dead on my feet through it all. To think it was all over me I am so sorry. I think it is fair to say it will never happen again, I have had a rude awakening I trusted too much, your forgiveness is of paramount importance to me where would I be now without you it doesn't bare thinking about. How is your own dear face? I see some bruising coming out. Will your Mother need to know?"

"Darling Emma one question at a time, I will be mending, as long as we get rid of the bruising before our wedding, all will be well."

"What a lovely word that is, wedding, Emma smiled Our Wedding Neil, now we can go ahead without this awful dilemma, us two how lovely a new chapter, I am fully ready to close the book on the old chapter to start a

brand new page. We will fill it with our love bring into it all of the family, colour and sparkle with a wonderful way to live. First I will take you over to the Ford to see where I was brought up; I was reluctant to do this but with all that has gone on it is the only thing to do. It is far from posh but it has stability, family love and trust. I thought all these things were readily found, I trusted the wrong people now I know my family are my strength I want to share that strength with you. I wonder if Aunt Polly will notice a difference in me, for surely I have changed although I say it myself, for the better."

Neil pulled her up from the chair his arms went around her.

"My own darling Emma how I love you, I want to be part of your family, you my dear are very welcome to be part of mine, Mother loves to sit and talk to you, you bring life to her elderly mind, when you are not around she talks about the time that you have spent with her. Now while I mend my bumps and bruises we will continue our search for a place of our own, the world is at our feet Emma, let us use that fact wisely"

Emma looked lovingly into Neil's eyes and said,

"Loving you Neil has become part of my

existence, the time I have to spend without you is wasted. We will put away all thoughts of yesterday, leaving only the future to look forward to." Sealed with a kiss they each made their promises; life would be sweet as they trod the path together.

"Get your coat, here let me help you."

Emma put her arm down the sleeve, pulling on the other sleeve she slipped and hit Neil in the eye, they laughed.

"Not trying to start another feud are you? He joked, like a couple of kids that is what Mother would say."

"Do you know Neil I feel like that, the light heart of a child where there is no thought of problem not counting the cost and no need to be running away. Knowing tomorrow will always come, that you always will be there in it my darling. Wherever you go I will want to be, oh Neil my life without you would have been so very different it will take a lifetime to show you how I love you" Neil kissed the top of her hair saying,

"It is a lifetime we have my dearest girl."

Chapter 44

Ada and Albert were bustling around the kitchen.
"Well it is this Sunday that Emma brings Neil to see us, I have tried so hard to make things look acceptable."
"I have told you Ada Neil will take us as he finds us. It isn't as though we haven't met him he knows we are not society people, the main thing is he loves our Emma." Putting coal on the black grate fire he said,
"I think our coal man is looking for a telling off, there is a lot of slack in this month's

delivery, good black shiny coal is what we order and what we pay for, but it is not what we are getting. This stuff makes too much smoke I hate it when the water for tea has been smoked it is a job to get it just right I know, smoked tea can go down the sink, that's my view anyway. It reminds me of kippers, I don't like those either!" Albert, almost talking to himself, liked to have a moan now and again.

Ada was on a different plain thinking about the tablecloth for Sunday.

"I am going to use the table cloth that has embroidery on it; Emma made it she will be pleased to see it in use, shall I put fresh flowers on the table Albert?"

"Do what you like Ada, as long as you don't ask me anymore. You know I am not experienced in matters of decor you always make a good job without my interference, be your usual self and that will suffice Neil would be the first one to agree with me."

"Wonder if they have chosen the colours for the dresses, Emma will make a beautiful bride, Ruby and Annie, will be lovely as Maids Of Honour, fancy Albert these are our lovely Daughters, I shall be so proud."

"Yes, our family has truly been a blessing to us, it is the love we have for each other not

many families have that bond, you should hear some of my mates going on about their children I feel sorry for them all, parents and children, they don't seem to even understand how family's work. We are lucky Ada I wouldn't have things any other way our girls have gone away to Polly's and the boys are growing up fast, time flies, next thing you know it will be us as Grandparents, ha, ha, ha, put the brakes on eh old girl." Ada had that look come over her; she was the central pin that the wheel of the family turned around. Dad knew when to chip in, Mother knew before the deed how to steer their ship. Neither Ada nor Albert would have it any different. A few rocky times when they had to hold on tight, then the balance, that made all secure again, one thing Neil could be sure of he would be able to count on his new family and they would be there for him at any time.

"Albert, do you think I could have a new dress for the wedding?"

"Crickey it isn't you who is getting married. I think perhaps you should contact Ruby and Annie they would make you one, we have to hold on to what money we have. Well I needn't tell you that, see what the girls say, write to them tonight then Emma can take the reply letter back to Polly and the girls, it will *be quicker that way.*

"Yes I could do that, as you say money needs to be used carefully, some of the shops are an outrageous price for the most simple of dresses. I have heard the girls are doing such nice work why didn't I think of that. I expect they will have their work cut out with all the other dresses that they have to make, I will see what I can find before I trouble them."
One up for Albert he did have his uses; he seemed to know just the right time to introduce his idea's into play. He had in his mind to buy Ada a beautiful corsage he would order it as a surprise as soon as they knew the colour theme. Ada may be plain, certainly not pretty, but now at this moment running through his mind was his one and only Ada and not even a Queen could surpass the image. All the toil worn parts of her body had been arrived at caring for his children and himself, what more is there to ask? He still loved her dearly.

Neil happily drove the buggy, his own horse Ned trotting along. He wanted to show Emma's parents the greatest respect. He knew where they lived, goodness hadn't Emma described it a thousand times. These, were Emma's roots, he would do his utmost to fit in. Arriving at the front door in Eadie

Street Emma with Neil made a fine pair. Neighbours had the net curtains peeked to one side to see the lovely dappled horse and the two-seater carriage it pulled. This was an accepted thing to do in Eadie Street, they were not being nosey, just inquisitive, it coloured their drab lives when something new happened, they could talk about the event between themselves.

"Here we are at last." Neil nodding towards the house said,

"Do we go in back or front? I see there is an entry that is the back way I presume."

"Help me down Neil, I can see the neighbours looking, we have to give them a good show. She smiled as she said it adding it is occasions like this one that brighten their lives is the only way our friends can get hold of a good yarn to gossip about". Emma, didn't mind, this was Eadie Street; she knew where she stood in Eadie Street. Putting her foot on to the step that assisted her going down to the pavement, she took Neil's hand. Moments later the front door was flung open.

"Hello Emma, hello Neil, comes on in, it is still a bit cold outside, it is this March wind it cuts you in two, I have a warm fire with flames half way up the chimney in the kitchen that is unless you would rather have

this room."
Neil replied
"Say no more, I will take the kitchen, I can smell something appetising going on in there, isn't that right Emma?" Emma replied,
"I prefer the kitchen it is always warm and homely and I think I can smell my favourite pie being baked, Mum is it shin of beef pie? Emma asked.
"Too true, although I said to Dad that you had it last time you came."
"Neil wasn't with me though was he? He will love it you can give it to me any time, I am very glad you cooked it for us. How long will it be in the oven?"
"Now then, give yourselves a chance to get through the door. Albert take their coats, put them upstairs out of the way, you will as you see realise there is not a lot of room, but what there is you are welcome to." Neil appreciated this welcome saying,
"A very warm welcome I would say, that is the best fire I have seen, the oven and the baking are a delight and I am so glad you asked me." Neil put them in no doubt as to their reception. Neil taking in the entire earthly atmosphere felt part of the scene already.
"So glad you wanted to come, Albert said,

Ada has been on thorns wondering if you would think of us as lowly, well I suppose we are compared to yourself, I told her if this fellow likes our Emma he would like us also, I sincerely hope I got it right."

Albert preened himself he was a proud man. Neil could see the pride and love Ada and Albert had for their family and said,

"Nearer the truth you could not be, I love Emma, wouldn't change a hair in her head, I am sure we shall all get along very well."

"A cup of Tea Neil, do you take sugar and milk?"

"I would love one. Now, what do I call you Mum or Mother?

"Mum will do nicely, I am very happy you want to call me that, as Albert said, I have been a little worried, now I feel in this short time we have always known you. The visits to the Hospital were short, we were all worried, now we can lay down firm territory and it is good to have you as part of my family Neil."

Emma noticed the tablecloth she had embroidered, that they had used on the table. She enjoyed the meal; all had gone so well she felt happiness spread over her. Leaving she felt a tug at her heart as she always did, this had been her home for all her growing up years, still loving Mum and Dad as always this being a different world to the one she now knew. Emma could carry the strength it gave her on to her own new life with Neil. Remembering the time spent at Mother's knee, teaching her to cook, to clean and to share her life with her Brothers and Sisters. Now she would share it with Neil who already filled her every thought. Both of them fell into a silence going back, savouring the moments that had been happily spent, the carriage candle lights had to be lit, the crisscross of many roads had to be driven, Neil thoughtful of his horse didn't want to give him a rough trail to trot along.

"Neil, why didn't you bring this your personal carriage, to pick me up in earlier days?"

"You were not well my love; I needed someone to drive so that all my attention could be dwelt on you, this time I thought you would like to show your parents that I was looking after you. So it was time for Ned to show you what he could do."

"Is that your horse's name, Ned?"

"Yes, he has been with me for many years, he is the favourite horse in my stable."

"I haven't heard you mention your stable either Neil."

"Now, what would you have thought if I had

told you I had a stable and a couple of horses? You would have thought I was showing off, that is the last thing I wanted, it was hard enough to get your attention in the first place and you wouldn't come to meet my Mother, no matter how many times I gave you an invite. Telling you about a stable and horses would have frightened you off all together. Perhaps I didn't do the right thing; if you had come to me sooner Jim would have never met you. It is all in the past now darling water under the bridge now we are really together no-one will ever come between us again." He left his hand on the reign; he took her hand with the other one she felt the luckiest girl in the entire World. The visit to Mum and Dad's had stabilised values, she could now talk to Ruby and Annie without picking her words. All could be in the open, and then she had a dulling thought, except her losing a baby, they must not know about that. It all being over she had a good chance of keeping this between herself, Doctor Pen and Neil that is how it must be. Now they were home, Neil parked; patted Ned's head and took Emma into her Aunt Polly who greeted them.

"Back again I see did you enjoy your trip?" Emma gave Aunt a hug saying,

"Seeing Mum and Dad was great I do declare they would have been glad to see you too. They send their fondest love to you."Aunt Polly smiled, she felt a part of her belonged to this her once removed family. There was nothing she wouldn't do for any one of them. Aunt wanted a quick goodnight saying,

"I am not going to keep you Neil it is quite late and you have seen enough of each other for today. Take your man to the door Emma to say goodnight. I will say goodnight Neil, I do declare I am tired out." Neil turned to Emma saying,

"Goodnight my darling Emma." Neil enfolded her in his arms as if to never let her go she being where she wanted to be, a rosy glow enfolded the couple. It took yet another call from Aunt to part them, he kissing her with all the love in his heart yet again said,

"See you tomorrow sweetheart sleep well." Standing at the front of the shop, the door still open, Neil unhitched his beloved Ned, patted him, said a word of kindness in his ear and got into the carriage. Waving as he pulled into the carriage lanes his heart rejoicing. All was well.

Emma couldn't believe how the experience of the past few months had changed her life, in fact ever since she came to Aunt Polly's the change had been quite drastic, where was the girl that lived alongside Mum and Dad in Eadie Street? Now learning new things every day, dropping the old, remodelling even her innermost thoughts Emma was becoming a Lady.

Chapter 45

Now not a cloud in sight Emma and Neil could plan their wedding. Ruby and Annie had to make up their minds about what colour they would wear.
"We have been given the opportunity to choose Ruby, so what shall we wear?"
"I think it has to be a follow up of the shop colours, so pink is my choice."
"I was thinking on the same lines, or lavender, we will stick to pink, as you say it is the colour choice for the shop, so Aunt will be pleased, it was pink we chose in the first place wasn't it Ruby?" Ruby replied,
"Emma wants us to make her dress, white of course, alter neckline with a small veil, pink roses in her bouquet and a little Lilly of The Valley, all done ha, ha, at least we can get on with the making, that will take us a few weeks even though there are two of us. When we go to get the materials we should bring a few choices, the satins have some really nice detail in them and Emma could choose which ones she likes best"
Annie said,
"Do you think Emma has been quiet these

last couple of weeks?"
"Come to think of it yes, she is not bugging us about the dresses for one thing."
"We'll see how she is this week when we produce the material, if she is stand offish then we will have to ask her what is wrong." Annie said,
"It is a delicate time for her I for one do not want to upset Emma and I know you feel the same way. I am glad the embroidery is ready for Lady Faversham, also her friend's initialled handbag we mustn't take any more orders, unless it is for a time after the wedding." *Ruby and Annie had it all laid out in their mind, the discussion with Annie was only to check they were both thinking on the same lines, Annie always left Ruby to do most of the planning Ruby was good at it, getting things into an orderly fashion wasn't Annie's best thing to do. The two girls worked very closely together chit chatting as they sewed, showing each other the detail to be worked on it was a delight to see. Aunt Polly happy in her choice, these three lovely girls of Ada's had given her so much pleasure and she was contented that Emma had chosen the right way for them all to follow, never did Aunt think they all would settle down as well as they had.*

"Annie, is this piece all right?" Looking at the embroidery with a trained eye scrutinising the way the colour had been blended in Annie replied,

"Yes Ruby, you will find when you get on to the next colour blend it will be right. I think the same at times, the customer always thinks it is lovely, so it must be good I love it when they come in to fetch their completed goods for their eyes to see our work and admiring the way it has turned out. That I suppose is what keeps us going the very fact that these items are going to be worn to elaborate functions may I say it is like taking a piece of our skill, then showing it to perfection," they smiled.

Of course Emma had been quiet she was afraid to speak openly in case she slipped up and told about the fight between Neil and Jim, and the fact that no one knew about the baby, or the fight, two hard things to keep secret. They had made a promise to each other Neil and herself, this information would go no further than Doctor Pen he being the Doctor in charge of the illness that caused the abortion and Jim, it was obvious Jim would want to keep all of this secret he had Nanette to deal with. That was it, no one else knew. Now with the trauma that had gone on Emma thought the least said the better. Ruby and Annie had picked-up on this; they were used to Emma talking about the daily family news it was bound to be missed. Emma must keep quiet to fob them off, the pretence of not feeling too well was readily accepted, it was an excuse that would have to stand until Emma was ready to move forward, Neil as her first thought, was all she could contend with. Not knowing how Jim was didn't really concern her, it was his own fault. I want to give my undivided attention to our wedding, Emma thought, in fact that is exactly what I must do and getting preoccupied with other matters has to be thrown to the winds. I will ask the girls if they have settled on a colour tonight, that will please them, also see if they have any material for me to look at. Perhaps if I do that, I won't come across as being vague. I know the girls have looked at me a few times wondering at my lack of interest, the shock of all that has gone on has put me in a spot. Tonight I will squash any thoughts the girls might be harbouring about me not being enthusiastic. Then show them I have nothing else on my mind, but the wedding. That will right things a bit, as the days go by all will become reality again and I will have no need for pretence. Emma's thoughts were interrupted by Aunt coming to see her saying, "Oh here you are Emma, it was so quiet in here I didn't think you were in the shop, are you all right dear?" Here it was again, somehow she had to gain her Aunt's and her Sister's confidence, it was obvious they had her welfare in question; she had to take a firm grip so that they all would stop the inquisition then all would be well again. The guilty feeling had to be put to the back of her mind. Her future with Neil being of paramount importance, regretting the time she had wasted with Jim. That now was water under the bridge, she was lucky to have come out of the trauma alive, come to think so was Neil, it all could have been very different, Tears welled up in her eyes. Thoughts ran through her mind once more, Aunt was left standing waiting for Emma to continue their conversation. Emma just had to have a minute her mind still evaluating her position. Jim was an infatuation that swallowed me up I can't bear the thought of him now. How very strange Neil has been my rock in all of this, yet I pushed him to one side in the beginning, thank God he loves me enough to forgive me" Aunt now getting impatient said, "Emma where are you now I declare you are

not in this room, you are miles away!"
"Sorry Aunt I was just lost in thought."
"Emma come on, we are in the kitchen waiting for you," called Annie.
"I am coming must lock the shop door, I won't be a minute." Emma down to ground level again went in; never had she appreciated her family more. How good it was to have stability and trust surrounding her she had took it all for granted, she never would again; the meaning of love had taken on a completely different concept. Coming from the loving family in the beginning had not prepared her for the world outside, too trusting, she thought everyone worked in the same way, to find out the truth in this matter had cost her dearly. Emma and Aunt joined Ruby and Annie in the kitchen, Ruby said,
"The patterns are here Emma, you don't seem at all excited, and here we are can't wait for the day." Annie's eyes too were shining saying,
"Has Ruby told you? We have decided on pink it co-ordinates with the shop colour, which has already become a part of who we are."
"I haven't been told that the patterns were here, of course I am excited, I just haven't had a moment," Emma said with enthusiasm.

This was not strictly true, but served the purpose to be excused.

"Shall I go and get them? Said Ruby?"

"If you like, this evening we could go over them together, Neil has a meeting so I have a little free time." Evening came, still in the kitchen to spread the cloth samples on to the kitchen table, the patterns became scrutinised. Emma now seriously deciding said,

"They all have their own merit, I keep going back to the one with the "Lilly of the Valley" embossed on it, the satin carries it very well. I could have a few of the flowers in with the pink roses as my bouquet I decided to have the Lilly of the Valley sprigs in with the pink roses so the embossed satin sounds about right, I don't want anything over done, simple and sweet that will be for me, I think Neil will readily agree. I could go in my shop clothes left to him as long as I am there Ha, ha. You are the important one not the dress," he would lovingly say. Annie said,

"Ruby and I think the plain pink satin, with a small lace hat and lace Muff in white to reflect your white, all of that we could make between us, we need not have flowers to carry."

"I like the sound of that it is all progressing

very well, what shall I have? Auntie Polly said looking, over the girl's shoulders. She needed to get her outfit sorted.

"How about if you also had pink, but in a much deeper shade, as befits your age group, you could decide whether you wanted Ruby and Annie to make it. In any case I am sure they would make your hat and then you could choose exactly the style you wanted." Emma wanted to please her Aunt.

"Hmm, do you think girls you could cope with all the work that has been discussed, it seems a lot to me," Aunt being sensible had thought it out for herself. Ruby replied

"Yes of course, we wouldn't mind working evenings and Sundays. It is a job for our family which we would be proud to achieve it would also advertise The Pink Perfection Embroidery and Fashion shop, plenty of jobs would come in from that."

"Ha ha; laughed Aunt Polly we will be taking on more staff at this rate!"

The pleasure that this evening had brought was immeasurable. Emma had been so engrossed in her own world and the events that had shaken her these past few weeks! She had forgotten how it felt to be at one with her Aunt and Sisters. A heavy weight had been lifted from her shoulders, feeling light-

hearted, flippant again and something other than misery to talk to Neil about, Neil's Mum too, she also was waiting to talk about the design of the wedding, even she was feeling left out, not knowing anything about the trauma that had taken place it left her wondering if all was going to plan. Emma could now open up, put her mind at rest knowing everything was now falling into place, she could be open, happy, yes contented, a wonderful feeling. Telling Neil's Mum about the prettier side of the occasion would be such a pleasure.

The dresses were now taking shape the Men's suits were almost finished. Doctor Pen had been asked to be Neil's Best Man. The day in June was soon now approaching the fever pitch only just surmountable. The hustle and bustle trying on, pinning up, gathering together fitting, all with good humour, much devotion and smiles for everyone. Customers wished Emma all happiness. Neil was getting his suit sorted and a pink rose button hole flower organised (yes in a man's eye view a button hole for him and his best man Doctor Pen took organising) Neil tried to stand back to let Emma have her choice when big decisions were about to be made. So many things to be planned, the time chose 2pm. at Saint Mary's Church, the bell ringers, the Vicar and the Church choir, flowers for the Church, the catering, Church Hall; it was near with no problem as regards transport but the décor had to be worked out and the layout of the tables. It was a very nice Church Hall well appointed and taken care of, had they thought of everything? The invitations had been sent some weeks ago, no one had declined and it made a round figure of 100 guests. Some had already brought to Emma wedding gifts; Emma shared the opening of these with her family and again with Neil and his Mother. The oddest item received was a stone ornament for the garden, a stone shell on a stand with a fountain top. Eventually they would have the garden for it to take pride of place in.

Still deciding on the dwelling, having gone to look at several houses for sale, they kept coming back to the same one, it being within the area of commerce, easy to get to, pleasing to the eye. Not a cottage but it had dormer shaped windows on the upper level, making it look like a cottage yet with more space. Enough room for children that they both wanted, a study for Neil as he was used to having his own space at home. This would give him privacy to do his accounts and to smoke an occasional cigar. Emma was glad of that because she didn't want the house and her fabrics to get the smell of tobacco. To Emma in her small way the house was a colossal price. Neil took it in his stride and he had a few alterations in mind that would be good space for a family. "First things first, Emma said with a smile, she was quite aware of what ran through Neil's mind, approving although wanting to slow things down a bit. Let's get the wedding over first eh," She laughed. The house was another story that would take time to complete, windows to drape, carpets to choose, before they ever thought of furniture, life with Neil was not going to be dull. He was already positioning a stable for his beloved Ned. There was never any time left to mope, so Jim's upset got pushed out, Emma became Emma again lively and caring full of her own ideas as Emma always was. Neil's Mother never had a dull moment either caring for Emma as she did; it made her very happy that Neil had chosen well. All Mothers miss their Sons when they leave home, but when the result is good and the Son and the new Daughter are happy, soon the heartache is a thing of the past, the visits from Neil and Emma would be constant, so a heart is soon eased.

"We will look after Mother, won't we Emma?"

Of course, we will, I love the company of your Mother, what made you ask that?

"I suppose it is because I think a great deal about Mother and want you to feel the same."

"Have no fear Neil your mother already has a secure place in my heart, together we will delight her, so that she will be happy too. She is so very easy to please and has taken to me without a qualm I would do anything for her.

Chapter 46

"What about your Mum girls, has anyone asked what Ada would like to wear to the wedding?" Aunt didn't want Ada left out. Emma said,
"I thought about that only yesterday and wrote a letter, I am posting it this morning, I have asked for a quick reply, I think though our Mum will want to do her own thing, she hasn't had many places to go that require special attire I have told her the theme is pink, so we will see what she says." Annie said,
"The dresses are all ready you know Ruby and me have spent every waking hour on them. I would like you to have a final try on Emma to see if you need anything altering perhaps tonight, would that be all right? Emma replied,
"Yes, we will drop the shop blinds then all of us can try on in the sewing room. We need plenty of space, the kitchen fire is too near we don't want to get singed or rather the dresses get singed!" In a good humour feeling all was well they went to tea, each one of them had something to say, they talked more than

they ate.

They all came back into the sewing area, the blinds had been closed so that complete privacy was enjoyed and got on at once trying on their dresses.

"Oh Emma, you look lovely," Annie exclaimed, Ruby was touching the back of the veil putting it steady on Emma's head. Ruby said,

"Neil will be so proud of his bride, now it is so soon here I find the waiting all the more difficult. Are the caterers taking the cake straight to the Church Hall, or will it come here first?" Emma in control now said,

"I am going to have the cake delivered here the night before the wedding, I want a good look at it before the guest's lay claim to it as they will no doubt. I want to remember, keep it in a little corner of my heart before it is sliced up, just one chance to do this special thing, I don't want to miss it."

To take Emma with Neil to and from the Church Hall where the reception was being held, friends and even Doctor Pen had bedecked the two-seater carriage that faithful Ned had pulled all the years with pink and white wide satin ribbon, even Ned's harness had pink roses entwined in it. An appealing pink umbrella frilled at the edge was to be placed in the carriage either for rain or strong sunlight, photos would be able to be taken with more advantage, a frilly umbrella never did any harm in event could be very useful.

A letter came from Emma's Mum telling her not to be worried about her dress yes; she did understand Aunt Polly would be looking her very best.

"Dear Emma,
"You are not to give my dress a second thought Emma dear I won't let you down, but I will require a subtle dress, one I can wear after the day, when I go out with Dad. As you well know, I am not one for waste, luckily I found a dress to fit the bill in a down town sale. I know you and the girls will look extra special, it is how I would want it, I will follow your pink I know you will like that. Dad and I have ordered flowers to wear they will be pink roses. Dad had ordered me a special corsage as a surprise, I put my foot in that one by finding out, but still I appreciate his thought. Dad has had a new suit in grey pin stripe, he protested but I must say he looks very smart. You will be proud of your old Dad, as he will be proud of you when he takes you down the Aisle to Neil. I told him how long it has been

since he went to the tailor we argued the toss! Ha, ha, I won. What Dad called his best suit is at least twenty years old! He was about due for a new one don't you think? Hope all goes to plan, my love is always with you.
See you in your Bridal White, on your special day."
Mum Dad. Xx

It was June the sun was shining, the beaming smiles told the story. Emma had seen her Mum and Dad at Aunt Polly's and they both looked very smart. All the dresses were fitted with care, thanks to Ruby and Annie. Pink roses were just the thing for this gathering. Emma's bouquet had pink roses with lily of the valley in a shower design trailing down to the hip line, the Lilly of the Valley design repeated in the dresses embossed pattern. Her Maids Of Honour Ruby and Annie looked so pretty. The men collected around in a group at the foot of the Alter giving a definite distinction to the scene. There was an air of sanctity, and reverence about the gathering. Neil a very happy man, this is the day he had been praying for.
Excitement filled the air. Emma walked down the aisle to Neil on her Dad's arm her gaze wandering across the well turned out

relatives and across the pews. It came like a blow, for looking straight at her were Nanette and Jim! Emma felt herself go limp she trembled. Dad looked at her with concern but she could only go forward to play her part in the destiny designed for today. Hoping the day was not about to be spoiled, surely Nanette and Jim were not going to step forward to spoil this oh so special day, they walked to, "Here comes the Bride" slowly with elegance.

Arriving at Neil's side going from her Dad to her future Husband, Neil took her hand giving it a squeeze of confidence. Emma wanting to whisper something to Neil obviously she couldn't, Emma was the keeper of this uneasy knowledge about Nanette and Jim being in the Church. The vows were exchanged, signing the register Emma tried to get a quiet moment with Neil. It was hopeless, there were too many people and the focus was set on the happy pair. Soon they had grouped the procession. Emma clung to Neil as they went back down the aisle; forward they went to be received with hands full of confetti at the Church door. They stepped into their carriage for the short distance to the reception hall. Once in the carriage Emma told Neil very briefly that

Nanette and Jim were among the guests, he said,

"How could they be, they were not invited." Neil the news fresh to him was indignant. Emma and Neil settled at the front door of the reception hall waiting patiently to receive their guests, Neil told Emma not to worry,

"They will have gone by now," he said as the surge of guests came up to the door, Emma's heart was thumping. Kissing and hand shaking and saying the words of welcome, thanking individuals for the wedding gifts the guests filtered through. Then all at once the moment was upon them.

"Congratulations Emma and to you Neil, forgive us for coming into the hall with no invite. Jim and I just wanted to say thank you for your help when Jim was attacked, I don't know how Jim would have got himself out of that savage situation, if you hadn't come to his assistance. A small gift, Nanette offered a gift-wrapped parcel Emma could feel Neil fidgeting by her side. Jim didn't come forward to say a word. His face as he stood behind Nanette was evil. Jim, Emma, Neil all knew the true story; it was hard to go along with Nanette and her belief. All in that momentary company knew the true story except Nanette, she understood Neil had been

there to help Jim during the surprise attack, none of them made the effort of denial so the moment passed. Nanette smiling insisted,

"Jim didn't want to come to see you although he is very grateful, I wanted so much to say thank you and wish you every happiness, Jim is slowly getting better although you won't find him saying anything today, his face is still very painful if he tries to talk, no-one was ever taken to task about the attack so we will have to learn to live with it. I mustn't take any more of your time I do hope you like our small gift." Jim stood directly behind Nanette, Neil and Emma could see his face, but not Nanette, Jim's eyes flashed daggers sending a personal message of his own, as he was behind Nanette she didn't see his face. He was recovering somewhat, but still had a lot of dressing on his cheek. Dying to get away and out of the limelight, he gave Nanette a meaningful nudge. With that, they went towards the open door, waving once before finally retiring out of sight, Emma turned to Neil and said,

"Thank God! Neil it is over, Jim dare not deny the things his wife has just talked about because the truth being fact could not be disclosed, the other side of this story was appalling," Jim needed Nanette and now the

truth must be buried.
Feeling so very much better Emma and Neil sat with all their guests eating a lovely meal. Speeches were made, now it was time they cut the beautiful cake, three tiers high again all white with pink decoration, the roses fashioned to tumble down from tier to tier, eyes shining smiles all around. The future was at last theirs for the making they both had each other that being all they needed.

Author Sylvia Jackson-Clark:
© 19.4.2013

Printed in Great Britain
by Amazon

43768912R00228